M000279906

Verge

Nadia Attia

———

First published in Great Britain in 2023 by
SERPENT'S TAIL
an imprint of Profile Books Ltd
29 Cloth Fair
London ECIA 7JQ
www.serpentstail.com

Copyright © Nadia Attia, 2023

1 3 5 7 9 10 8 6 4 2

Typeset in Tramuntana Text by MacGuru Ltd
Designed by Nicky Barneby @ Barneby Ltd

Printed and bound in Great Britain by Clays Ltd, Elcograf S.p.A.

A CIP catalogue record for this book is available from the British Library.

ISBN 978 1 80081 015 0
eISBN 978 1 78283 971 2

FSC
www.fsc.org
MIX
Paper from
responsible sources
FSC® C018072

For Gina Attia (my north), Ibrahim Attia and Felicitas Riley

1

23 April

———

ONE FOR SORROW. Rowena remembers the magpie standing brazenly over the rabbit trap, a soft, glistening eye dangling from its beak. She, too, had taken a treasure of her own that day, whispering thanks before crunching her cutters through bone and placing the paw in her pocket for luck, knowing she could still get a good price for the other three, along with the fur and meat.

Twenty minutes later, her pa dropped down dead in front of her. Perhaps the luck didn't have time to work its way in? She touches the bump in her pocket as her mother flits from kettle to sink to stove in the farmhouse they've shared for seventeen years, the words from her mouth becoming a wash of noise. Rowena can picture her pa's eyes rolling back in his head, him crumpling to the ground, folding in on himself like a pack of cards. How the grass held his shape even after the body was taken away. Three days ago he was here, she thinks, and now ...

Her mother's voice cuts through, making Rowena sit up in the hard kitchen chair. Even the highland lilt that's lingered since childhood can't soften Tessa Murray's words: 'You did this. That curse of yours has become a danger.'

Rowena opens her mouth to reply—

'The day you were born two hundred and fifty starlings dropped out of the sky and slammed into the main road.' Tessa lights the

1

grease-thick burner on the stove. 'The lucky ones died on impact. The villagers had to rake up all the little bodies and burn them. If that's not a bad omen I don't know what is.'

For years Rowena thought all this talk of omens was simply Tessa's way of keeping her daughter at arm's length, and because her pa's affection came easily Rowena never bothered to chase her mother's love. Tessa started pointing out signs to her only child as soon as she was old enough to listen: the position of the spoon when it fell from her chubby little fingers; the crow that called her by name from the roof; the curdled milk that was fine before Rowena touched it ... When Rowena got sick and had to be home-schooled that was another sign – one that marked her as different, as something to be kept apart. Whenever she asked her pa about it he laughed it off, said her mother was raised by eccentric folk and to pay her no mind. He pretended not to hear Tessa's superstitious whispers, was careful to divide his time between the fields and the bottom of a beer glass and keep Rowena's focus on the sheep, her books and her riding lessons. But Pa's not here now, Rowena thinks. Tessa's all there is. And maybe she's right after all?

A passing cloud dims the room, turning everything stone-grey. Tessa shifts from foot to foot, gnawing on the ragged skin next to her fingernails. She clicks on the radio as she waits for the whistle of the kettle. There's a strange energy to the place now that he's gone, and they both feel it. The radio announcer rattles through the news: more rioting at the ports where food is being burned due to the latest soured trade deal with Europe; claims of a postcode lottery for medical treatment; environmental groups asking why the government isn't reintroducing pollinators or building flood defences instead of border fences ...

'The Split happened eleven years ago,' Tessa tuts, 'and the whole Kingdom's still bawling about it.' She changes the station to a comedy quiz show.

Rowena studies the thin lines around her mother's mouth, the red-tinged lashes distorted by the gelatinous curve of her glasses, the strands of wiry hair slipping from the nest at her neck. 'Do you really think it was me that did it?' she asks her.

Tessa presses her spine against the sink and gives the slightest nod. 'Death touches everyone you get close to; first that boy you were running round with, the one who'd shag the back out of an old coat, and now your pa. What if I'm next?'

Rowena worries the paw in her pocket, finding the claws with her thumb.

'I've written to my mother and you're to go to Culcrith,' Tessa says. 'I'd have sent you there long ago but your pa wouldn't allow it. And look where that got him.'

Tinny laughter spills from the radio.

'What?' Rowena looks up. 'Why? His ashes are still warm and you're kicking me out?' She's never spoken so boldly to her mother and the words prick her tongue.

'It's for your own good – your gran's the best healer in the north and she might have a chance of undoing this thing before you turn eighteen next month.'

'Why, what happens then?'

Tessa stares at her daughter – eyes wide and round, like the rabbit's. 'The curse is likely to fix and settle as you'll be a woman grown. And if we've not lifted it by the time the solstice rolls around it'll be rooted too deep to shift. You'll be too far gone.' She starts pacing again, making the window blink each time her body crosses it. 'Death has marked you, clear as day, Rowena, and It's getting bolder, working up to something. You know I'm right. Unless we undo this now, everyone you ever love will die.'

'There's no one left for me to love,' Rowena mutters with a shiver.

Applause bursts from the speakers.

'There's a healer in the village, why can't I try her?' she protests. 'I've never even set foot outside this *county*, let alone travelled across the whole Kingdom to somewhere like Culcrith.'

Tessa's face hardens as she stops still in the middle of the kitchen. 'What do you mean "somewhere like Culcrith"?'

The kettle starts to huff and whisper.

'That's my family home you're talking about – land fed by the bones of our ancestors, worked with blood, sweat and tears. Our heritage. A sacred land.'

Rowena swallows, gets that twist in her gut that tells her a storm's coming.

'Your pa spoiled you,' Tessa says, jabbing a finger. 'Turned you into a bloody fool: you sit there mewling like a baby when you should be thanking me for sending you away so your gran can fix you. And it's only a matter of time before Lord Northwood catches you poaching on his estate, and we know how that'd turn out for us!' She flares her nostrils and lowers her brow, like a bull about to charge. 'As long as I'm legally responsible for you you'll do as I say, and I say Culcrith's the best place for you now.'

The kettle screeches. Tessa lets it.

Rowena scrapes her chair across the flagstones, leaps up, flings the door open and runs outside before the first tear falls.

Someone slams into Halim as he's halfway through the gate.

'Watch it!' It's the most he's said to Rowena Murray all year – since her mum hired him to shift livestock before lambing kicked in.

'Watch what?' she snaps, flashing her grey-green eyes. She stomps off up the slope in her mud-caked socks, the wind catching her hair like a red-gold Medusa.

Her mum yells from the farmhouse door. 'Rowena, I want you packed up by Sunday evening!'

Halim bends down to pick up the phone that was knocked from his hand, then watches Rowena disappear into the leafy copse. She's a strange one, he thinks, clanking the gate shut behind him. He nods a greeting to Mrs Murray, hands her his job sheet, thrusts his fists into the pockets of his jeans and gazes up at the storm clouds as they unfurl like smoke.

'Is it true what I heard about Lord Northwood raising the land rent?' he asks.

'News travels fast.'

The first fat drops of rain bounce off his shoulders.

'You've been working on and off for us about a year or so, haven't you, Halim?'

'Yes,' he says, worried that she's about to cancel all future contracts.

'And you're good pedigree – you sound well educated, I mean?' Mrs Murray turns to him and sucks in a breath before he can reply. 'I've a new job for you.'

'Really? The pigs are all safely up at Hungerden and I was planning on heading across the border to Sinkhurst's in time for—'

4

'I can pay you double. Half now, half on delivery. Should be enough to pay off that precious truck of yours.'

The first grind of thunder sounds in the distance.

Halim scratches his chin. 'What's the stock?'

'My daughter.'

2

28 April

———

HALIM LEANS AGAINST HIS TRUCK and watches Mrs Murray tuck a sprig of something green into the pocket of Rowena's backpack. She takes her daughter's face in both her hands and says something. From this distance it looks more like a doctor's examination than an embrace. He straightens up as they break away and Rowena heads towards him.

'Take a picture why don't you?' She chucks her bag into the cab and herself in after it.

Mrs Murray comes over and presses a brown envelope into Halim's hand. 'Here's a bit extra for food,' she says. 'Green stuff, not junk food. And no booze. Make sure she earns the rest and doesn't act up – she needs eyes on her, that girl.'

This sounds more like babysitting, he thinks, and he's about to say as much when Mrs Murray continues.

'And remember: this is a job not a holiday, and you've got your reputation to think of.'

Halim frowns at the threatening edge to her voice.

'You'll get the rest of the payment on safe delivery. In one piece. Unsullied.'

He recoils. 'I wouldn't ...'

'I was young once, I know what young men are like; quick to take advantage of a situation.'

Halim clenches his jaw, turns his back on her and climbs into the truck.

Rowena scratches her nails up and down the seat belt, pretending not to care, but he can see her watching the old brick bungalow wobble and recede in the wing mirror as they pull away. Mrs Murray has already disappeared inside. When the curve of the hill smothers the farmhouse from view, Rowena sniffs and stares out of the window. He worries that she might cry and considers turning around – then remembers how much he needs the money.

Rowena pulls something out of her pocket, something small and furred like an animal part, and works her fingers over it.

Halim clears his throat. 'You okay?'

The livestock container behind the cab clanks and rattles as they bump down the track.

'Um, let's see: I killed my pa eight days ago so I've been sent away with some random farmhand to get "fixed" by a woman I've never met, and until I turn eighteen in about four weeks' time I get fuck-all say in the matter.' She starts picking at the rubber window seal.

'I heard it was a stroke,' Halim mumbles.

'What?'

'I said I'm sorry for your loss.'

'He's not lost. I know exactly where he is.' She stares out the window at the sluggish curve of the river, the pockets of sheep doing their best to graze the sodden meadow beyond. 'What did my mother tell you about me?'

'Nothing, it's none of my business.'

'Except it is though, isn't it? This is business. Didn't she just hand you a wedge?'

'She gave me some money, yes.'

She narrows her eyes at him. 'You're not gonna chuck me in a ditch somewhere, are you?'

Halim winces as the gears crunch. 'I get paid the rest on delivery – so no, that would be counterproductive.'

Rowena snorts. 'What kind of man tears a grieving girl from her family home for the sake of a few quid?'

Halim doesn't answer, wishing he'd never spoken up in the first place.

'You're not good with people, are you?' she continues. 'The

shearing boys always say you're stuck up, that you don't like talking to them 'cause they're beneath you. Do you want me to go sit in the back like one of your little lambs?'

'That's not a bad idea, actually.' He edges the truck onto the verge and brakes, waits for her to open the door. Here's your chance to turn back, he thinks, I won't give you another.

When she unclips her seat belt, grabs her bag and leaps out he curses to himself in Arabic.

He leans over to see if she's really gone and finds her stood in the middle of the road, her oversized cardigan slipping off one shoulder. They're more likely to come across horses than cars these days, but he watches for them anyway. He realises that she's staring at the 'Welcome to Pickbury' sign that marks the edge of her village. He doesn't remember ever being attached to a place, and part of him envies her sense of belonging.

Her back suddenly becomes rigid and her body jerks as if she's been hit: a heartbeat later a crow bursts out of the trees and swoops low, screeching a warning. The next moment she's opened the truck door and is sitting beside him again.

'We're being followed,' she says, her voice tight. 'Well, what are you waiting for? Drive, for fuck's sake!'

He frowns, checks the mirrors, sees nothing, releases the hand-brake and pulls away.

They thread their way towards the county border, settling into silence. As treetops and hedgerows slide past the window Rowena sighs and draws it out so long Halim wonders if she'll faint.

'So how you gonna get me across all those county borders?' she asks, the colour returning to her cheeks.

'I get travel privileges as a livestock driver, and Mrs Murray and I applied to get you listed as my assistant for the next five weeks.'

She turns to him. 'Five weeks? How slow is this heap of junk? Surely it only takes a few days to get up to Culcrith?'

Halim raises an eyebrow. 'You've never crossed a county border before, have you?'

'No, why would I? I can't even drive.'

'Five weeks is contingency time. It takes at least a day to issue permits for each crossing, even as a livestock driver, and by my count we'll need fifteen of them. Even if we do a couple of crossings a day this isn't a typical run, so I'll need to prove that I have con-tracts in place, and if a job falls through we'll be delayed.'

Rowena seems to shrink into the seat. 'We'll get to Culcrith before the twentieth of June, won't we?'

'It's the twenty-eighth of April now, so I'd certainly hope so.' The sooner the better, he thinks. 'In the meantime you're to work along-side me and cover your expenses.'

'Work? Really? I thought that was just a cover to get me the stamp.'

Halim's dark eyes dart over the mirrors.

She pulls out her passport and examines the fresh ink: 'Land Labourer. Status Approved 25.04.25.' She would have had to pass a physical and medical assessment for that classification. He imagines a line of people waiting to be conscripted like soldiers – off to fight a war amongst themselves, over a frigid land that offers increas-ingly meagre spoils.

'I have some savings to see me through,' she mutters, 'and I can do readings, sell charms and tokens for cash.'

Halim shakes his head. 'No. Some of these contracts depend on you working too.'

Rowena slaps the passport shut and rubs her forehead. 'When's the first one?'

'Soon.' He flicks the indicator, rankled by her huffing and puffing. 'I'm surprised your mother didn't tell you all this.'

'I'm surprised what a selfish prick you are.'

Halim's shoulders rise and fall as he pulls the wheel and swings them around the corner.

'If I'm stuck with you let's make some ground rules,' she sighs. 'Rule number one: you're not my keeper or guardian or boss, and this "assistant" arrangement is only for show.'

He checks the mirrors and accelerates.

'Rule number two: you can sleep in this shit-stinking truck if you want but I'm staying in hotels and that cost's coming out of the fee you squeezed my mother for. Rule number three: you don't ever touch my stuff, and when—'

He clicks the radio on and blasts away her voice.

Rowena gapes at him and then mutters an obscenity he's glad he didn't quite hear. She digs around in her backpack and fishes out a scratched-up dinosaur tin, a neon-pink lighter and some papers and lays them out on her lap.

'No smoking in here,' he says.

She waves her hand by her ear and shrugs over the loud music.

He twists the volume dial. 'Please don't smoke in here.'

'I need it to calm my nerves, otherwise I get hysterical.' Her fingers smooth the waiting skins. 'I'm not joking – proper mood swings, tears, the works. You really wouldn't like it.'

Halim scowls and lowers his window.

'Want one? You look like you need a smoke.'

'I grew out of it.'

'Really, how old are you?'

'Twenty.'

'In that case, you can buy the rum 'cause my fake ID won't work outside of Dunfordshire.'

'Not a good idea, I promised I'd keep an eye on you.'

Rowena licks her lips. 'Well, what if I were to phone Tessa and tell her that your eyes were on me a bit too much, lingering on all the wrong places?' She smiles and runs a finger over her collarbone, traces a line down her cleavage. 'I wonder, would that be a breach of contract?'

Halim's knuckles whiten on the steering wheel. Think of the money, he tells himself, think of the money.

3

'YOU KILLED ME, ROWENA.'

She looks down at her hand – in it, her curved skinning knife is dripping red, and below, sprawled on the floor of the truck, is a lamb with its flank heaving and pale tongue flopped out. Its slit-eye rolls up towards her, wide with terrible knowing...

Rowena's jolted awake by a bump in the road, her head and heart thudding. It takes a moment to figure out where she is, and as she glances over at Halim he raises an eyebrow.

'You were muttering in your sleep,' he says.

She closes her mouth, rubs her forehead where it must have knocked the window, and realises her armpits are damp with sweat. The earlier brightness has dimmed to an end-of-day gloom as the whole Kingdom unfurls before the truck's wheels: road signs to places she's never heard of; hills rising and falling like fists; other people's fences and fields, sagging under the weight of a recent storm. They must be miles from home now, she thinks. Only, Pickbury isn't home any more, not without Pa. The tugging inside her chest and the static in her bones confirm what she already knows: she won't be back this way again.

Halim looks over. 'We're approaching the border, Rowena, get your passport ready.'

She doesn't remember him ever speaking her name before – it

rolled softly from his mouth in his thick Egyptian accent, a contrast to how her mother wielded it.

'What do I say to the Border Guard?' she asks.

'Nothing, let me do all the talking. I'm the one who's secured the job contracts, and the one with the qualifications and licence, you're simply my assistant.'

'Whatever.'

Rowena's never been this close to a checkpoint before. The tarmac is confettied with gum and cigarette butts, and above them the Liberty Jack snaps in the wind next to two county flags heralding the one they're leaving and the one they're about to enter. To the right are hitching posts for horses and a low concrete building with horizontal slits for windows. The arrow pointing towards it calls it a 'Processing Unit' but it looks like a cell block. A few feet away a leathery-skinned man in a torn, knee-length duffle coat holds up a sign and eyes Rowena hopefully: 'Will work hard' it says in slanting black letters.

The truck shudders over rumble-strips and comes to a rest at the white line, on top of a giant pressure pad that throws red numbers to a monitor in the Guards' booth. A large, top-lit sign shouts orders at them:

PLEASE HAVE YOUR PASSPORT READY
AND REMOVE ANY HELMET OR ITEM OF
CLOTHING THAT COVERS THE FACE.

YOU MUST DECLARE ANY EXTRA CARGO
THAT IS NOT LISTED IN YOUR E-PROFILE
BEFORE CROSSING THE BORDER.

BORDER STAFF ARE LEGALLY PERMITTED
TO CONDUCT SCANS AND SEARCHES OF
YOUR VEHICLE. YOU MUST COMPLY.

Rowena gapes at the huge reinforced fence, striking far out into the distance like a silver blade cleaving the land in two. She remembers hearing that some landowners who can't afford professional fencing dig cavernous ditches instead and stick them through with broken glass or spikes, like sharp-toothed mouths.

She whistles. 'They really don't want us in there, do they?'

'They do if we have something to offer,' Halim says.

There was plenty of work in construction, land registry and surveillance in the early years of the Split, when county borders were made hard and had to be monitored for access – so much so that people thought the economy might withstand being cut off from the Continent. Yet as fast as these geological surgeons could add their steel scars to the map, more bits of land were dropping into the sea or being flooded beyond salvation.

Halim clicks off the engine, lowers the window and reaches across Rowena's knees, making her shift away as he hooks his passport from the glove compartment.

The man in the booth narrows his eyes as he's handed it, possibly surprised that it's in the Kingdom's colours. The Guard licks his fingers and turns each page, poring over the stamps, taking his time before actually scanning the chip. The other Border Guard ignores them, his balding head bent over a newspaper. Rowena notices the headline: 'Expect More Carving as Sea Levels Rise'. How long before we're all pushed further inland, piled on top of each other like pigs in the back of Halim's truck? she wonders.

'This vehicle is registered to a Mr Halim Hosny?'

'Yes, that's me,' Halim replies.

'And you've secured work in Wellshire.'

'Yes. It should come up on your system.'

The Guard sucks his teeth.

Rowena can sense Halim's body tense next to her.

'I'm part of the Seasonal Agricultural Workers' Scheme,' he says in a monotone. 'I've secured work with Mr J. Shand, and also Swanleigh Farm. Here are the references.' Halim holds up his phone for the man to see – one of the fancy smartphones, nothing like Rowena's vintage handset.

'Hmm. And so is this ...' the man leans forward, the computer sheen highlighting the pores in his face, '... Miss Rowena Murray?'

Rowena passes Halim her passport and sits on her hands, trying not to look shifty as the Guard scrutinises first it and then her.

'Miss Murray, do you confirm that you're working for this man under your own free will?'

Halim frowns. 'What's that supposed to mean?'

The Guard raises his hands as if Halim – through two sheets of glass and metal – were somehow a threat. The other Guard looks up from his paper.

'These are standard questions, sir, we've had a lot of child trafficking for cheap labour in these parts, a lot of Land Boys and Girls coming from—'

'I'm not a child!' Rowena yelps, making Halim flinch as she leans over him. 'If anything he's working for me, for my family. Jesus, what's your problem?'

Halim darts her a look but she stays where she is.

The Guard purses his lips and hands back their passports before pressing a button to turn the light green and raise the barrier. Halim starts the engine and the truck lurches away.

'Twat,' Rowena mutters. She sticks two fingers up at the security camera as they pass.

'You need to let me do the talking,' Halim growls once they've sloshed through the wheel-wash and passed the 'Welcome to Wellshire' sign, its 'Twinned with' part scrubbed out.

'*Child* trafficking?' Rowena sneers. 'I'm seventeen!'

'If you want to be treated like an adult you should start acting like one. I can't have you insult officials and risk my permit. If I lose my travel privileges, I lose my income and my truck, do you understand?'

She glares at him, puts bite in her voice: 'I might not know as many fancy words as you but I know how to speak to small-minded button-pushers like that. I know my way around those kind of people, I grew up with a bunch of them.'

'You sound almost nostalgic.'

Rowena curls her lip and turns away.

Halim flicks on the headlights in the yellowing dusk and turns the world into an etching. The truck bumps over something, throwing them both into the air, and he brakes hard.

'What the hell was that?' Rowena asks, a steadying hand on the dashboard.

They climb out of the cab to find a hare lying broken in the road, its hind leg in spasm, its domed eye flashing orange from the hazard lights.

It's another sign, Rowena thinks with a shudder. Coldness slides over her and the shadows become elastic – reaching out from the branches and thickets, creeping closer in the periphery of her vision.

'It's in pain,' Halim mutters. 'Step back.'

Rowena silently counts the number of times the hare's leg kicks out in spasm – one, two, three ... Her mother always said to pay attention to these things ... Seven, eight, nine. A beeping makes her look up – the truck is in reverse and heading towards her. She jumps back into the nettles.

The wheels crunch over the hare again, finishing the job they started. Rowena walks over and stares down at the mess left behind. The hare's body is split wide, a rib spikes through soft fur as if it were the dagger that tore open the rest of it, spilling its steaming guts onto the road and exposing the clutch of pink-jellied leverets she was carrying. Rowena watches the hare's silk-white belly turn crimson with blood. She crouches, grazes her fingers across the glistening tarmac. 'I'm sorry,' she whispers, as her own belly becomes wracked by sobs that rattle through her spine. She doesn't know why she's crying – she's handled and skinned countless animals before – but she can't stop.

Halim sounds the horn and calls out the window. 'Are you coming?'

Thirteen, she thinks as she takes her seat and slams the door. Her leg kicked thirteen times.

'I thought you were about to kneel down and skin it,' Halim sniffs as the truck pulls away.

Rowena keeps her tear-stained face away from him and levels her voice. 'You should never skin a hare, everyone knows that.'

The TV light glints off Rowena's pale eyes as she lies across the hotel bed with its too-tight bedding and takes another bite of burger. She nods to the tiny bathroom in the corner.

Halim clenches his washbag, heads inside and checks the lock twice. He leans over the sink and takes a few synchronised breaths with the guy in the mirror. A year and a half has changed the city boy, he thinks, roughed him up a little – but he's still not the *right*

Halim. Underneath the grime and stubble, the forearms tanned from driving, he's just a soft fruit with no stone, at risk of splitting and spoiling. I'll give it a bit longer, he thinks, I've come this far.

He unpicks his laces, places each sock in its corresponding boot, peels off his cable-knit jumper, jeans, boxers, the T-shirt that used to be a crisp white. He unclips the chain from around his neck and runs his thumb over the nine-carat-gold disc that was destined for the collar of a dog that never was. Then he sets the shower going, blasts away the stray pube in the corner and steps into the flimsy cubicle, letting the water press his eyelids shut. He stands there for a few minutes, steaming up the glass, feeling his skin breathe, the extractor fan purring in his ears. Then he unwraps the hotel soap, lathers his hands and reaches down to stroke himself.

The bathroom mirror whines as Halim swipes away condensation and leans closer to guide the razor across the contour of his jaw.

There's a knock. 'You done wanking off in there? I need a piss.'

He winces as the blade catches, his face turning almost as red as the blood dripping onto the porcelain.

When he opens the door Rowena is standing right there, an empty sort of look on her face. 'Thank you for letting me use your bathroom,' he says, nudging the damp hair from his forehead.

She ignores him, heads past and locks the door.

'Okay, well, I'll be in my truck.' The tap gushes inside. 'See you in the morning.'

As he turns to leave, Halim's phone rings: an international number. His mother, choosing to ignore the time difference again. He can't face her – and knows what she'll say – so he lets it ring out. His eyes catch on the soft dent Rowena's body left in the bed-spread, and then wander over to the three Tarot cards laid out on the formica side-table; grim images of a stabbed man, someone crying into their hands, and Death riding a white horse. He's never considered himself a superstitious man, yet for some reason there's a bad feeling scratching at his bones.

4

———

BACKSTABBING. TORMENT. DEATH. Rowena bites the inside of her cheek as she looks down at the three Tarot cards still lying there on their silk square, tainted by the TV light as Botoxed bikini girls spit curses at each other over her shoulder. Her mind races: it's a warning, like the shadow I saw at the edge of Pickbury, the hare that we killed ... Something's close, watching, waiting for me to screw up again. Is it the one who cursed me, or the curse itself? Maybe It wants *me* this time?

She perches on the edge of the bed, knocks on the table three times and turns over another card from the deck, hoping for some kind of consolation. A prickle shoots up her spine, followed by a hot flood of adrenaline. Death. *Again?* She shakes her head, rubs her eyes and turns over another: Death, the skeleton rider. She throws the silk over the cards with a quivering hand and they scatter to the floor. Were there really two too many? She doesn't linger to find out – without looking, she can sense something crossing the room, a distortion in the air. 'Halim?' Her voice catches: she knows it's not him. There's a grey flicker behind her in the full-length mirror, and now the beige walls are closing in and her mouth seems filled with woodsmoke, making her gag. She leaps up, pressing one fist to her chest as if that might stop the pounding as she reaches for the door handle and fumbles it with sweat-slick fingers. Behind her the TV blinks and then cuts out, leaving the room dark and silent. Silent, but not empty.

Rowena sits barefoot on the low wall outside the hotel, waiting for her breath to steady. A witch mark is scratched into the brick pillar next to her, shaped like the swirl of a marble. A failed attempt to ward off bad spirits and evildoers, she thinks, gripping her rabbit's foot tight. Who would have cursed a baby? And why me? She presses her thumb on the leathery paw-pad and looks up at the pinprick of stars, wondering if her gran is as good a healer as Tessa claims. When she looks back down she catches Halim's eyes from the cab of the truck where he's sat reading. He goes back to his book. Rowena shivers, pulls her cardigan tighter across her thin floral summer dress and slips off the wall.

'Shit!' Halim jumps when she taps on the window. He leans over, opens the door and Rowena climbs into the passenger seat. They sit there for a while in silence.

'Bad dream?' he asks, his question tinged with sarcasm.

'I left my boots in the room.'

Halim shrugs. 'From what I've seen, you like running around with no shoes on.'

Rowena looks over at the hotel – a converted old town house with a modern extension stuck onto it like a concrete barnacle, sucking out all the charm. 'Still can't believe you sleep in this poky truck most nights.'

'It's free, and – usually – it's private.'

'Sorry, but I can't sleep in that room, it reeks of cheap fucks and hairspray,' Rowena says, too embarrassed to tell him how scared she is to go back in there.

Halim clears his throat. 'Okay. Well, if you don't want it I'll have it – no point wasting the booking.'

'What? But I thought you'd ...'

He holds out his hand for the key.

Rowena frowns at him. 'I paid for it!'

'Are you going to use it then?'

She bites her lip, places the key in his palm and grasps the sleeve of his expensive-looking sweatshirt: she wants to ask him to stay, to tell him that she doesn't want to be alone – but he might take it the wrong way and that would be worse. 'Can you get my stuff, please?' she asks instead.

He must see something in her face because rather than protest he gives a quick nod and heads for the hotel.

Rowena puffs out her cheeks and sinks low in the seat. She looks around the cab. A half-eaten banana – a luxury import – lies discarded on the dashboard between a cup of something that smells and looks like pond-water and a book, *A Complete Woodworker's Manual*, canyoned up its spine from heavy use. Turquoise beads are looped around the driver's headrest, a striking contrast to the sea of grey-and-black plastic and metal. She exhales over the window and draws a large eye on the glass.

A while later, Halim opens the cab door and drops Rowena's boots and backpack onto the seat. 'If you pull this lever the seats recline all the way back, there are curtains on the side windows, an eye mask if you want it and blankets underneath. Don't run the battery down and remember: no smoking.' He grabs a few of his things, eyes her sidelong, then clicks open the glove compartment to swipe its contents into his bag.

Rowena tuts.

Crossing the tarmac, he looks back once and then melts into the gloom of the lobby. Rowena turns the rear-view mirror and wing mirrors as far out as they can go, in the hope that they'll reflect any negative energy, and then draws the curtains so that she can't see the jagged elbows and arms of the trees. As she reaches over to click on the radio her toes brush against something in the footwell. A square of white. She picks it up and turns it over. It's a photo of Halim as a boy with what must be his parents: a handsome duo looking stiffly at the camera, Dad with his hand on Halim's little shoulder, Mum trying out a smile. It looks like an evening do, full of twinkling lights and starched tablecloths, the sort of special-occasion photo you'd stick in a frame above the sofa. With a stab, Rowena feels the absence of her own photos. They were considered an extravagance in her family, reserved for births and weddings, and they had none of those in seventeen years. The only non-practical thing that hung on the wall of the bungalow was a small painting of the Murray family farm in Culcrith, amateurish in its brushstrokes, though probably accurate in its ruggedness, according to Tessa's descriptions. It always struck her as strange that her parents never bothered decorating the bungalow; it felt like a featureless stone shell, a practical temporary shelter and nothing more. Her mind turns to the pig heart she wedged up the chimney when she was eight, stuck through with pins – a protection against all the bad omens that Tessa kept finding and attributing to her daughter. It must be a shrivelled-up fist by now, Rowena thinks. She turns up the radio, grabs all the blankets and cocoons herself against the long hours of night that lie ahead. At 4.40 a.m. she finds herself rifling through the tourist leaflets in the enclosed porch of the hotel, a cigarette hanging from her lips.

'I want to go here,' Rowena says, waving a leaflet at Halim as he clicks in his seat belt and lowers the shade against the morning sun.

He looks over at the crude collage of a child's hand holding an ice cream, a deckchair and a family silhouetted at sunset and shakes his head. 'You've got a job fruit picking at Swanleigh Farm while I make a delivery.'

Rowena twists her mouth. 'See, thing is, I've never been on a road trip, so I don't wanna spend my time working, unless I *really* have to, and you've totally got it covered with your pig humping or whatever it is you do.'

'It was your mother's idea,' he says, starting up the engine. 'You'll need to earn your keep. I'll pick you up at Swanleigh in three days.'

'No, you won't, because I'll be here,' she taps the photo of the beach. 'So when you're done with your delivery you can collect me from one of these seaside hotels.' She scribbles on the leaflet and thrusts it under his nose. 'Here's my number. It's not a smartphone like yours, but I've got credit.'

'There will be some contracts that require the two of us, and I expect you to pull your weight.' Halim's dark-brown eyes narrow as he slams the handbrake down. 'And I'm not covering your hotel bills so you'd better have the money.'

'I appreciate your heartfelt concern, but don't worry about me, I can look after myself. Have done for years.'

He huffs.

She holds the leaflet steady.

He takes it, throws it on the dash and then backs them out of the parking bay. 'I'll text you my number. The minute you check in let me know where you are. No running off – do you promise?'

'Why would I run anywhere when I've got a chauffeur?' she smiles. 'Besides, they say the sea air is healing and that.' Her voice trails off as she loses herself in the strange new world sliding past the window, and tries to push the dregs of fear down below her gut, as far from her brain as possible. 'Can we stop at a café?'

'Didn't you eat at the hotel?'

'Food looked shit,' she replies, knowing that she didn't want to set foot inside that place.

Halim sighs. 'I'm not getting paid enough for this.'

Blue neon announces the Haven Café & Fuel Station, one of those old petrol stations that had to diversify when the Split inflated the cost of vehicles and the liquid gold that kept them moving. Other weather-worn signs screwed to the wall promise a warm welcome, a postal point, Wi-Fi, fresh coffee, home-baking and local ingredients – as if the latter were a treat as opposed to a necessity. When Rowena steps outside she stretches and drinks in this fresh new air – sweet relief from the musk of animals and Halim. It makes her realise how much Pickbury has been suffocating her: how the hills she grew up with seemed to crowd in on her as she got older, and the sky formed a lid; how the well-worn tracks were all pinched and narrow, like the faces at the windows. Like her mother's face.

She rolls her shoulders back and follows Halim into the café.

Four men with blacked-up faces, in black outfits with knee-length socks and sashes, sit at one of the tables, their blue-and-white feathered caps perched next to a scattering of teacups. She notices Halim scowling at them. They notice too – their eyes like hard, white cue balls.

'They're Nutters,' she whispers, 'part of the annual Nutter Dance. You always see them out and about in late April.'

'They're fucked up is what they are,' he says a little too loudly.

'It's just an ancient tradition. The costume's supposed to hide their identity from the bad spirits they're driving away.'

'Oh, like how racist scum hide behind pointy white hoods with eye holes?' Halim shakes his head and makes for the service counter.

Rowena doesn't know what to say, so she starts picking up a rainbow of chocolate bars, then adds a packet of salt-and-pepper Bear Claws to the pile she's making on the counter.

Halim raises an eyebrow. 'That's your breakfast?'

She drops a packet of breath-mints onto the heap. 'For you,' she says.

'That everything?' the shop assistant asks. The book he's laid flat shows a scantily clad girl on the cover, too busy simpering at the hero to notice there's a dragon right behind her.

'A coffee too please, black,' Halim sets down his thermal cup.

The guy pours the filmy liquid. 'Sweetener's over there,' he says, looking directly at Rowena, while pointing elsewhere.

She rolls her eyes.

'What's the traffic like today?' Halim asks.

Rowena's heard about this from the farmhands back home – there's never any real 'traffic', not these days, it's driver code for asking where the easiest border crossing is, or if there's a stop-and-search ahead.

'Pretty good. Avoid the A-road heading west from four p.m.'

'He's paying,' Rowena announces as she scoops up her snacks.

'The local Lord needs foundation diggers – are you and your girl looking for work?' the guy asks.

Halim swears as he burns himself trying to fix the lid on his cup. 'She's not my girl.'

The shop assistant calls out after Rowena as she heads for the door. 'You'll get fat eating all those chocolates, sweetheart!'

She flips him her middle finger.

'Do you usually eat that much sugar?' Halim asks as he catches her up. 'Do you get tired easily, or weak or dizzy? If you have a condition you should let me know.'

She shrugs as she chomps down on a Bubbly Bar. 'Why? You're no white-coat.'

'White-coat?'

'Doctor – you know, the ones who rip us off with their overpriced medicine?'

Halim frowns. 'The cost of medicine isn't their fault, and no, I'm not a doctor but I did study biology and took a course in animal husbandry so—'

'I'm just a pig or a cow to you, aren't I?'

'Don't think so highly of yourself,' mumbles Halim as he unlocks the truck.

Rowena notices the crumb trail down her front and brushes it off.

'What now?' he asks, as she stomps back towards the café.

'I need to change my tampon,' she yells over her shoulder.

As Halim drives off down the coastal road, Rowena enjoys the salty tang that teases sea. She takes a quick inventory by patting down her pockets: phone, lighter … Hesitates, checks her jacket, rifles through her backpack, unzipping everything.

'That sneaky fucker!' She looks past the sand dunes to where the truck disappeared. Halim's taken her passport. He must have lifted it when she left her things in the hotel room, a guarantee that she wouldn't ditch him and run away.

She re-packs and heads for a little gift shop, its window filled with rainbow wind-spinners and witch bottles. Rowena makes a beeline for the drinks fridge, selects a local sparkling wine, grabs a map of the Kingdom and, as an afterthought, a blue-and-yellow stick of rock with 'YOLO' written through its centre. After placing her things on the glass counter she fumbles in her backpack, unscrews the urn that holds her pa's ashes and – to the horror of the woman at the till – pulls her money stash out of it. Shaking a note from the plastic pouch, Rowena hands it to her and smiles.

The sand feels incredible between her toes as Rowena strolls towards the waves, her heart skipping at the hushing sound, at the kiss of sun on her face, the breeze stroking her goose-bumped skin. A vague memory comes to her of a red bucket and spade, her parents backlit by the sun, but it could have easily been something she'd pieced together from hotel leaflets, nothing but a patchwork of stock images. It's pre-season so it's only her and a couple of dog walkers. She swigs from the wine bottle, belches, and then drops her pack to run into the water. The sea-sculpted bumps of sand massage the soles of her feet as she pushes through the cold surf. Seaweed slathers around her ankles and her hastily rolled-up jeans drink in the spray. This is what it means to be alive, she thinks, her senses firing. If my curse means that Death is now coming for me, I need more moments just like this, I have to collect them and hold them close. She takes another swig, the wine's too fizzy to drink quickly but she tries – waiting for the bubbles to hit her brain and soften the worry from her brow. When her feet go numb she relents and heads towards the shelter of the cliff, collecting the prettiest pebbles and shells along the way to make charms for selling later.

'Watch out for them rock falls.'

Rowena's pulled out of her trance by the old man who's sat himself on a flat rock a few feet away and is busy lighting a pipe, his creased hand cupping the flame. He flicks the spent match onto the sand. 'I'n't the best place for a nap,' he says with a pleasing West Country drawl.

Rowena cranes her neck to look up at the cliff towering above. I dare you, she thinks, I dare you to end me right now.

Nothing happens.

'If I'm gonna die this is as good a place as any,' she sniffs.

The old man chuckles out a cloud of smoke. 'I'd say it's a better place than most.'

He's right, she thinks, this place is beautiful: untamed and ever-changing, not stagnant or fenced in. She watches the gulls scrying for their next meal in great wheeling circles.

The old man puffs away, his cheeks hollowing and filling like sails. 'Besides,' he says, 'we're all dying sure enough. The minute you're born, you're dying.'

Rowena pictures her Tarot cards again, imagines herself kneeling under the white horse's hooves begging to be saved – and then she's the rider, carrying the black flag in her skeletal fist. 'Yeah, but some get there quicker than others,' she says with a shiver. 'Some are pushed towards death.'

The old man raises his bushy grey brows but keeps his face to the sea. 'If you're ill, we got a healer in the village, you need to ask at the Bosun's Locker – pub at the top of the high street yonder. Bet he'd be glad of the business to be honest, not much else going on round here.'

'I don't think he can help me, but thanks anyway.'

The old man wipes his rheumy eyes as he turns towards her. 'Don't s'pose you want to buy some cockles, do you? Crab claws maybe? They're nice and fresh.'

Rowena shakes her head.

He smacks his lips and turns back to the blue-grey horizon.

'Are you a fisherman?' she asks.

'Was. More a shore-trawler now.'

'What's the Continent like?'

'Never made it that far, kept to Kingdom waters like we're told. These days most of the boats are used for sightseeing, or border patrols, no big catch around these parts.'

Rowena pulls her jacket tighter and downs the dregs from the bottle.

The old man watches her unfold the map and lay it across her lap like a blanket. 'Nowhere for you to run to,' he says, knocking his pipe on the rock to empty the bowl. 'Each place is much like the other – folk busting their bones to make ends meet, fighting over land like dogs over scraps.'

'There's always the Wilderness,' she shrugs, pointing to the space on the flipside of her map – not important enough to be drawn in properly, just a thin web of lines, a ghosting of place names, too far north for anyone to care about.

A gull screeches overhead.

'Well, if you can rest your head there you're a braver soul than I.' The old man gets up and cracks his spine. 'Good luck to you, young lady, may the road rise up to meet you.' He doffs an imaginary cap at her and ambles up the zigzag path.

Rowena stares at the Wilderness scratched on paper, then out at the wilderness scratched in salt water.

5

29 April

———

HALIM FOLLOWS THE VOICES TOWARDS the cowshed, a jumble of corrugated iron and rotting timber. Two men are leaning on the gate as a third hoses down the concrete. They stop their conversation and look at him.

'Halim Hosny, livestock driver. I'm looking for Mr Shand.'

'You found him,' says the tall, white-haired one.

Halim offers his hand but Shand doesn't take it. The other man watches, his arms still slung over the gate as the hose hisses in the background. Halim takes out his passport and job sheet. 'I'm booked for two days, Saltmere to Crincey. Sorry I'm late.'

'Traffic bad, was it?' Shand asks.

The man next to him chuckles.

'Job's changed, just a day run now, to take some parts up to Clatworth for us.'

'But the agreement was for three days, that's what I came all the way to Wellshire for.'

The men remain silent.

'I'm a Class One driver trained in animal handling Level Two,' Halim continues, 'and I took the SHAD assessment end of last year – I can send you my CV again if you want to check—'

'Job's changed, boy, that's the nature of farming. Do you want the work or not?'

Halim gives a sharp nod.

Shand points to the younger man with the hose, a skinny thing with lank hair, all knees and elbows. 'Joe here'll help you load the gear and give you the address, everything's stored up in the barn.' He signs the job sheet. 'Seventy quid should cover it.'

It wasn't a question: Shand's already stuffed a few crumpled notes inside Halim's passport and placed the documents on the moss-covered wall between them.

Pick your battles, Halim tells himself, it's only seventy but it helps, and maybe I can eke out the fuel. He follows Joe up the track, and when he looks back Shand's leaning on the gate again, but the other man is scattering what looks like salt in the area by the wall – the exact spot where Halim had just been standing. Halim's neck bristles as he grinds his teeth. He takes his anger out on the grain sieves and combine belts as he hefts and slings them onto the tarp in the back of his truck.

When he's well away from the farm Halim slams the horn, sending a shock of sparrows into the air from the hedge hugging the road. He hits it again. And again and again – jolting his bones all the way up to his shoulder until, breathing hard, he pulls over and stops. He reaches behind his ear to the turquoise worry-beads wrapped around the headrest – the ones his grandmother used to rub between finger and thumb as she'd indulge his stories, his dreams, his rants and ramblings, only stopping him long enough to drop a nugget of advice, scold him or push another bowl of koshari his way. 'You chose this bullshit,' he says to his thin reflection in the windscreen, 'so rise above them and get on with it.'

A blackbird lands in the scrub on the steep bank next to the window, a maggot unfurling from its yellow beak. The bird snaps once and the maggot is gone.

Halim sighs, retrieves his notebook from the glove compartment. The numbers don't look good: he'll struggle to make this month's instalment on the truck and incur a government fine – they won't make an extension this time. He slaps the pages shut and stares out of the window, pinching the bridge of his nose, and then checks his phone: still nothing from Rowena. He calls her but it rings out.

'*Khara!*'

As he dials his voicemail something unpleasant squirms inside his chest. He sits back and waits for his mother's voice. She's speaking Arabic – something she only does when Halim's father's not around, since he's of the opinion that English is the language of refinement and business.

'Halim,' she says, 'where are you now?' A pause. A TV murmurs in the background. 'I hate talking to these machines, it's like I'm talking to your father,' she sighs. 'He's discovered t'ai chi and it works wonders for his temper – if you wanted to reach out, now would be a good time. Are you okay for money?' There's the sound of a glass being put down. 'Please don't embarrass us, you've made your point, *habibi!*' She only calls him that when she wants him to do something, usually something to placate his father and make her life easier. 'You must come home now, you turn twenty-one soon and you know what that means. He won't change his mind. Well … you know how to reach me.' The message ends.

If he loses the money from Rowena's delivery too, that'll tip the scales – he might as well book a flight and slink back to his parents, tail between his legs, apologies in his mouth. He'd have to look up at his father's pointed face and praise his wisdom and benevolence, admit that driving a truck around a broken Kingdom was no life for a young man of his upbringing, and once again take up the manicured path his parents have paid others to cultivate for him. It would be easy to give up on these parochial people and seek the comfort of money, he thinks – but too hard to confess that he's nothing without it.

'You can't bring that in here.' The barmaid nods to the strawberry ice cream dripping down Rowena's knuckles.

Rowena looks around at the dull, sticky furniture, the green-glass floats and crab pots threaded to the wall with cobwebs, and the ancient PC in the corner – a prerequisite of the pub licence so that locals can do their banking and book jobs. The barmaid waits.

'Fine,' Rowena says, upending the sloppy cone into an ashtray on the bar. 'I was told this town had a healer and that I should ask at the Bosun's.'

It's the barmaid's turn to look Rowena up and down. 'We used to have one but he died. Turns out he weren't as good a healer as we thought. Now can I get you anything, or have you just come here to make the place look messy?'

'Babe, you can't talk to customers like that.' A young man has abandoned his friends in the corner and taken up a stool next to Rowena.

'I'm not your babe, Griz, and in case you hadn't noticed I've a business to run.'

'Pint of Spindrift then, please.' Rowena holds her nerve, knowing that confidence gets results when you're under-age drinking. As the barmaid busies herself, Rowena unzips her backpack.

'I got this,' the man next to her says, sliding a note across the bar. He's wearing the usual pub camouflage: flannel shirt and jeans, fake Redwings, unshaven face. The whole look entirely forgettable.

'Thanks.' Rowena offers him a brief smile, turns away and unlocks her phone. There's another message from her mother, checking up on her. She thumbs a quick reply – 'All fine. Fruit picking. Hard work' – and hits send.

'So, you in town for business or pleasure?' the man asks over her shoulder.

Rowena rocks back on her heels and sniffs, coating her tongue in stale beer and damp carpet. 'I'm here to exchange money for drinks, so I suppose you'd call that business.' She digs her hand into the bowl of stale crisps on the bar and shoves some into her mouth.

A chill wind has picked up, cutting through some of the alcohol-fuzz in Rowena's head as she struggles to walk around the cordgrass and find the path through the saltmarsh as it fades in and out. She stumbles again and falls forward, her hand thumping into the spongy ground. The golden lights of her seaside hotel wink in the distance, but the sky has greyed so much it's taken the edges off everything, making the flat landscape blend upwards into nothing. And the nothing of it seeps into Rowena, empties her of all the joy she'd found earlier in the day at the beach. She's texted Halim, but is tempted to curl up here, among pillows of sea lavender, and sleep it off for a while …

A sound turns her head.

The grasses dance and whisper ... but there's something else moving there too. Imagining the worst, Rowena stands up and quickens her pace as she heads for the lights. Glancing behind, she sees that the flat lines have grown a shadowy hump, and the hump is moving closer, steady and unhurried.

She takes out her phone and dials Halim. He immediately picks up.

'I'm at the hotel and they say you haven't checked in,' he says. 'What the hell are you playing at?'

'Chill out, I'm just a few minutes away on the marsh path, it's full of ditches and lumps and stuff and one of the lumps is moving and it's taking ages to walk around—'

'What do you mean one of the lumps is moving?'

Rowena snorts. 'I dunno, I'm just drunk and – *ow!* Fuck it!'

'What was that, I heard a splash – are you okay?'

'My foot's wet.'

'I'm coming to get you.' He hangs up.

'Okay.'

Rowena climbs back up the knoll and It's waiting ... A shadow bound to no body, a too-tall figure made of darkened mist, its hands bleeding into feathers that flicker and move like static. The thing she saw in the road at the edge of Pickbury. The familiar seaweed smells turn acrid and her eyelids flutter as her mind races through sayings and superstitions. Has she strayed below the tideline? She looks down: no. When she looks up again the shadow-man has slunk closer and Its inky arms have spread outwards like the branches of a dead tree. The thing is faceless but she knows It's staring at her, keening in silence, singing of her death. She could let It take her, then she might join her pa and Drew – but her heart pounds against her ribcage: '*not now, not now, not now*'.

Not knowing what else to do, she grabs the rabbit foot from her pocket and holds it up, but the fur and flesh have rotted away and in her fingers is a beige husk with claws, stringy and withered like a dirty rag. She drops it. 'Who cursed me?' she hisses. 'Name yourself.' She knows there's power in a name, if only she could speak it and banish the shadow.

Something thin and cold tries to slip into her hand and grasp it.

She drops to her knees, scoops up seawater from a rivulet and flings it into the air: north then south, 'away, away', she yells. East then west, 'away, AWAY'. When the figure leans forward she shrugs her pack off her shoulders and gets ready to swing it.

'Hey! Easy now, it's only me – Griz. We met at the Bosun's, remember?'

Something more solid stands in front of her now, a flesh-made man, his hands raised up. Rowena's wild eyes dart around, her mouth forms words that never come.

'You really shouldn't be out this way on your own at night,' Griz says, 'it's dangerous if you don't know the lay of the land.'

He comes closer.

She blinks. It's definitely the guy from the pub. She wants to ask him if he saw the shadow-man too but her jaw is suddenly stiff.

'It's not uncommon for folk to get lost in these flats,' Griz continues. 'Only takes a moment for the sea haze to come in, mud sucking at your feet, holding you there for the tide to rise up and swallow you. Not a nice way to go. Not nice at all.'

'I'm okay,' she manages. 'I'm going to that hotel over there.'

'Are you now? 'Cause to me you seem a bit lost.' The bulk of Griz's body seems to grow.

She hears the crack of a shell under his boot.

'You know, I bought you a drink but I never did get your name.' He's close enough now that she can see his breath, slipping like ghosts from his smile.

Rowena's seen that look in a man before and doesn't like it. She touches the place on her hip where her hunting knife used to hang and is surprised to find the fur of her rabbit's foot jutting from her pocket – whole and soft again. She swallows, takes a few steps back, edging towards the sea.

Griz cocks his head. And watches. And waits.

When she trips, he's on her.

'Get off!' She tries to knee him in the balls, jabs her fingers at his sweaty face, but they can't find his eyes and instead she rakes his skin into her nails and leaves ragged red lines down his cheek. And then he's pinned her arms with his knees and his hand is over her mouth.

'Shhh! You're okay,' he whispers. 'I'm here now. I won't let you drown.'

The cold stings her skin now, piercing through the drunkenness, and the realisation of how little control she has terrifies her. She tries to bite his palm, writhes under his weight as he leans forward to sniff her hairline.

Then, to her relief, he jerks back – releasing her completely.

Rowena rolls over, heaves and vomits up a hot bile of crisps and beer.

Next to her there's a beast with two heads now, a twisting mass of limbs and muscle, exploding with guttural almost-words as it beats itself with moonlit fists again and again and again. The blur settles and she realises that it's Halim with his fist raised, and it's Griz breaking away, legs and arms bent over himself like a carapace. He's bleeding, his face mushed up like the marshy ground.

Good, she thinks, spitting into the dirt.

Griz staggers to his feet, his eyes bulging as he stumbles away. 'You'd better watch that one,' he says to her, a shaking finger directed at Halim. 'His smoke goes against the wind.'

Halim's still on his knees in the wiry grass, his body tensed, chest rising and falling. He yells. It's just a long, ragged sound but its meaning is clear enough.

Griz runs.

Rowena watches him go until he's nothing but a charcoal smudge in the distance. Her cracked lips taste of blood. She frantically picks at her fingers, tearing her own nails as she digs out Griz's skin from beneath them and washes him away in salt water.

'Thank you, Halim.'

He doesn't seem to hear her. He sits back on his heels and stares at his wet, red fists with a look that still sparks with anger.

6

HALIM WAVES HIS HAND in front of Rowena's stone-like face. 'Are you hurt? Can you hear me?'

She's a bundle at his feet, staring mutely at the sea mist lolling on the waves, now only a few metres away. His father warned him about Kingdom girls and their love of drugs and alcohol. At least she's breathing, he thinks, but her eyes are glazed over and he wonders if she's taken something. He runs through his animal-handling training, but it doesn't seem appropriate to stick his fingers down her gullet, so he takes her by the arms instead and guides her to her feet.

She leans her body into his as he picks a way across the marsh, avoiding the ruts and channels where the water laps and slathers. He tries to ignore the split skin and bruises across his fist as he thrusts out the torch beam from his phone. I could have carried on hitting him, Halim thinks, I *wanted* to. I could have killed him.

'Aren't we going to the Wilderness?' Rowena's voice is thin. 'If we leave now we can be there before dawn. It won't reach us there.'

He's heard people refer to the Wilderness before, as a faraway place where 'bad people go', something to threaten naughty children with. 'I'm taking you to your hotel. When my next contract kicks in we'll continue north,' he says, 'then you can go where the hell you want.'

'There's darkness here,' Rowena whispers, her sour breath grazing his cheek. 'It's all over you.'

Halim sighs and fights the urge to just leave her there. 'Look, Rowena, you've never been outside your home county so you don't realise what the world is like, what people out here are like. You need to be more careful.'

She snorts and taps her breastbone. 'They need to be careful of *me*. I'm the one they need to fear. I'm cursed.'

'Ya rab sabarni,' Halim mutters.

'Give me my passport and I'll be gone, I'll be someone else's problem.'

'Well, it's in the truck, which is parked outside the hotel.' Halim pulls Rowena on but she shrugs away.

'I'm fucking *sick* of people controlling me!' she spits, her eyes like cut glass. 'For the first time in my life I can breathe, I can do and say what I want – so just let me!' She claps her hands to punctuate her words, making the darkness seem to jump away with each snap. 'If I can't be fixed this is all there is – don't you get it? Aren't you meant to be the smart one?'

Halim can feel his pulse behind his ears, the blood still coursing with adrenaline from the fight. 'Honestly? I don't care what you do, as long as it doesn't jeopardise this contract I have with your mother: if I don't deliver you safely I don't get my money, and I'll not only lose my truck but the reputation and life I've spent years trying to build up despite being the outsider,' he says. 'So sort your shit out and face it: you're not cursed, your mum just doesn't want you around any more.'

Rowena's scowl drops. She stares at him, wipes her nose with the flat of her hand. 'You're worse than that beast who attacked me,' she says, striding off on unsteady legs.

Halim takes a breath and worries that maybe she's right. He follows, catches her as she stumbles over a knot of mud.

'Tessa sent me away to save me,' she slurs, jerking her arm back. 'She paid for all this even though we don't have much money. That's her own kind of love. But you wouldn't understand 'cause who have you got?'

A bat cuts through the mist, swerving Rowena's head, making her flinch. 'Just get me to Culcrith before something worse happens,' she mutters.

*

'You didn't have to stay in the room with me all night, but thanks,' Rowena says, stabbing her fork into the yolk and watching it spill gold across the plate.

'You asked me to,' Halim says, rolling his shoulders and cricking his neck.

'Did I?'

'And I wanted to make sure you didn't choke on your own vomit.'

'Nice,' she says, trying to swallow a chunk of hash brown. 'What you did for me out there on the marsh ... I can normally look after myself, you know, but my mind's been a bit all over the place lately, so ...' She draws a huge breath and glances around the café. 'I guess I appreciate you looking out for me.'

'I shouldn't have to.'

'I know. And I'm not asking you to.'

'I also had to lie to the woman at the desk and tell her that we were a couple, and that you were just tired from a long hike.'

'And I bet you found that harder than beating the shit out of someone,' Rowena mutters into her steaming tea. She takes a gulp. It burns her mouth and snakes a line of fire all the way to her gut. 'Don't tell me you've never been pissed before.'

'I've been many things before, but evidently I have a higher threshold than you. Young women should know their limits.'

Rowena spits out some tea as she laughs. 'Have you heard yourself?'

'I mean physiologically: women's bodies are built differently.'

'As if you'd know.' She notices Halim's cheeks flush, and smiles.

He shakes out a newspaper, creating a monochrome wall between them.

Something on the financial page catches Rowena's eye – a face she recognises from Halim's family photo. The caption reads 'Mr Ahmed Hosny, CEO of Messis International'. Huh, she thinks, leaning closer, seems like Halim's dad has his own company, something to do with pharmaceuticals.

Halim catches her reading and twists the paper around. When he sees the picture he tenses, folds it shut and tosses it onto an adjacent table.

Rowena turns her attention to the large window next to them.

Through the condensation the grey waves are rolling in, sending her mind back over what Halim said about her last night – the words that struck out through the drunken fog like a lighthouse beam. 'You know, my mother might not show love the way you soft city types do,' she says, adding her breath to the glass, 'but this is her way.'

Halim sips his coffee.

'And although I was mostly home-schooled I do have friends. Some folks cared for me.'

Halim crunches down on his toast.

The waves fold in and slide away.

'We used to have moots in the woods next to Robin Hill. That's where I met Drew, my kind-of boyfriend. It was after the Beltane party, almost a year ago, that they found him at the bottom of Steep-side, tangled up in a barbed-wire fence. He'd broken his ribs in the fall and one had punctured his lung. They say he must have struggled there for hours before giving up. Probably drowned in his own blood.'

She catches Halim's gaze and holds it.

'They didn't find him for two days,' she continues, 'so the crows got to his body first. My mate Rags told me that Drew was on one that night and he'd taken something. But we'd had an argument and I'd gone home so I wasn't there when ... I wasn't looking out for him.' Rowena's voice trails off. She adds more sugar to her tea and scrapes the spoon around the bottom of the cup. Really, she thinks, it wasn't the fall or the crows that got him, it was my curse. It all seems so clear to me now.

The waitress appears next to them, places an egg on the table – shell and all – and raises an eyebrow. 'Now, you sure we can't cook this for you, love?'

Rowena smiles up at her. 'Nah, this is fine, thanks.'

The waitress shrugs and heads back to the kitchen.

Rowena takes up the egg and cracks it over her glass of water, being careful to keep the yolk back as the white slides in.

'Do I even want to know what you're doing?' Halim asks.

She takes a breath, studies the wisps and swirls in the water, holds the glass up to the light. 'I'm trying to see the face of the one who cursed me.'

'You don't really believe you're cursed, do you?'

36

'I didn't at first, but then my pa dropped dead right in front of me, barely a year after Drew died.'

They get looks from nearby diners.

Halim winces and puts his toast down.

Rowena peers through the bottom of the glass, spilling a little as she tilts it to study the viscous mess within. She tries closing one eye, tries squinting. Nothing. She puts the glass down and slumps in the plastic chair.

Tired of waiting for Halim to finish his breakfast, she digs out some half-made poppets from her bag and starts weaving the straw into shapes – anything to hide the shake in her hands. Her nails are still pink and sore from where she tore at them after scratching Griz's face. As she twists the straw her mind runs through all the other ways she could have hurt him, each one darker than the last.

After a while Halim's curiosity gets the better of him and he breaks the silence. 'What are the dolls for?'

She doesn't look up. 'They're love tokens I'm gonna sell. Someone else might as well get some joy around here.'

'Isn't this all just nonsense for gullible people? Don't you ever stop to think you're taking advantage of someone's vulnerability?'

'Would you say the same about folk who accept the wafer as flesh and the wine as blood?' Rowena threads in some of the shells she collected from the beach. 'Our ways were around long before any of these organised religions, and there's practical sense in the way we draw strength and energy from the land. Besides, everyone – even you – believes in something, and if you believe in something hard enough it becomes real. *Powerful.* That's true magic.'

Halim doesn't look convinced.

Rowena puts down the poppet, pushes the dirty crockery to one side and fetches something from her bag. On the table in front of her she lays out the photo of Halim as a young boy with his parents.

He sits up. 'Where did you get that?'

'It fell out of the glove compartment. I was gonna use it to bargain with, in exchange for my passport,' she says, smoothing the corners of the glossy image.

'Give it back.'

'I will – but first I'll speak a spell over it.' She holds up a fork and mouths some silent words.

'What are you doing?'

She stares at him as her mouth continues working. She moves the fork over the photo so that it hovers above his mother's image.

Halim tries to snatch the picture back but she bats him away and sucks in a deep breath. 'Question is – should I pierce her head?' The silver prongs touch the photo, dimpling it. 'Or her heart?'

'Stop it. *Now*.' Halim bares his teeth like a wolf.

She presses the fork there a moment longer before letting it drop and sliding the photo across the table towards him.

'Chill out, Halim, it's just nonsense,' she smiles.

7

30 April

———

ROWENA STANDS ASIDE, WATCHING HALIM and the farmhand drive the pigs up the metal ramp and into the container on the back of his truck, bound for the slaughterhouse. Must be nice to be oblivious to your own death, she thinks, watching the beasts nod and shuffle and grunt. With each passing day she's tried to ignore the sense that the curse's grip is getting tighter – 'taking root' or 'settling' her mother said, like a virus, or a cancer being sucked into her marrow. She looks at the pigs, snout-to-arse, a pink mass of fat and flesh, and shudders as she remembers Griz's bulk above her, his breath huffing at her face.

When the pigs are loaded, Rowena stubs out her cigarette on the wall and climbs into the cab next to Halim.

'The slaughterhouse is across the border in Somerton,' he says, 'just outside of St Cross. Should only take an hour or so.'

'It's the thirtieth of April,' she says. 'Do you know what that means?'

Halim shrugs as the truck pulls away.

'May Day Eve. It means there'll be some fun to be had somewhere.'

'Look, I know you've been through a tough time recently, what with your dad ... passing, but don't you think you've had enough fun for a while?'

'You think getting attacked by a stranger is *fun*?' she frowns. 'Boarding school must have really screwed you up.'

'All I'm saying is perhaps it's time to slow down and take stock.' He fixes her with a level gaze, his unblinking eyes deepened by long black lashes and thick, dark brows.

'I'll slow down when I'm dead,' Rowena says, looking away.

They overtake two young girls on horseback, swigging from plastic bottles. The girls smile at Rowena as they slide past her window, but as the late-morning sun flickers through leaves, it tweaks their faces and for a moment their smiles turn to wide, toothy snarls. Rowena twists around in her seat but loses them behind the bulk of the truck – instead, through the narrow window into the container, she sees rows of little pink heads nodding in time with the rise and fall of the road. Shaken, she lowers the passenger window for air. Her reflection in the wing mirror is dissected by a spiderweb that shudders and comes unstuck as the truck picks up speed, moves to a slip road, and then onto a near-deserted motorway.

When Halim meets Rowena outside the B&B that evening she's wearing a short flowery dress with a mustard cardigan and her dirty brown boots, their soles worn down on their outside edges. Her red-gold hair hangs down her back in one thick braid and her cheeks and lips look as flushed as the evening sky. Unable to reach the comfort of the chain around his neck, Halim tweaks the collar of his shirt. He hasn't spent much time around women outside of the occasional wine-bar fling, and his boarding school was single sex, so Rowena holds a strange fascination – a creature to be studied. A thing to be wary of.

She gives him a cursory glance. 'Come on, let's go.' She walks ahead with her cutters, stopping to snip at blossoming hedges or at flowers in front gardens, dropping the clippings into a drawstring bag. After the third house, Halim gives up trying to dissuade her.

'It's for May crowns,' she insists, 'every Beltane celebration needs them. They're worth good coin, you'll see.'

When they reach the Black Rabbit in St Cross it's already busy, full of noise, bustle and body heat, the herby smell of home-made gravy and the tang of hops. They order pie and mash and take a small, rickety table in the corner. It feels strange to be around this many people after so long and Halim's not sure if he's okay with the proximity to others. As he sips his berry tonic, Rowena starts threading her stolen blooms into the hoops of willow she's brought with her, her nimble fingers combining pale blossoms and gold flowers, creating a froth of colour like the yolk and white of an egg. Voices pipe up near the bar, singing something about the turn of the wheel.

When their food arrives Rowena digs in, but Halim gets lost in a new song, and watches the glowing faces of its singers, fascinated by the easy camaraderie of young and old alike. He picks over the meat and rakes his fork through minted peas as he follows the cadence of the melody and the unfussy lyrics ...

'You gonna eat that?' Rowena points at the chunk of pie left on Halim's plate as he gets up.

He shakes his head. 'It's getting stuffy in here, I'm going out to get some air.'

Rowena shrugs and drags his plate towards her.

Halim sits on a low flint wall in the pub garden and looks out over the meadow beyond the fence where two large stacks of wood, about ten metres apart, wait to be lit. A few locals stand around the stacks, chatting and laughing. The sky has deepened to indigo and the lights from the pub cast bronze rectangles onto the lawn. There's a fizz nearby: some kids have lit sparklers and he watches them draw rune-like shapes in the air, giggling as the sparks shoot like stars to land at their feet.

None of it moves him.

It should – he knows that. Perhaps by now I've seen too much of the bad in people to be able to appreciate the good? he wonders. Or perhaps I'm not looking hard enough?

Rowena appears and sits next to him on the wall, making him shuffle up. 'I'm surprised you came, to be honest,' she says. 'I didn't think Beltane was your kind of thing.'

'It isn't, I'm just here to make sure you don't get into any more scrapes.'

Rowena sniffs. 'I don't know what fire dances you've been to, but "getting into scrapes" is all part of the fun. Look – if you're gonna be my bodyguard or whatever I don't want you dragging me down with your face like a slapped arse.' She leaps up before he can reply, hooks her arm through the flower crowns she's made and starts passing from table to table, her face beaming as people hand over their money.

She returns a while later with two bottles of strong ale and offers him one.

He waves it away. 'I'm not a big drinker.'

'Do you even know how to have a good time?'

I did once, he thinks, but the initial kick at defying my parents, defying the natural order of my life, seems to have lost its edge.

'Come on,' she says, 'these are my last days of freedom before I'm handed over to another Murray matriarch – least you could do is have a drink with me.'

Halim takes the bottle and nods his thanks.

'Hey, look – the fires are lit!' Rowena flies off and he has to jog to catch up.

A ring of people now surrounds each of the fire stacks. On the far side of the meadow local farmers have let in some cows and are driving them towards the gathering, shooing them on with crooks or sticks. The pale beasts lope through the gloaming like a procession of cave paintings come to life. Halim drinks down the nutty ale, wonders if it's the alcohol that's stirring something in him, or if it's the bizarre sight of bovine worship. The crowd parts as the cows pass between the fires, accompanied by applause, and then someone takes up a fiddle. Then the beasts are herded away again, their part seemingly played.

Halim frowns at Rowena. 'Was that it? Was that the fire dance?'

She snorts. 'Oh boy, I could tell you anything right now and you'd believe me – this is too easy!' She must have seen the look on his face because she softens. 'The local farmers drive their best heifers between the flames to bless the herds and bring prosperity to the farms. Fire purifies and protects.' Her eyes suddenly brighten. 'That's why we should pass between the stacks too.'

'What?' He looks over at the crowd, drinking and laughing, their kids flitting about like moths, dogs barking ...

'Do you have somewhere better to be?' She grabs his free hand and leads him forward.

The music gets louder and a jaunty folk song dances on the breeze.

O come the maiden, mother and crone,
Amongst the leaves so green-o,
With luck for the barrow, the bushel, the beast,
Let nothing but harmony reign in our breast.
Amongst the leaves so green-o.

O sing a song of summer strong,
Amongst the leaves so green-o,
Let neighbour and neighbour be ever at rest,
With cups charged with wine, and only the best.
Amongst the leaves so green-o ...

Heat slaps Halim in the face as they approach the fires. He tries to pull his sweaty hand away but Rowena is surprisingly strong and soon they're between the stacks and around the other side. Rowena wafts smoke over the both of them.

'Oh, yeah, I feel much better,' Halim coughs, rubbing his eyes. He spots a smudge of soot on Rowena's freckled nose as she shakes her head at him. Truth is, he does feel a bit better; the tenseness of the past few days is loosening its hold and shedding from his body.

'What are you going to do with your dad's ashes?' he asks. 'I saw the urn in your backpack when you left it at the hotel, next to the mini soaps, sewing kit and flannel.'

'Wow, mood killer.' Rowena gulps down the last of her ale, grabs Halim's empty bottle and produces two more from her shoulder bag. She cracks them open and hands him one. 'I'm taking my pa with me to Culcrith – he's from there so I figured it'd be nice for him to return. It probably sounds a bit weird to you but I quite like having him around. Who knows? You might get to meet him tonight – the veil's thin on Beltane Eve, under the Mother's moon.'

A flicker of fear crosses Rowena's face, but Halim can't be sure – she never seems to stand still long enough for him to figure her out.

She knocks the top of his bottle with hers, making it erupt and froth over his hand, then she turns back towards the fires.

8

Beltane Eve

THE OLDER FOLKS HAVE LONG GONE, and the younger crowd – about a dozen of them, probably every teenager from St Cross – have made their own fire in a far corner of the meadow and are watching it paint the night sky with a confetti of ash and embers. Elderberry wine is being passed around by ruddy-faced revellers as chart music blasts from tinny speakers. The home-made concoction tastes sour and kicks Rowena from the inside as it fights its way down her throat – she hopes it's enough to help her forget that it's one year ago today that Drew died.

'Don't you think you've had enough?' whispers Halim, sat next to her on the grass. His hair and shirt are dishevelled, but his brow still betrays the conspicuous lines of a worrier.

'Why, do *you* want some more?' She offers him the bottle.

He takes it and hands it off to a passing girl, ignoring Rowena's eye roll.

A boy who looks barely thirteen approaches, his hands thrust into the pockets of his navy bomber jacket. He crouches down next to Rowena. 'I've got some molly if you want,' he says. 'Or gummies? County line's pretty strong round here.'

'Nah, you're all right, thanks.' She tries to push away thoughts of Drew's last hours, how his drug-curdled mind led his feet down a deadly path. Perhaps a secret part of him wanted to go there?

'Suit yourself.' The boy stands, takes a run and hurls himself

44

– split-legged – over the fire as everyone hollers their approval. Others leap the flames too, and a rhythmic chant is taken up, powered on by handclaps and bottle taps: '*Summer is a-cumin' in, summer is a-cumin' in, summer is a-cumin' in* ...' Soon Rowena and Halim are the only ones who haven't crossed the fire and all eyes are on them.

Rowena shrugs off her cardigan, stands, takes a run and flings her arms up as her feet leave the ground. Her body cuts through the yellow tongues unscathed and she lands with an exhilarated laugh. The clapping continues as everyone looks towards Halim.

'We'll be here 'til winter if you wait for him,' she calls out. The voices loosen and fade, the music's turned up – and just like that the moment's gone. She catches Halim's eye across the fire and he looks away. A pretty brunette with brazen cleavage approaches him with a bottle and he takes it.

A popular song comes on and Rowena joins the Beltane dancing: bare feet bounce off the dew-kissed grass, smiles catch the firelight and are passed around like little gifts as arms tangle with the stars. The fire throws their freakish shadows across the meadow as distant trees sing back to them and bats swoop overhead, performing acrobatics that drunk eyes can't follow. Rowena has never felt this free and untethered: her lungs are so full she feels as though she might float away like one of the embers riding the thermals, or burst from the joy of it all and come to rest in little pieces, scattered across the earth like—

'Watch out!' A shout wrests her from her thoughts.

'Her dress!'

'You're on fire!'

Rowena looks down at the flames licking a fold of her dress. In the back of her skull she registers that something's wrong but is unable to move, mesmerised by the twisting glow ...

She's knocked hard to the ground.

Halim's boozy breath is in her face as he curses in Arabic and mashes her dress into the dirt. There are cheers and whistles as he leans above her, panting, and for some reason it makes her laugh. He grabs a big bottle of water and throws it over Rowena's legs, silencing her.

When Halim moves away another face replaces his – tiger-striped with mud and crowned with oak leaves.

45

The Oak King helps Rowena to her feet. 'You okay?' he asks.

She looks down, inspects the redness on her thigh and the charred hem of her dress. 'I think I prefer it in black,' she sniffs.

The Oak King grins and strips off his shirt, revealing a broad chest with a dusting of hair and a skull tattoo. He lets out a howl as a ring forms around him.

Rowena notices Halim join the circle, swigging wine as the brunette does a fake 'fuck-me' laugh and rests her hand on his back.

The music stops as a slim, dark-haired young man with a holly crown and a wool-topped blackthorn branch enters, waggling his tongue in response to the jeers and boos. The Holly King and Oak King circle each other, hefting branches like clubs, tensing and flexing the peaks and valleys of their muscles. The revellers holler, creating a wall of noise as the branches are raised and knocked together, pausing only to cheer each blow from the Oak King. The fighters wrestle and shove each other: coming together, breaking apart, shouting, snarling, branches snagging and tearing skin to reveal the red beneath. And then a real blow lands – but it's Rowena who stumbles backwards ...

It's her pa's face that she sees under the holly crown – stunned, contorted with pain and confusion, looking exactly like he did the day he died. As he picks Rowena out from the circle every sound seems to fade, even though she knows that everyone's still cheering, their proud-veined fists pumping, spit flying from their mouths.

'I'm sorry,' she mutters through her fingers.

Her pa tries to say something but his mouth freezes as his lips fold in on themselves, tugged into a grimace that makes his face look like a death mask. He shakes his head – in frustration? Or is it disappointment in his daughter for killing him? She can't tell.

He tries again, and this time he wheezes out a plume of ash that falls and gathers at his feet, and when his eyes roll back in his head Rowena can't look any more and backs away.

Night sounds creep back in: the crackle of the fire; hushed voices; the sound of her own quickened breath. That's when she realises that the cheering has stopped. She turns towards the throng to find them all looking at her, and among them is a tall, faceless shadow with ragged arms.

'No,' she whines, falling to her knees. The burn-blister on her thigh splits open and weeps but she doesn't feel it: all around her the bodies of the partygoers are crumpling too, thudding to the ground to lie there, limbs splayed like fractals of flesh.

'I choose the fire-kissed maiden as my May Queen,' a voice booms, cutting through her terror.

Rowena lowers her trembling hands to see the circle part and everyone turn towards her as if nothing's just happened, their faces bright and very much alive.

The Oak King steps forward to claim his prize, a flowered crown in his pink-grazed hand, one of the ones Rowena made. Everyone cheers as he helps her to her feet and places it on her head – everyone except Halim and the pretty girl, who stands there with her arms crossed. Behind her, the Holly King is a young man again, swigging beer and proudly touching his fingers to a bloody cut on his forehead. The Oak King leans in to kiss Rowena full on the mouth – and as she turns her head away she catches the pretty girl's eyes again and they pierce her like a dagger.

The music restarts and bodies find each other. The Oak King grabs a bottle and leads a dazed Rowena towards the river. 'You ever been to Beltane fires before?' he slurs.

She stares at the sinuous lines of moonlight on water, swallowing down her nausea. 'Hmm? Yeah, course, it's my favourite night of the year.'

'Really?' he raises an eyebrow. 'You should tell your face that.'

She shakes herself and forces a smile. 'Sorry, I was just spinning out – from the wine and that.'

He tilts his head to appraise his strange queen, sweat glinting beneath the oak leaves at his hairline, heat rising from his body like smoke in the night air.

She would have jumped on him at this point if her head wasn't wild with thoughts of her curse, if the Oak King hadn't reminded her of Drew. 'Look, I'm honoured and everything but I can't do this right now, you should choose a different May Queen.'

'Is that guy you came with your boyfriend?'

Rowena hesitates. 'Yeah, he is.'

'So, do you think he'd mind if I kissed you again?'

She blinks, gets a flash of Halim kneeling in the saltmarsh, panting, staring down at his bloodied fists ... 'Actually, yeah, I think he would.' She takes off the flower crown, places it on the Oak King's head and curtsies.

'Lucky bastard,' he concedes with a grin. He wolf-whistles to the others as he sprints off back to the fire, leaving Rowena alone at the riverbank. For a long while she looks for answers in the watery depths, scours the ripples for words, a message, anything to tell her if that was really her pa or just the curse playing tricks.

By the time Rowena returns to the fire the dancing has stopped and most couples are lying in the long grass, enjoying the touch and taste of each other as the sky grows milky around them. She finds Halim sat under a tree with the brunette, smoking. 'I'm heading off,' she says.

With a sheepish smile, he slips away from the pretty girl's arm and follows Rowena as she strides across the meadow, her boots dangling from one hand, her dress blackened and frayed.

'I thought you didn't smoke,' she mutters as Halim catches her up, a cigarette end glowing from his lips like a rosebud.

'You're a bad influence,' he shrugs.

9

May Day

——

A FEW HOURS LATER, with thick heads, bloodshot eyes and shower-damp hair, Rowena and Halim find themselves at the green in St Cross, where the maypole has been erected and a handful of pot-bellied folk musicians have just finished a set. Six dancers festooned in white silk ribbons and flowers pass by. Halim recognises one of them as the brunette from last night whose name he can't remember. He nods a greeting but she scowls and whispers something to her friend.

He gazes up at the maypole and takes a big bite of a meat pasty, its hot, tacky filling coating his tongue. 'It looks like a giant penis,' he says through a mouthful of flaky pastry.

'I think that's the point,' Rowena yawns, 'this whole thing's about fertility, Mother Nature getting knocked up and that.'

Halim checks his phone again to see about a job posting in Wendelshire, the county to the north of here. Still nothing. There's a new text from his mother, though: 'Board members are asking questions again. Only so long we can lie for you. Call me.' I never asked you to lie, he thinks, deleting the message and slipping his phone away.

'Looks like we've missed Mad Jack,' Rowena says, scanning the cobbled street, 'but we might still catch the procession if we're lucky.'

I suppose I should pay more attention to all this, Halim thinks, I might not get the chance to observe these quaint sort of customs again, not if things don't work out as planned. On the wall next to them, a poster created by Somerton Council boasts about crop yields and prize-winning herds – in each photo the smug white face of a farmer smiles out at Halim from a sunlit, pastoral setting.

People start lining the pavement and gathering on the old stone steps of the Buttercross. 'This place is ripe with tourists,' Rowena says. 'I'm gonna flog some more of my charms and posies.'

'I'll wait for you by the bakery there,' Halim says, not wanting to follow her into the throng.

He watches a horse-drawn wagon trundle by, its spokes wrapped in ivy. Children with colourful hats made of card and tissue paper sit atop it, smiling and waving, seeking out the cameras of their parents. People wave cloth banners. Somewhere, an accordion belches a merry melody. A man in a top hat on a bicycle almost runs over Halim's toes, forcing him to jump back – attached to his bike frame are two crudely made dolls with oversized heads that nod to Halim as they pass. He shivers, touches the gold dog tag around his neck. Someone pushes him roughly aside, knocking his pasty to the pavement: a man more foliage than flesh, bells jangling with each stomping step as he waves his head around, making people dodge the jabs of his antlers with squawks of delight. It's like a bad dream, Halim thinks, dragging himself back into the bakery to replace his breakfast.

Waiting for him when he comes out are four men with narrowed eyes and puffed-out chests, all wearing what must be their best suits.

'That him?' the long-haired one asks, pointing at Halim.

The pretty brunette from last night nods. 'Yeah, he's the one who gave me this when I refused him,' she raises her voice for the benefit of the others and indicates a blueish swelling under her left eye.

'What?' Halim gapes. 'I never laid a finger on her!'

'Oh, *really*?' she says. She's stood behind the men, alongside her fellow dancers, their eyes drilling into him. 'Him and that weird ginger girl crashed our Beltane party and started kicking off,' she continues. 'Proper mashed up, they were, and giving us the evil eye.'

The dancers start muttering something and flicking their hands towards Halim.

The long-haired man strides forward and shoves him towards the wall.

Another man reaches into his suit pocket and pulls out a penknife.

'That true?' the long-haired man squares up to Halim, his fleshy nostrils flaring. His hands start flicking too, as if shaking off water or dirt. 'Know what? I don't care – we don't want scum like you in our town. You've outstayed your welcome.'

A few passers-by avert their eyes as music trills on down the high street.

'I chatted to her at the party but I don't even know her name,' Halim protests. 'Have you tried asking her friends what happened last night before accusing random strangers?'

'Bang on!' the man with the knife says, his fingers flexing and releasing. 'You're a stranger. Why'd we trust you over her?'

'What's going on?' Rowena elbows her way through and places herself between the men and Halim.

He tries to move her back but she stands firm.

'This one got a bit handy with our girl here, so now we're gonna get handy with him.'

'What are you on about?' laughs Rowena. 'He's my boyfriend and I was with him all night. The only girl he'd dare touch is me!'

'You calling me a liar?' the brunette pipes up.

'Come on, leave it, Jess,' the Holly King has joined the gathering, the dry, prickly crown still clinging to his brow. He tries to pull her away but she shrugs him off, tearing her white dress at the shoulder.

'There was plenty going on in the meadow last night,' Rowena says, 'she could have gotten that bruise anywhere.'

'Step out of the way, bitch, or you'll get one too,' an older man draws close, his wiry body buzzing with nervous energy.

'We were leaving anyway,' Halim says, still clutching the paper bag from the bakery. 'Everyone just calm down, and we'll be gone.' He manages to shift Rowena aside, but that's when the wiry man slams into Halim and knocks his skull against the brick wall, sending a shockwave of pain through his temple. Stunned, Halim tries to find his footing and grits his teeth as something warm trickles down his face. He knows if he collapses they'll pin him down so he presses his spine into the wall to stay upright.

Rowena's shouting and swearing, and before he knows what he's doing, Halim's put all his weight behind his fist and jabbed it under his attacker's ribs, sending the man stumbling back, gasping for air.

It's far enough for Halim to grab Rowena by the arm and run.

'Fucking get 'em!' someone shouts.

'Oi!'

The four men give chase, feet pounding the concrete close behind. Rowena and Halim duck into a side street, dart between bollards and race across a small wooden bridge curtained by a weeping willow.

'Over here,' she pants, heading for a food market set up in a car park. Halim follows her lead as she ditches her bright green cardigan and slows to a brisk walk. She begins to weave in and out of the shoppers, moving between the stalls, crates and carts. Halim glances behind – the men have dropped back and are splitting up to search the crowd. He's never, until now, felt relieved to be surrounded by so many people as he and Rowena jostle and slide between bodies and canvas.

A bus pulls into the stop nearby and Rowena drags Halim onto it and drops some coins on the tray. They have to squeeze themselves past a row of people in the aisle. She's pressed so close to him that he can feel her heart beating against his chest.

'You're bleeding,' she whispers.

'I dropped my pasty,' he says.

'Hopefully they haven't reported us,' Halim says as he starts the truck. 'We'll need to cross the border as soon as possible, in case word gets to the Guards and we're detained here. Luckily that job at Farley Farm came through, so it should give us clear passage.'

He barely draws breath between words and Rowena can tell that he's shaken up but trying to hide it.

'What did you do to piss off that brunette bitch?' She takes a bite of the nectarine she pocketed from the market, its juice drips down her chin, filling the air with a sweet perfume.

'Nothing, and I think that's why she had it in for me. Or it could have been your doing.'

'Me?'

'She didn't take too kindly to you being chosen as May Queen, an outsider. And you know what they say, a woman scorned ...'

'A woman scorned what?'

Halim accelerates, pressing Rowena's spine into the seat. Hawthorn blossom and bindweed unfurl like white garlands along the roadside, blurring as the truck speeds past.

'You don't like women much, do you?' she asks. 'You think we're only put on this Earth to fuck you and clean up afterwards.'

'On the contrary. I just prefer my women with a bit of dignity – the ones who get pissed and throw themselves at me soon lose their attraction.'

Rowena narrows her eyes. 'That's what you think I did with the guy on the marsh, isn't it? That I somehow deserved it?'

'What? No, of course not. He was scum, one of the many arseholes who plague this increasingly fucked-up Kingdom.'

'We're not all arseholes,' Rowena sniffs, 'besides, if you think so low of us why don't you just piss off back to your rich folks?'

Halim glares at her and wrenches the gear stick. 'I didn't peg you for a racist.'

'I'm not. I'm a realist.'

He draws out a long sigh and she readies herself for a lecture.

'I know I come across a little harsh sometimes,' he concedes, 'I'm pretty sure that's my father's influence. In his eyes men and women aren't exactly equal, and his beliefs have this insidious way of getting under my skin. I assure you, I can be just as disdainful of men. I don't discriminate.'

'Oh, well, that's okay then,' sneers Rowena as she unfurls the rest of the loot from her pockets – two apricots and an orange. Expensive fruit.

'Where did you get those?'

'Where d'you think?'

Halim shakes his head. 'We don't need any more trouble.'

'They were just a bunch of townies throwing their weight around, I don't know why you're freaking out so much.'

'They had knives.'

'Shit.'

'Yeah.'

'If I'd known that I wouldn't have stepped in to save you.'

10

ROWENA SITS BOLT UPRIGHT IN HER SEAT, drawing Halim's eyes from the road.

'Look!' she says, pointing to a field on the left. 'Standing stones! Pull over, let's check them out.'

'We should just press on to Farley's now that we're over the border, I'm pretty tired and it'll be dark in a few hours.'

'Oh, come on! Have you ever seen standing stones up close?'

He checks the time and then steers them onto a small, stony track dotted with pheasants who seem reluctant to flee from the truck's wheels. I could do with some air anyway, he thinks as they get out and cut through cobwebbed nettles, jump over a small stream and continue on over a lip of raised earth towards the stones.

There are nine of them, some squat, some roughly his height, standing in a circle like worn teeth in green gums. The field is surrounded by low-lying hills, its grass kept short by a handful of sheep who, seeming to know that the weather's turning, are huddled together under a stand of oak trees, eyeing the two newcomers.

In the middle of the circle Halim scuffs his boot across a scorched patch of grass, betraying the site of a recent fire. Amongst the black debris he spots something white and bends closer. A tiny skeleton lies there, a toad, he thinks, totally intact except for the pelvis.

When he looks up he sees Rowena standing with her palms on the largest stone, which rises a foot above her head – a wash of watercolour greys with a skin of shaggy blue-green lichen.

'They're like the bones of the land,' she mutters, as he comes over. 'What does this circle mean?'

She shrugs. 'I think it's something to do with energy: a circle gathers you into it, encloses you, focuses you. That's why stones like these are used to celebrate the cycle of the seasons and turning of the year. Like a wheel.' She presses her ear against the stone and gazes past him. 'I also read that some stones were used as boundary markers for plague villages, a place where farmers would leave food and things, and the infected villagers left coin in return.'

'Doubt that would happen these days,' scoffs Halim, thrusting his hands into his pockets. He clears his throat. 'About earlier: I really wasn't implying that you're like other girls, *women*, I mean. You're ...' he tries to find the word, '... different. I just, you know, wanted you to know that.'

Rowena's pale eyes find him and a smile tweaks her lips. 'Stop it, you flirt!'

Halim's face prickles with heat. 'This isn't – I'm not flirting, I was just—'

Rowena's laughter cuts him off, and she offers a hopeless shake of her head. She takes out what looks like a crumpled thistle from her pocket and lays it at the base of the stone.

'What's that?'

'Burdock. My mother gave it to me, it's protection for travellers. I'm making an offering of it.' She bows her head and whispers. 'I ask for your blessing and cleansing on this day of fire.'

Halim looks up at the stone. From this angle it has a gnarled human face, contemplating the ground below as if figuring out how it came to be there.

'Go on, put your hands on it,' Rowena says.

He does. It's cool and crinkle-rough beneath his touch. His fingertips find a crack and he digs in, as if trying to split the stone apart.

'Feel that?' she asks. 'That energy, the oldness of it – the things it must have seen, absorbed, all soaked into the rock and held there, vibrating like a tuning fork. Maybe you can hear it?'

He shakes his head.

'Close your eyes. Go on – close them!'

With his eyes shut, Halim's other senses come alive: the murmur of the green-leafed oak trees; the soft questioning 'who-who-who?'

of a wood pigeon; the breeze smoothing his brow, bringing with it the leathery scent of soil; the soft caress of sunlight as a cloud passes. He takes a peek at Rowena, but she's got her eyes shut and is nestling into the stone like it's an old friend. That's when he notices the sudden silence. The hair on his head and neck stirs. There's no more wood pigeon, the sheep are nowhere to be seen and the air is so still it's as if the whole valley is holding its breath, waiting for something. A red glow appears above the hills, unlike any sunset he's ever seen – more like the reflection of a great, distant fire. Halim's hands begin to tingle and at first he thinks he imagines it but then they grow warm. And then they *burn*. A burst of intense heat rips through his skin, making him draw back with a gasp. His palms are raw and blistering, a mottle of crimson and pink with a weeping of amber. The scald marks disappear the moment he blinks. His stomach lurches as he presses his hands and feels no pain; then he raises his head to a cool, eel-grey sky.

'Did you feel anything?' Rowena asks. 'Did the stones talk to you?'

'What?' A skittish laugh escapes him. 'No, nothing.'

It's only rock, Halim reminds himself, it's just sediment packed solid over thousands of years. Geology, nothing more. 'We need to get back on the road,' he says, striding towards the truck.

Halim is relieved to see that Farley Farm is one of the better ones with a well-ordered, logical layout, neat outbuildings, security cameras – you can tell a lot about a farm in the first fifteen metres. There's money here too: a couple of recent-model tractors are parked up in the yard, and they have solar panels, water pumps, tidy stables and a freshly painted farm shop. How ironic, he thinks, that a place like Farley Farm is beyond my reach, yet a few calls could see me in a thirty-fifth-floor apartment with its own infinity pool.

'Hi,' he says to the young woman stood at the farmhouse door. 'Halim Hosny and Rowena Murray to see Jade Flynn. We're booked on a three-day job from tomorrow.' He shows her the confirmation email on his phone, cross-referenced on his job sheet.

'Great! I'm Susie, Jade's daughter,' she says with a bright smile. 'I'll show you both to your lodgings.'

She leads them to a dorm block that has a slight whiff of detergent. 'You'll be in this room, Rowena, and Halim, you're right next door. Shared bathroom is down the hall, and to the left is the kitchen. Help yourself to communal tea, coffee and oat milk, but please don't use the items that are labelled as they're other people's food. If you need anything call this number,' she points to a laminated poster. 'I'll leave you to settle in, and we'll see you guys tomorrow in the yard, bright and early, okay?'

'Yeah, sounds great!' Rowena says, holding her smile a bit too long.

Susie doesn't notice, she turns to leave with a toss of her ponytail, her black jeans swishing as she walks.

Halim drops his bag onto the tightly tucked bunk bed. If I hadn't had this job to Culcrith, he thinks, this is exactly the kind of place I could have settled for a while, racking up a good solid wage. Though he knows that would take longer to pay off the truck, and time is something he doesn't have.

'Pass me that post,' Halim says to Rowena as they're almost done mending the fence in the north field. 'And put your gloves back on, a cut out here might need treating.'

'Aw, it's so nice that you care.' Rowena blows a strand of hair from her forehead.

They work on in silence for a while, hefting out rotten, water-damaged posts and boring holes for the new ones. He welcomes the flex and tug of his muscles and the pull on his lungs. Just as he's getting into a rhythm it's interrupted by Rowena's voice.

'Pa used to get me to help out around the farm back home,' she says. 'Well, when I was strong enough. I almost died from meningitis when I was seven, then I got measles, which basically ended up with me being home-schooled. I say home-schooled, but I basically just had a load of library books dumped on me and—'

'I work quicker in silence,' he cuts in.

'Don't you find this kind of work boring?'

'Yes. That's *literally* what it is,' Halim nods to the long metal tool in his hands, its corkscrew point plunged deep into the soil.

Rowena sniffs. 'Got a comedian here, folks.'

'I guess we could take a break,' Halim sighs, cricking his neck.

They sit with their backs against the truck and gaze out over a sweep of gold, the rapeseed almost in full flower. Rowena gets out her dinosaur tin and rolls a cigarette.

'If you're expecting to be healed don't you think you should pack that in?' Halim asks, sipping coffee from his flask.

'What do you care, as long as you get paid? Look, I'll try not to die on your watch, but I can't promise anything.'

Halim winces at the realisation that he's starting to sound like his father, treating everything and everyone as a business transaction, turning people's lives into profit. 'If you're sick, why didn't your mother invest in medication, or some kind of therapy? Why pay to send you all the way across the Kingdom?'

'Firstly, I *am* "sick" as you call it and I don't give a toss if you believe me. Secondly, there are some healings that white-coats and their precious pills can't do. Ones that involve the soul. You'd understand if you had one.'

'Look, I know we don't have to get on, but it would make our time together a bit easier, don't you think?'

'Sure, whatever.'

He notices the sausage of ash teetering at the end of her untouched rollie.

A loud screech above makes them both look up. A bird with a russet belly and forked tail glides past, arcs, and comes back around, so slowly that Halim wonders how it doesn't simply drop out of the sky.

Rowena keeps staring at it, enraptured, a slight tilt to her head as if she and the bird were sharing some sort of secret language. She shivers, drops the dead cigarette, leaps up and thrusts her hands back into her gloves without a word, leaving Halim to wonder what's wrong with her soul.

11

4 May

———

ROWENA GROANS AS SHE WAKES before the alarm again. It's only her third morning at Farley and already her muscles are aching from the labour, much more than they ever did on the smallholding at Pickbury. She misses her clandestine trips into the woods, the simplicity of her traps and the heft of her skinning knife. She rubs crumbs of sleep from her eyes and prises them open; the light, caught halfway between night and day, barely touches the room and does nothing to banish the chill. Somewhere in the back of her mind she registers a flutter at the window and turns towards the curtains. Standing at the foot of the bunk bed is a dark figure, partly obscured by the wooden frame. Its lower half is shadow-thin with overlong arms ending in twig-like fingers that hang at its sides. Rowena is rigid with fear, it feels as if the figure has reached right into her chest, latched onto her heart and in that moment is deciding what to do with it. She tries to raise the covers – a futile gesture as the shadow-man's arms catch fire and blast the room with light. A heartbeat later, she finds herself pressed hard against the wall, tangled up in the duvet, panting. As the flash of firelight burned onto the backs of her eyelids fades she realises that It's gone. She rubs her face, feels her damp vest sticking to her, her bladder screaming to be emptied. That was too close, she thinks, too real to deny.

*

Rowena's still trembling when she reaches the stables, her hair a knotted mess, extra layers on to try and stop the shivering. Nobody's up yet, but she jumps at every sound – even those made by her own boots. She inspects the horses and spots a shiny brass plaque with a name and owner etched into it: 'Captain. Lord Croft Esq.' Perfect, she thinks. She approaches Captain, rubs his nose in greeting, and with soothing words she makes swift work of bridling him, not wanting to waste time with a saddle.

She loosens up on the short ride into town: the hedgerows yawn their morning breath towards a blushing sky and the chatter of birds helps steer her mind away from what happened barely twenty minutes ago. She enjoys being on horseback again, and recalls her pa's encouragement when she was learning to ride as a child: 'I'm right here, Ro,' he'd say over and over like a mantra. Three simple words that steadied her every wobble – even those she had when she was older and grown. Rowena's eyes prickle, she pinches her nose to stop the tears and spots a couple of kids at a bus stop, clutching baskets filled with juniper berries, still glistening with dew.

'Hey, does Greater Wendel have a healer?' she asks, pulling up in the street next to them.

'Yeah,' one of the boys replies.

'Care to tell me who it is, and where I can find them?'

'What's in it for us?'

'A quid.'

They laugh.

'Okay. How about a bird skull?'

'Cool! Show us it!'

Rowena takes out a cloth pouch, opens it and reveals the blackbird skull she found a couple of days ago and polished up with vinegar.

'He's called Pappa Red,' the other boy says. 'He lives at forty-three Lark Street.'

'Great, thanks.' Rowena kicks Captain into a trot, still clutching the pouch as the boys shout after her.

'I don't take deliveries for neighbours,' comes a smoker's voice through the door.

'I'm sorry, I know it's early but I'm not a delivery person, I'm – well, I can pay you, I have money. Or charms,' Rowena says through the letterbox. 'Please, Pappa Red, I really need your help.'

She hopes those kids haven't pranked her ...

When the door opens, a barefoot, middle-aged man with red lips and a long crimson kaftan is staring at her.

'Are you Pappa Red?' Rowena asks, already knowing the answer.

The man gathers up his straw-coloured hair and pins it in a bun. 'They do call me that. Who are you? You're not from around here.'

'Rowena Murray. I'm from Pickbury, in Dunfordshire.'

Pappa Red narrows his eyes for a few seconds and seems to focus past Rowena, into the street. 'Well, now that I have your name you'd better come in. Boots off, please.'

Rowena follows Pappa Red down the hall and into the front room. The net curtains over the bay window add extra gloom to the flock wallpaper, burgundy carpet and age-scuffed furniture, all of which seems to be pushed up against the walls. Pappa Red slides the adjoining door shut, but not before Rowena spies the shiny white breakfast bench, marble-topped units and a flatscreen TV.

'Um, should I put a light on?'

'No, no, it helps me see better when things aren't shouting in my face for attention. Please take a seat, Rowena. I would offer you tea but I just ran out, and I don't drink coffee unless it's got whisky in it, and I've run out of that too.'

A cat swaggers in and rubs its lean, striped body against the glass coffee table. When it reaches a paw to swipe at the dusty crystals lying there, Pappa Red shoos it away. He drags over a wicker-backed rocking chair and sits opposite Rowena, so close that their knees are almost touching. Over his shoulder a gargoyle-like creature stares out from the wall, its stone head skewered with spent incense sticks.

Rowena bites her lip and sits on her hands, trying not to over-think or project anything, or stare too much at the make-up line around Pappa Red's jaw.

'I always put a face on first thing in the morning,' he says, somehow guessing her thoughts. 'Especially when I'm expecting a visitor. Oh yes – I saw you coming from the clump of ash stuck to the grate, it all flew *upwards* when I clapped my hands.'

Rowena glances around the room but doesn't see a fireplace.

'Now, what can I do for you? A reading? A balm? Where does it hurt?'

Rowena steels herself. 'I have these nightmares, but I keep seeing things when I'm awake too. Dark-grey shadows. Sometimes creatures, birds. Sometimes ...' she swallows, 'like a man. I think It's Death and It's getting closer. I need to know how to escape It, or at least slow It down or something.'

'Pish! You know I can't tell you that. Nobody can!'

'Well, can't I protect myself somehow, buy some time?'

'Sure, with the right medication – is it cancer? I don't see any sickness in you. Except maybe around the head area.'

Rowena wrinkles her nose. 'No. And I don't want expensive medicines.'

'Good, because I don't deal in black-market. Not any more.' Pappa Red sighs, rocks back and forth for a while and then taps a soft, manicured hand on Rowena's knee. 'I can tell you're scared, sweetness, but you can't stop Death, all you can do is live like it's your last day and draw strength from those around you. Focus on viriditas – a greening of the soul. Green wood doesn't burn so easily.'

Well, this was pointless, Rowena thinks. Is this what my gran will be like too – some showy pseudo-psychologist spouting words from greetings cards?

Pappa Red reaches over to the bookshelf and picks up a tea light. He spits on it and rubs his finger over the wax to scoop out the dust. 'Here,' he says, holding it out. 'Take this and make an offering tonight under the full moon. Bury a toad bone if you have one, ask for protection. It'll keep the shadows at bay for a while. Better than any old rabbit's foot.'

Rowena frowns, checks her jacket pocket to see if the rabbit's foot is poking out. It isn't.

'Here then! Take it.' Pappa Red waves the candle under her nose.

Rowena takes it, gets up and places a crumpled ten-pound note on the coffee table.

When she heads into the hall to put on her boots Pappa Red follows, the cat twining around his legs, batting at the fringing of the kaftan. 'There's a young man you travel with, isn't there?'

Rowena tugs on her laces. 'Yeah.'

'There's always a young man,' Pappa Red sighs. 'Especially with one as bright and wild-eyed as you.'

Rowena fumbles the door latch. 'Thank you for your time.'

'You can choose, you know – to be the lamb or the knife.' Pappa Red smiles as the door narrows and closes, leaving Rowena on the doorstep, unease rising in her chest at those strange final words.

'I'm sorry, Halim, you're a hard worker and honestly it pains me to do this, but I've got to let you both go. It wasn't just that she was late for your shift, it was the fact that she "borrowed" the Lord's horse. We can't have her set a bad example to the other workers, or tarnish our reputation as a livery.'

Rowena bites her lip as she peers through the gap between the frame and the door of Jade Flynn's office. Flynn sits at her polished wooden desk with a wide-eyed Halim hovering nearby.

'Could you at least keep the job registered on the system, to give us enough time to find something else in the next county along?'

Flynn shakes her head. 'Again, I'm sorry, Halim, but we have to follow the rules at Farley, we've spent far too long building this place up. The council does random checks to make sure everyone who's here is meant to be here.'

Halim nods. 'Yeah. I know. I understand. Thank you, Mrs Flynn.' Head bowed, he clutches the payment receipt.

Rowena jerks back as he breezes past her and out into the yard. She jogs after him. 'I don't understand – she seemed nice enough when I explained I needed time off for a medical emergency.'

Halim stops and turns on her, jabbing the receipt in her face. 'That's just it, Rowena, you don't understand how the world outside Pickbury works because you think everything revolves around you! Tozz Fiiki!' He stomps off to the dorm.

Rowena's gut churns as she realises she might've pushed him too far this time, that he might ditch her – or worse, take her back to Pickbury. The stuttering clack of a magpie draws her attention to the roof of Halim's truck where it bobs a little dance; another bad omen.

When she catches up with Halim in the corridor he has his bag slung over his shoulder. 'Pack up your shit,' he says, 'and meet me at the truck.'

'I'm sorry, Halim. I just needed to find someone to tell me everything would be okay. Honestly, I didn't mean—'

'No, you never *mean* anything, Rowena! You talk in riddles and turn everything into a stupid fucking sign or superstition. You can't keep hiding behind some predetermined destiny,' Halim's face darkens as he throws his hand in the air. 'You have to own your decisions and take responsibility for your actions because they affect other people too – so stop being an annoying, selfish bitch. No wonder your own mother wanted rid of you!'

Rowena slaps him hard across the cheek.

Before she can blink, Halim's pinned her against the wall and they're eyeball to eyeball with his hand at her throat.

Pappa Red's parting words flash through her brain.

She's about to retaliate when Halim's eyes seem to clear and he realises what he's doing. He releases her and backs away, shaking his head in disbelief.

He turns, runs up the corridor, kicks open the door and disappears.

12

___

IT'S BEEN ALMOST EIGHT HOURS, far too much petrol, and Halim's eyes are tired from the strain of peering at every crease in the hills, every tree, every speck that turned out to be another sheep and not Rowena. The world is becoming dull and pretty soon he'll have to put the headlights on. '*Khara!*' He smashes his palm against the steering wheel, sickening regret coursing through him, for what he did, and for driving away from Farley Farm and leaving Rowena there. They said she'd left on foot, so she couldn't have gone far. It's a knife in the gut when he pictures her cowering on the saltmarsh again, and recalls the look on her face as he pinned her to the wall himself, no better than the brute who attacked her.

He swerves the truck onto the scrub next to one of the freshly ploughed fields, turns off the engine and jumps out, sucking in air until he feels his nerves slacken. There isn't enough passing traffic to have hitched a ride and he's tried all the farm tracks now – she must have gone off-road. If I have to search every forest, field and barn in the county I will, he says to himself, I can't leave it like this.

'Rowena!' Her name is swallowed up by the furrows of soil, a static sea of brown that he knows he shouldn't set foot on. He cups his hands to his mouth: 'ROWENA!' A few birds are startled to the air. He watches them tessellate above as he strides towards the hill for a better view.

The wind buffets Halim, making his nose run as he reaches the crest. He notices ridges carved into the earth a few metres below, remnants of an Iron Age hill fort. Below, crop fields unfold like a patchwork blanket, dusking at the edges where night is skulking in. An empire of dirt, he thinks. A Kingdom passport wouldn't be enough to convince the Lords and councils who own most of the land to sell me a scrap of it, he sniffs, they consider me a cuckoo looking to steal the livelihoods from 'good honest locals'. Fuck them, they can keep their poor soil. He unzips his jeans and takes a piss next to an uprooted tree, then continues to circle the summit, looking for anything Rowena-shaped below.

When he stubs his toe on a conical pile of rocks, a cairn to mark someone or something, one of the rocks tumbles down the slope and a glimmer of orange catches his eye in the direction it comes to rest. There's a smudge of dark grey in the sky: someone's lit a fire in the clearing down there. Please let it be her, he thinks as he jogs towards it, almost tumbling down the steep bank in his haste.

The smoky meat smell hits him before the firelight does and reminds Halim, with a burst of saliva, that he hasn't eaten since breakfast. In the clearing, Rowena is sat at a fire holding a skewer of what looks like pheasant, dripping fat into the hissing flames. A tightly woven lean-to is nestled between the trunks of two birch trees nearby.

He's so impressed he can barely get the words out. 'Um, hi,' he manages.

Rowena doesn't look up.

'I went back for you but you'd gone already. I've been searching for you for hours.'

Rowena turns the skewer and tests the meat with the point of her hunting knife.

Halim approaches the fire, his hands in his pockets.

'Watch my salt circle!'

He freezes mid-step as Rowena points to a line of white across the ground. 'I'm deeply ashamed of what I did,' he says, widening his step. 'I didn't mean to hurt you. I'm so, so sorry.'

'Are you sorry for what you said too? Or did you mean every word?'

'I'm also sorry for what I said. I worry that I sound like my father sometimes. I'm trying to shake him off, but it's hard.'

'I know that feeling,' Rowena mutters. 'Well, at least you came back for me. Eventually.' She picks the meat from the pheasant and drops it onto a plastic picnic plate, next to one that's already piled high with what looks like a whole packet of crisps.

'I understand if you don't want to continue with me to Culcrith,' he says. 'If you want, I could contact your mother to make alternative arrangements.'

'This arrangement is fine.' Rowena looks up at him, her eyes narrowed. 'I just need to know that you're not a danger. I've seen your temper and what you can do with your fists.'

He draws his hands from his pockets, the shame rising hot to his face. 'I would never hurt you, I swear it.' I've fucked it, he thinks, shaking his head.

Rowena gestures for him to join her.

Grateful, Halim sits cross-legged and starts warming his hands near the fire.

Rowena divides the meat and crisps, adds some green leaves that Halim doesn't recognise, and passes him a plate.

'Thank you,' he says, 'this looks delicious.'

'You don't have to suck up, Halim, I've already forgiven you,' she says through a mouthful of crisps. She glances at Halim's untouched plate. 'Go on, it'll get cold.'

They both sit there chewing, crunching, sucking their greasy fingers until their bellies are full and the only sounds are the crackle of the fire and the shuffle of nocturnal creatures moving along hidden pathways. Rowena scrapes the bones and skin from their plates into the flames.

'I don't know why ...' Halim begins, unsure where this is going but needing to redeem himself. He looks away, scans the birch trees that zebra-stripe the darkness and starts again: 'Sometimes it's like there's a lava flow creeping along inside me, and it burns and it builds, then it catches on something and splits open, and everything comes spewing out. Anger, frustration, resentment. I should have controlled it today and I didn't.'

'We're not robots, we all make mistakes, and sometimes we need to get shit off our chest.' Rowena picks up a stray feather and runs it through her fingers. 'That's why I took the horse and snuck out to Greater Wendel. I never meant to get us fired, I just needed to do something, to talk to someone.'

'And you'd rather risk our job than come and talk to me?'

She raises an eyebrow. 'You're not exactly the most approachable person I've met.'

'I suppose misanthropy runs in the family.'

Rowena darts him a look.

'It means a dislike of others: you were right to point out that I'm no good with people, I just thought I was better at hiding it.'

'So ... what you're telling me is that you hate everyone, including me?'

'I hate you a little less than everyone else,' he concedes, with a tilt of his head.

'Well, there you go, that's progress!' she laughs. 'I push people's buttons, I get it. That's why I learned to keep my mouth shut around Tessa and stay out of her way. I'm used to being my own boss, I guess, working to my own schedule.'

He follows her gaze upwards: above them, the stars are competing for attention across a velvet-blue sky.

'Truth is, I'm glad you found me,' she continues. 'I was dreading spending the night out here on my own.'

'Why? You seem more than capable of taking care of yourself.'

She hesitates and he wonders if he's said something wrong.

'I keep getting these nightmares and visions, and I know you don't believe me but it's hard to shake this feeling that something's watching me. I can barely sleep and I'm so fucking tired of it all, and it could be weeks before we reach Culcrith, so I hoped Pappa Red might help banish the shadows or undo this curse.'

'Pappa Red?'

'He's a healer – they always give themselves names like that, it helps with prestige and marketing.'

'Can I ask what he told you?'

'He told me to get on and enjoy life.'

'And you paid him for that?'

'Of course! You should never stiff a healer, trust me. My mother thought she'd upset the local healer once and made me paint lamb's blood on the walls and windowsills outside our bungalow. At least, she told me it was lamb's blood – I was six, she could've told me anything and I'd have believed it. I thought it was all a game.' She starts picking at the dirt-filled crescents of her fingernails. 'I can still remember the smell though, I washed my hands for hours and couldn't get the stink off.'

'Maybe this Pappa Red's right, you can't tie yourself in knots over something that's unknown. We all die at some point.'

'Yeah but my cards, my nightmares, my very bones are telling me I'm dragging death along with me,' Rowena sighs. 'I know you think it's all stupid and I wouldn't expect you to understand our ways, you're not from around here.'

Halim winces and rubs his forehead. 'I was born in the Kingdom almost as soon as my parents arrived from Egypt twenty years ago and I've lived and studied—'

'That's not what I meant. You're from the city – you're all well spoken with your fancy phone and branded clothes and that truck. You city types put your faith in stock markets and banks; here in the countryside the only thing we can trust is the land, and when that fails we seek help the ways our ancestors did, before governments and county councils were even a thing. And fuck them anyway – they don't give a shit about country folk even though we feed their fat faces.'

Halim stokes the fire with a stick.

'What are you doing slumming it in that smelly truck anyway? Why aren't you lording it up in a mansion somewhere with your CEO dad?'

'Because I never wanted to be that city boy. And I certainly never wanted to be like my father.'

'What, rich?'

'Lacking in morals. Ruthless. He's done some shady things to get to where he is, stuff that would get him arrested, ruin the family name.'

Rowena looks half-impressed. 'Are you from an Arab crime dynasty?'

'No. And I'm Egyptian, African,' he says, shutting her down. 'I'm from a life that hardens you if you let it, if you get swept up in the race for supremacy and to own things, own people. I've seen the way my father talks to my mother and treats his staff, and although

69

I'm mostly misanthropic by default I wouldn't want to see someone suffer just so I could have my penthouse suite and Napoleon cognac.' He continues jabbing at the fire. 'I know what it's like to be treated like shit. I never want to be the one dishing it out. That's why I stayed on in the Kingdom after boarding school, skipped uni, bought the truck on hire-purchase with my own money and just ... got away from it all. Away from them.'

Rowena reaches over and takes the stick from Halim. 'I think you've killed that flame already.'

'Sorry,' he sniffs, trying to think of something to steer the conversation away from himself, keenly aware that he's never opened up to anyone like this before. 'So, Murray is Tessa's family name, isn't it? Is it not tradition for you both to take your father's surname?'

'My folks weren't technically married, and for some reason my mother insisted on me taking her name. Dunno why, I'm more like my pa than her. I get the feeling that they didn't plan for the life they got landed with, that we were all just kind of stuck there together in Pickbury. I'm not even sure they loved each other by the end.'

Rowena gets out a blue-and-yellow stick of rock from her bag, snaps it in two and hands him half.

He holds it up and reads the word through its middle: 'YOLO. Very apt.' He licks it. It doesn't taste as bad as he expected. 'So, are you planning on camping out tonight, or would you like to sleep in the truck? I could sleep out here if you'd feel more comfortable, I'd understand.'

She leans back on one hand and sucks on her piece of candy, her cheekbones sharpening, her lips forming a pout. 'It'd be a shame to waste the fire, and it's a nice night. But you'd have to stay here with me to prove that you're sorry, and scare off the shadows with that nasty face of yours.'

'That I can do,' Halim smiles and runs a hand through his hair. 'Just don't expect me to build a shelter or anything, I'm not resourceful like you. All I've known are pre-made boxes of concrete and glass.'

Rowena shrugs. 'Well, if you think about it, this is all the same sort of stuff, just the original elements, the raw materials. You work with what nature gives you, depending on the season. It's simple.'

'Not to me.' He gets up to stretch his legs.

'I saw that woodworking book of yours in the truck,' she says. 'I could teach you some basic craft skills, if you like, enough for you to get by out here, on the road.' She hugs her knees to her chest, and licks the sugar from her lips. 'Idle hands and that.'

'I'd like that,' he says, his eyes dancing in the firelight. 'I'd like that a lot.'

13

5 May

———

ROWENA'S PHONE PINGS. Another text from her mother, up late again. 'News says bad storms on the way, are you okay? Where are you now?' Rowena thumbs a message back: 'Am fine. Been fence-mending. Midlands somewhere.' She adds a kiss, but then deletes it and hits send right before the battery dies. It's weird, she thinks, how much more Tessa seems to care about me now that I'm gone.

Rowena steels herself, reaches into the dying fire and gasps as it bites her skin. She manages to hook out the charred wishbone – burned clean of pheasant meat – and carries it on her open palm into the birch trees, past the lean-to and on through the darkness, ever alert to any patch of dark that looks thicker than the rest. Whenever a twig snaps it sets her on edge and stutters her step. She finds a spot where the moonlight breaks through, next to a carpet of stitchwort, the flowers trembling like a fallen constellation. A fox banshee-cries in the distance.

She kneels down, places the wishbone next to her and scrapes aside damp, clingy leaves, releasing the heady smell of decay that was locked in the soil, before plunging her fingers into the cold earth to dig. She lights the little white candle that Pappa Red gave her and lifts her face to the moon for a few breaths, letting its sooth-ing light wash over her. 'I seek peace, I seek respite. Let my fear melt with this wax. This is my desire. This is my will. Let it be done.' She places the candle next to the hole and takes the delicate wishbone in her fingers. A sudden rustle in the leaves at her elbow startles her and the jerk of her body travels down her arms to her hands, snapping the wishbone in two.

'Shit!' Rowena sits back on her heels and wonders if it's another sign – that she won't get what she wants and that she'll never be at peace. It's almost enough to make her cry. She tosses the fragments of bone into the hole anyway and covers them up, thumping the earth firm. Another noise draws her attention and this time something flits past her. She gets out her hunting knife and swipes at the undergrowth, decapitating white flowers, chopping down fern stalks, slashing wildly at anything that moves. 'I'll kill you!' she hisses, baring her teeth, hacking away until her arm aches. 'Just show yourself again, I fucking dare you!'

By the time she's returned to the camp it's started to rain and Halim has huddled closer to the freshly stacked fire like a soggy, beaten dog.

'What are you doing, you idiot?' she asks, her loud voice stirring him. 'Get under the lean-to with me.'

He sits up. 'How's your hand?' he asks. 'I saw you stick it in the fire.'

'It's fine, forget it,' she mutters, climbing under the shelter. 'Now are you coming or what?'

After an early fuel and Wi-Fi stop they reach the county border. There are trucks using the lay-bys to turn around, horse riders being waved back and a sign flashing a warning: 'BORDER CLOSED DUE TO FLOODING. SEEK ALTERNATIVE ROUTES.'

This isn't good, thinks Halim, the only reason he secured this new contract was by saying he could make the pick-up today. He comes to a stop behind a van at the booth and lowers his window to listen in on what looks like an argument between the driver and the Border Guard.

'Why the hell wasn't this announced on the radio, or on the junction signs?' the driver yells.

'Only just closed,' the Guard replies. 'We had a month's worth of rain in a few hours. Best I can do is issue you a detour stamp.'

'World's gone to shit,' the driver says as he hands the Guard his passport.

'Hi. How do we get into Mershire?' Halim asks when it's their turn to approach the booth.

'You've got GPS, don't you?'

Before Halim can respond, Rowena's grabbed their passports, jumped out and approached the hatch. 'Excuse me, sir, I know you're really busy but I have an important contract that's time sensitive and a man like you must know the area well, so I was hoping you could help me find the quickest route?' She looks up at him through the glass, making her eyes wide. It starts to rain again, smoothing her hair to her face.

'Take the B31 heading east through Glynbury, cross the toll bridge, then into Pendleshire, you can try a border from there,' the Guard says, stamping two detour passes and handing them to her.

She smiles at him. 'Thank you!'

'And that's how easy life is if you have the right face and skin,' Halim mutters through gritted teeth as she climbs back into the cab. 'That detour will take hours,' he says, shoving the steering wheel through his hands, jerking the truck into motion as Rowena fumbles with her seat belt.

'Will we make your new job in time?'

He scowls at the road as they move off.

'I guess that's a no, then ... Can't we try somewhere else, there are "unofficial" places to cross, aren't there?'

'What good would that do if the place is flooded? We'd get the truck stuck, get caught – no, I can't risk it.' He presses on the accelerator.

'Well, if you drive like this we might still make it,' Rowena mutters, as she fishes out a chocolate bar from her backpack. 'Want some?' She holds a piece towards him but he waves it away and flicks on the radio. He turns it up loud enough to rattle the windows.

They cross the border at Pendleshire, a rugged county of hills and heath with the occasional village crammed into the cracks of a valley. They make good progress but Halim knows that time's running out if they're to make the pick-up; he grips the steering wheel tighter, weaving around potholes in the empty streets. Next to him, Rowena's staring through the window at the boarded-up shopfronts, burned-out houses, warning signs and padlocks – as if the residents might one day return and reclaim their abandoned property.

'It's like a ghost town,' she says.

'That's exactly what it is.'

Rowena looks like a caged animal glimpsing the jungle for the first time. He'd forgotten that, until now, she'd never been out of her home county. How small her world must have been.

'So where is everyone?' she asks.

'Moved away to towns the government deemed worthy of investment and chose to save – towns with a post office, a school, services for the community. The smaller villages get left behind and eventually the residents give up on them too. I've seen it plenty of times.'

They drive past a burly, hooded man leading a shire horse and cart onto someone's front lawn. The cart looks more like a skip, loaded with lead strips peeled from roofs and windows, metal from old drainpipes and guttering.

'A Sally,' Rowena mutters.

That's what they call salvage men and women, remembers Halim, the ones who thrive on others' misfortune, taking anything not welded down – they probably make a better living than me.

He checks his phone again but there's still no signal, and the clouds are splitting open again, the rain giving everything a slick, grey patina. A flash of lightning blinds him for a second, followed by a great boom of thunder.

'Shouldn't we try to find somewhere to wait out this storm?' Rowena asks, a tremor to her voice. 'We're in a big metal box.'

Another flash. He counts the seconds before the thunder.

On a small rise on the outskirts of town he pulls in next to the carcass of a church, its windows extracted, doors unhinged and removed, and its guts emptied out. Only the graves lie undisturbed.

'Oh, great!' Rowena claps her hands together. 'Let's park on a big old hill and wait for the lightning to skewer us.'

75

'I won't be long,' Halim says as he pulls up his hood and jumps out.

He walks around, holding his phone in the air – still no bars. The grass in the graveyard is alive with snails, bubbling spit from their shells, and everything smells of wet dog. Leaflets cling like rags to the church noticeboard, and underneath a carving of what looks like a flower within a circle, someone has scratched 'RIP Helmslow'. Another flash of lightning backlights the spire, creating a black shard against the sky. Halim tries turning his phone off and on again. The next grind of thunder actually vibrates his skeleton.

He heads around the side of the church and freezes: strung between two yew trees is a huge figure, its torso made of beer crates, its arms and legs comprising branches, its head a mouldering stump with large eye-holes bored into it and a spray-painted mouth that drips on one side. The rain drums on the ivy that binds the hideous green man together and to Halim it's the sound of his quickening heartbeat. He's about to turn away when he sees, stuffed into one of the central crates, a lump of something red and glistening ...

14

HALIM TOUCHES THE GOLD CHAIN around his neck and tears his eyes away from whatever dead thing is lying inside the belly of the green man.

'The job's as good as gone by now,' he says to Rowena as he jumps into the cab and starts the engine. 'We might as well find somewhere to spend the night.'

She frowns at him. 'Are you okay?'

'Fine.' He jerks the truck into gear and speeds off with a squeak of the tyres.

'At least that booking got us across another border,' she shrugs.

'It's not just about that: you forget that my reputation's at stake – I have to show up for the jobs that I'm booked for.' Halim swipes droplets from his face and peers through the wipers, looking for any decent stopping place off the main road. Two screwed-up jobs in the space of days, he cringes. I should have planned this whole thing better. I've been careless. Distracted.

Rain pelts the windscreen, fracturing his view. He feels a tug on the steering wheel as wind catches the side of the truck and tries to nudge them off the road.

'Do people ...' he hesitates. 'Do some people practise human sacrifice? Is that a thing?'

Rowena snorts. 'Not that I'm aware of, why? What the fuck did you see out there?'

'Nothing. I think it was nothing.'

A brown tourist sign appears ahead – he flicks on the indicator and swings the truck towards a place called Dingle House as the dreary grey heath eventually levels out into fields.

The headlights glide across acorn-topped gateposts and catch a tangle of trees as they turn into a long, serpentine drive. Through the grain and flicker of rain, a large mansion comes into view, its roof spiking the low, dark clouds, seeming to snag them in place.

'Wow!' Rowena gapes.

'Try not to steal anything,' Halim says, only half-joking, as he follows parking signs and pulls up next to an abandoned car with weeds curling up through its windscreen and its petrol cap cracked wide.

'At least the place looks open.' Rowena points to the glow coming from the thin arched windows either side of an ebony front door.

They leave their things in the truck, brace themselves against the weather and dash towards the house.

No one answers the bell. Halim goes to knock, but the door's unlocked and his fist pushes it wide. They step into a black-and-white-tiled hallway. Two oil lamps flicker in the draught, giving light to walls choked with winter coats and framed flower pressings. Dirt-crusted boots of many sizes nose the skirting boards.

'Hello?' Halim calls out.

Rowena wrings droplets from her hair as Halim wipes his feet on the doormat. 'Close the door, I'm freezing my tits off,' she says.

They pass a roped-off reception room with a silent grandfather clock and an elaborate fabric sofa, its seat dotted with pinecones, and continue on past the wooden staircase, towards a light at the end of the hall.

Halim knocks on the door, hesitates, and then enters what must be the dining room.

An older man, maybe in his late thirties, is stood near the open French doors with a towel wrapped around his head. In too-tight black chinos and a blouse unbuttoned to his navel he looks like a Renaissance vampire, thinks Halim.

'Oh, hello there! Welcome!' The man's smile is crammed with crooked nicotine-stained teeth and his voice rings with public-school clarity.

'Sorry to disturb you,' Halim says, 'but we needed to get out of the storm and I thought this place might be open to the public.'

The man rushes over and grasps them both by their elbows, gently drawing them inside towards the wood-burner. 'Yes, yes, Dingle House is still open to the public, but I took over management from the Trust a year ago and I insist on no visiting hours or fees. I think of it more as a free haven for weary travellers – much like yourselves.' He smiles again and offers his hand to Rowena. 'I'm Oscar.'

'Rowena.'

'Wonderful.' Oscar brings her hand to his lips and kisses it.

She raises her eyebrows.

'Halim,' he says, grateful for only a handshake.

Female laughter sounds from the garden, and that's when Halim notices the silken nests of dresses and knickers lying discarded on the floor.

Two attractive young women – completely naked and glistening with rain – tumble into the room.

'Oh, we have company,' the taller one smiles. She takes off her sunglasses, seemingly unashamed of her nudity. 'Don't mind us, we were just rain-bathing – would be a crime not to on a night like this!'

Halim drags his eyes away from the wet tongues of black hair sticking to their flawless dark skin and they settle on a cluster of decanters on the sideboard.

'I would do introductions,' Oscar says, 'but seeing as we're all a bit damp, why don't we get some towels in here before the parquet rots?'

Halim continues his appraisal of the crystal bottles with their silver tags as the two women head for a side door, moving through the air as if it were water. He can feel Rowena's eyes on him and imagines the grin on her face.

'Are you both hungry?' Oscar asks. 'We have a cheeseboard, or perhaps you're thirsty?'

The women return, wrapped in towels that squeeze and bolster their cleavages. 'Here you go, handsome,' one of them says as she hands Halim a towel. She holds herself as if she's posing for a painting, he notes.

Oscar gestures towards her: 'This lovely creature is Agatha, and the other beauty is Kezia. Ladies, we have two new guests, Halim and ...?'

'Rowena,' she says, accepting a towel. 'This place is amazing.'

'Isn't it? The house has been in my family for five generations.' Oscar pours them red wine from an earthenware jug on the dining-room table. 'I inherited it a year ago and decided to move straight in.' He presents two glasses filled to the brim.

'I can't, I'm driving,' Halim says, wondering how much it must cost to import Argentinian wine.

'I'll take his,' Agatha says.

Oscar reaches across Halim to hand it to her. 'These two have been staying for – how long is it now?'

'A couple of months,' she replies, also helping herself to some blue cheese. 'We were hiking the old pilgrim routes and came across this place. We were only supposed to stay for one night, but you know how it is when the mood takes you.'

No, Halim thinks, I don't. He moves aside as Kezia approaches the wood-burner and starts combing her fingers through her long, damp hair.

'What a storm,' she says, catching his eyes.

'Yes, and it's not passing any time soon,' Oscar adds, his hands on his hips. 'You two might as well spend the night – we've plenty of rooms, it'd be good for them to see some use and get an airing.'

'Sounds great, thank you,' Rowena jumps in before Halim can reply and turns to him. 'Makes sense, doesn't it? We can get our bearings in the morning, then pick up Wi-Fi in a pub or something.'

Oscar whistles through his teeth. 'Ah, no pubs anywhere near, I'm afraid, cable doesn't run here any more and the phone signal's AWOL since the mast got pulled down.' He shrugs. 'Do you know, I quite like not being plugged in, there's something liberating about it – a detox from all the white noise of the world. We do, however, have hot water from the boiler stoves if you'd like to get out of those wet clothes and share a bath.'

'Oh, we're not ...' Halim shifts to a different foot. 'We're just trav-elling companions.'

Oscar places a hand on his shoulder and gives it a squeeze. 'Well, friend, take a break from all that travelling, you seem a tad knotted up. Besides, it probably isn't safe to drive in weather like this.' The squeeze turns into a massage.

Halim steps away. 'Well, yes, I suppose it is getting late and we can't really push on until tomorrow. So, thank you – we'd be grateful for your hospitality.'

'Well said,' Oscar decants another glass of wine and hands it to Halim, clinking it with the signet ring on his little finger. '*Santé.*'

Halim takes a sip as Kezia and Agatha drop their towels and shimmy back into their dresses. The wine tastes of plum and spice, but for some reason he finds it hard to swallow. A shimmer of amusement crosses the faces of the women and at that moment he hates himself more than ever.

'So what brought you to this desolate old county of Pendleshire?' Oscar asks, oblivious.

Halim clears his throat. 'A detour. Flooding. I missed out on a contract because of it, so I'll need to get online early tomorrow and secure something that will take us over into Langtonshire. We can pick up our route from there.'

'Floods,' Oscar sighs loudly. 'You know, this county used to be famous for its lavender farms, there were vast fields of the stuff – a sweet-smelling, bee-humming purple haze. Sad thing, what's happening to the Kingdom. Soon we'll all be seeking higher ground and lifting our skirts from the rising waters.' He gazes thoughtfully at the rain trails on the windows.

'You two could always stay on here a bit longer,' Kezia says, directing her words at Halim as she leans against the sideboard and runs her tongue along her teeth. 'You know, recharge, slow down for a bit. Dingle House has amazing healing energy.'

'Yes, of course, you're more than welcome,' Oscar says as he swills wine around the bowl of his glass.

Halim shakes his head. 'We can't afford to slow down, I have a delivery to make about four counties away.'

'He means me,' Rowena says. 'He's taking me to Culcrith and we need to get there before the twenty-sixth of May.'

'Culcrith? Never heard of it, is it up north?' Kezia asks.

Rowena nods. 'It's where my grandmother lives, an old family farm.'

'And what happens on the twenty-sixth of May?'

'I turn eighteen.'

Kezia's face lights up. 'Ooh, so your gran's throwing you a big party, is she?'

'Not if she's anything like my mother.'

'Oh, you've not met her? Well, I hope for your sake she's nice.'

Agatha leans back in her chair as she turns to Halim. 'So if Rowena's off to see her grandmother,' she says, 'what does that make you – the wolf or the woodcutter?'

'I can't imagine those soft hands hefting an axe,' Kezia adds, her head tilted, 'but I bet there's a wolf under that shy exterior.'

'What was your name again?' Agatha asks.

'Halim.'

'Halim,' she smiles, turning his name over in her mouth. 'We're just jesting, Halim, don't mind us.'

'Speaking of wolves, who's hungry?' asks Oscar. 'Aggy, I think we have some leftover potato pancakes and apple sauce.'

Agatha sighs like a sulky teenager as she gets up and heads to the kitchen.

'We grow all our own fruit and veg but, unless you can catch it and kill it, meat is a rarity, I'm afraid,' Oscar says as he gnaws and sucks on a cheese rind.

'I can hunt,' says Rowena. 'I was a gamekeeper back home.'

Halim sniffs, amused that she's promoted herself from poacher.

'Really?' Oscar pulls a chair over. 'That is a very useful skill to have, you'd do well in Pendleshire. Perhaps you could take my air rifle out tomorrow and rustle up something for our larder?'

'We'll be leaving in the morning,' Halim says.

'Oh, that's a shame. It's always nice to have new faces around here, it gives the place some extra vim, brings the old girl to life.'

'I could take the gun out early,' Rowena says, ignoring Halim's glare. 'Dawn's the best time anyway.'

Rowena's room is dark and chilly but she's been issued with an oil lamp, a pile of blankets and a pair of moccasin slippers. She sniffs them – gags – and drops them by the door. Halim's been put in the room opposite, and her relief in knowing that he's nearby annoys her. On his advice she locks the door, even though Oscar, Agatha and Kezia have been nothing but nice to them since they arrived. Rowena places the oil lamp on the bedside table and takes a look around. The chalky magnolia walls are crumbling in the corners, the arched windows make it feel like a place of worship, there's a dried-up bunch of roses hanging upside down above a crusty basin in the corner, wax spots on the carpet, and the plug sockets don't work. She loves it. She's never been anywhere so big, so old and impressive. She jumps up onto the sleigh bed and sneezes. A fading cloud of white on the cold glass of the window catches her eye – too far away to be her own breath. Her heart lurches. She takes out the rabbit's foot and presses it between her fingers as she climbs down and edges towards the window.

Outside, the rain has slackened. Gravel glints below, pine trees tussle with each other in the wind, and the lightning's been relegated to a distant flicker of torchlight behind thick clouds. Rowena shivers. This is the furthest I've ever been from Pickbury, she thinks, from all the overgrown tracks and snickets Pa and me used to make our own secret ways – shortcuts I'd memorised by the time I was twelve so I could sneak out to midnight moots. She remembers the night she met Drew – she was thirteen and he was fifteen, bent double, puking up the hooch his gramps had made. Those times and places seem so thin and distant now – memories fading like sun-bleached postcards. Memories that will die with her.

She comes away from the window, lets the blanket drop from her shoulders and studies herself in the full-length mirror: the soft curve of her hips and breasts through the thin cotton of her charity-shop dress; the annoying bump on her nose; the way her freckles make smudges under her eyes in the half-light. An *almost-*May Queen. She pinches the hem of her dress and spins, returning full circle to see a pale face reflected behind her.

Her pa smiles, and it breaks her heart all over again.

15

___

ROWENA GOES TO TURN AROUND but her pa's reflection holds his hands up, his eyes widen and he shakes his head 'no'. She freezes, wondering if it's merely a trick of the light, a warped refraction in the old glass. With every fibre, every mote of energy, she wills it to be real. How long have they got? Holding her breath, she races through all the things she could say, knowing that she might lose him again any second ...

'Was it my curse?' Her voice is barely a whisper and her question a dagger – hanging in the air between them, pointed at her heart.

Marcus's head moves a fraction and his eyes dart away, as if he's heard something beyond the room.

Rowena fights the instinct to turn around. A chill creeps up the nape of her neck. Fear and love tumble and churn in the space between her lungs as her heart tries to wrench itself out of her, and her soundless mouth forms the words 'I'm sorry' and 'I love you'.

In the mirror, her pa's face softens and he smiles at her like he used to, but already he's out of focus and they both know they don't have long.

'Don't go!' Rowena whimpers, surprised to find a deep, rough voice breaking from her – more his than her own. 'Please – don't go!' She's pretty sure it's *his* mouth moving in the reflection behind her, *his* head that's shaking. 'Listen,' he says – and she's trying to, but when she blinks there's an empty space over her shoulder where he stood just moments before. She scrunches her eyes shut, hoping to see the negative of him on the backs of her lids, the ghost of his ghost. There's only black.

'Pa?' Her voice is her own again.

She turns and looks, a painful lump in her throat, her face hot with the coming of tears. There's no one there, just flickering shadows from the oil lamp – a draught perhaps.

The rain picks up again, like fingers drumming on the window to be let in.

Rowena fetches the urn from her backpack and sits on the floor, holding it to her chest. 'I lit you so many candles,' she whispers. 'I put drops of dill, vervain and St John's wort on my pillow every night for days after you died, hoping to dream of you, but you never came. Why now? Why here? What were you trying to tell me? I'm here, Pa, I'm listening.'

She sits there for what seems like hours, but no reply ever comes.

After a long and restless night, Rowena emerges from her room pre-dawn and almost bumps into Halim in the hallway.

'I heard you getting up and thought I'd join you,' he says.

She tries to smooth down her bed-scuffed hair, wonders if her eyes are red. 'I don't need babysitting, I've used a gun before.'

'I know, that's why I want to come, to learn from you. You promised to teach me things. Survival-type things, remember?'

Rowena scratches her collarbone and looks him over. 'Well, for a start, you need to put on darker clothes and wash off that disgusting cologne.'

'Oh,' he says. 'Give me a minute.'

He darts back into his room. Through the open door she sees him unpeel his red cable-knit jumper and catches a flash of brown skin and muscle when his T-shirt gets caught up. She looks away.

When he's ready, they head to the room behind the kitchen, as instructed by Oscar. The chunky table, sloping floor and large hooks suggest it was once a butchering room and meat store. There's a note pinned to the box of pellets: 'Happy hunting! x'.

'Do you think he's got a licence?' Halim asks.

'Don't need one for an air rifle. Besides, it's his land anyway.'

'So he says.'

Halim watches her check the scope and silencer, then clean and load the rifle – listening as she explains every careful action. His attentiveness gives her a secret kick.

They head into the walled kitchen garden, where everything's a silhouette against the silvery sky. At least it's not raining, she thinks, flicking on the torch. The herbs are all thinned and bowed by the recent storm, but the rose garden beyond looks lush and well tended, with budding stems trained to wooden arches and a scroll-work trellis. She waves the torch to the right and it picks out a hunched figure. She gasps.

It's nothing but an absurd-looking scarecrow: a waistcoat with brass buttons, a purple silk scarf knotted around a mould-spotted sack head, a pipe dangling from a tear where its mouth should be. Rowena rolls her shoulders and takes a steadying breath.

'He's a bit weird, isn't he?' Halim says.

'Doubt the crows care.'

'I mean Oscar.'

'I think he's nice. Quite fit for an older bloke.'

'He smiles too much, it's disconcerting.'

'You only think that because you don't smile enough,' she sniffs, heading towards the field at the end of the rose garden. 'This one's too overgrown, we need to find one that's grazed, better for hunting.'

'What about the two girls, what do you make of them?' Halim asks.

'I think Agatha and Kezia are friendly, beautiful *women*.'

Halim mumbles something.

'Why?'

'They're insincere. They're the type of girls – *women* – who constantly look over your shoulder to see if someone better has entered the room.'

'They're just confident.' Rowena turns and deliberately shines the torch on Halim's face, making him squint. 'And that scares you, doesn't it? You're not used to women who speak their mind – I've seen the look you get when I say stuff sometimes. Now, keep your eyes peeled,' she says, walking on. 'Look for any dull-brown lumps on the ground.'

'So how did you learn to shoot?' he asks, catching her up.

'My pa used to take me out every Sunday, it was mainly an excuse for him to swing by the church without Tessa knowing. They didn't exactly share the same beliefs. I think that's one of the reasons they never kept in touch with their families up in Culcrith.'

'You went to church every Sunday?'

She can hear the surprise in Halim's voice. 'Nah, I stayed out exploring the woods on the Lord's estate and practising my aim. My cathedral was one of trees. Pa never pushed me, he wanted me to make up my own mind about things.'

'Hmm,' Halim mutters. 'You're lucky, he sounds like a decent man.'

'He is. *Was*.'

They reach a wooden gate, marking the barrier between fields. Rowena stops halfway through, blocking the way for Halim. 'You know why they call this a "kissing gate", don't you?' she asks, her eyebrow raised. 'It's bad luck if we don't kiss at the midpoint.'

Halim frowns, his jaw clenched.

She bursts into laughter. 'The look on your face!' She steps through, letting the gate swing back and hit him.

The clouds are cracking open in the distance, revealing the pink flesh of dawn, and birds are stirring in the ragged crooks of hawthorn and hazel. 'I'm turning off the torch now,' she whispers. 'We'll follow the hedge-line. You'll need to keep quiet, and stop slapping your feet through the mud.'

Halim keeps close to her side, pausing whenever she does, his eyes scanning the meadow. Rowena can feel the shape of him against her arm.

Her boot squashes through a mushroom clump as she stops and raises the rifle in one slow, controlled movement. The rabbits are nothing but smudges, betrayed only by the twitch of an ear or the white wink of a tail. They're upwind and have no idea that she's nestling into the recoil pad, lining up the shot, breathing in … holding it …

*

Rowena and Halim hear the panting of the dogs before they see them. Two hulking German shepherds emerge from the scrub at the edge of the dell, followed by the two men walking them. The men look thin, in their early twenties – probably not much older than Halim, except that life has roughed them up a bit. Their dark-circled eyes narrow as they note the brace of rabbits dangling from Rowena's shoulder, and the air rifle dangling from Halim's.

'Hold up. I believe those belong to us,' the man in the red beanie says, stopping a few metres away.

'How d'you work that out?' Rowena frowns, sensing the change in their body language. The dogs have sensed it too and are looking up at their masters and straining on their ropes.

'Well, you and the darkie ain't from around here,' the other man says, 'and we are. Born and bred. So those,' he points to the rabbits, 'by rights, are our supper. Our land, our goods.'

'This is Oscar's land,' Halim says, drawing himself taller, 'and we've permission to be here.'

'Oscar who?'

'He owns Dingle House,' Rowena adds, not knowing his surname. 'We're on our way back there, if you'd like to check with him.'

The man in the red beanie shakes his head. 'No, sweetheart. See, this is common land for the locals – so it ain't *your* way, or Oscar's way, it's *our* way.'

The other man bends down, whispers in his dog's ear and ruffles its neck as its tail thumps the dirt.

'Outsiders need to pay up to use these paths,' red beanie directs his words at Halim, whose face darkens as he grips the butt of the rifle.

Rowena catches Halim's eye and shakes her head. She runs through a quick mental map of the area as the weak morning sun prises its fingers through the hedgerows and skims the tops of molehills.

One of the dogs starts to growl.

'Well? What's it to be, we ain't got all day.'

'Thing is, if we give up our rabbits our friend with the gun over there won't be happy,' Rowena says, pointing to the trees behind the men.

When they both turn around Rowena yanks Halim into a run. 'Follow me,' she hisses as they race off along the hedgerow.

The men shout after them. The dogs add their barks to the din as their leads are unclipped and finally they're loose.

Rowena finds the narrow gap and shoves her way through the brittle branches, bursting out into the adjoining field – this one fallow, choked with hip-high grass and cow parsley. The barking comes in bursts now as the dogs focus on the chase. Rowena knows they can't outrun them, so they might have to stop and shoot at close range, but the air pressure's low and there are maybe two pellets left before they'll need to reload.

'Head for that ditch at the field entrance,' she gasps, trying to sprint through clingy stems and slicks of mud, the low sun blinding her.

The dogs are close; she imagines their teeth sinking into her ankle at any moment, tugging and twisting it loose with a crack ... She stumbles over a stone, regains her balance and crashes on, the weeds thinning as they reach the edge of the field.

'Just give them the bloody rabbits,' Halim hisses between bursts of breath.

'Get behind me but have the rifle ready, aim it like I showed you.' She can taste blood – her throat ravaged by the cold air tearing up and down it.

Halim does as she says and points the barrel towards the waving grass, his chest heaving.

Rowena cuts the string binding the rabbits together and slices into their flesh to expose their still-warm innards. She grips her hunting knife in one hand, holds the dripping carcasses high and waits.

The thumping of paws gets closer, almost as loud now as the pulse in her ears.

A few seconds later the dogs explode from the grass, jaws gaping, tongues flapping like flags.

She whistles and waves the rabbits, drawing their attention. The dogs pull up short, skidding in the mud as their heads snap upwards, teeth bared. Salivating, eyes sparkling, they ready themselves for a leap.

Rowena tosses the rabbits into the ditch behind her and jumps away.

The dogs' dark muzzles follow the arc of furry bodies, and in a flash they've launched themselves after the carcasses.

Their piercing yelps are like nothing Rowena's ever heard before, turning her stomach and weakening her legs.

Halim darts her a look. He lowers the air rifle and goes towards the ditch but Rowena holds him back. 'Don't,' she says, knowing full well that its floor is embedded with sharpened spikes. She swallows hard, takes the rifle from him and stands over the pit, ready to end their misery with a swift shot to the head.

Below her, both dogs lie skewered and broken, spines split, fur ripped through by points of wood and jagged shafts of metal, now slick with blood. They're already gone. A spike pokes through one of the dog's skulls and its stilled jaws are cracked wide open, tantalisingly close to a rabbit. Its weeping eye looks up at Rowena accusingly: she stares back and imagines what the points might feel like through her own skin and flesh ...

A sharp whistle from the far side of the field shakes her free and she turns to Halim. 'That tree's our way out,' she says, pointing to the oak thrusting up from the tight-knitted hedgerow. 'Up and over. Hurry!'

Rowena shoulders the rifle and scrambles up the rough-ridged bark, finding handholds in knots and forks. She swings off a branch and drops down on the other side.

Halim doesn't land well and stifles a cry as his foot turns over.

She helps him up and takes some of his weight as he limps alongside her, sweating and flinching. She checks over her shoulder every now and then, but they're not being followed. The men will soon find what's left of their dogs, she thinks with a shudder.

Rowena and Halim eventually make it to the grove of pines at the edge of Dingle House. Only then, in the muffled shadows, does she allow them to stop and rest. Halim slumps down on a damp log, grimacing, his fists clenched.

'Is it broken?' she asks, leaning on her thighs to catch her breath.

'I don't know, just sprained I hope.'

Somewhere in the canopy the rooks scream to each other like electric buzzers.

'How did you know about that ditch, Rowena?'

'I spotted it through the gap in the hedge on our way out. You should always be aware of your surroundings in an unfamiliar place. My pa taught me that.' She spits on the needle-padded ground. 'I never thought it would come in useful though – Pickbury was all there was and I knew every inch of it.' Her legs are still trembling and she knows it's not just from the running.

Halim heaves a great weary sigh. 'I don't think I'll be able to drive.'

Rowena gazes through the trees at Dingle House and wonders if her pa is looking back at her from a window, if he somehow meant for this to happen, and for her to remain there, with him.

16

6 May

———

THAT EVENING, AS HALIM RESTS in his room and Oscar sleeps off a hangover, Rowena shares a smoke with Kezia, the two of them sitting cross-legged on velvet cushions at the French doors. A paddle-shaped dulcimer lies next to Kezia's lap and every now and then she reaches over to stroke a string or two. 'No offence, but you look like shit, Ro,' she says.

'I didn't sleep very well, and then we had a pretty rough day.'

'Don't worry about the hunting thing, we're hardly going to starve.'

'Yeah, but I insisted we went out shooting because I wanted to show off, basically, and now Halim's screwed his ankle and we're stuck here.'

'Perhaps it's the world telling you to take a pause?'

'It's just that I need to get to Culcrith before my birthday. We only have twenty days to get across all those borders and cover the distance.'

Kezia smiles and narrows her eyes. 'Are you and Halim running away together?'

'What? No, he's just my ride.'

'Then what's the rush?'

Rowena gazes out at the glistening lawn, dressed in pearls of water that catch the moonlight. She's embarrassed to confess that she's cursed, touched by Death and a liability to everyone. 'I'm ill,' she simply says, 'my gran's a healer and the sooner I get there the quicker she can help me.'

Kezia leans back and exhales a curl of smoke like a question mark. 'Oscar's got a whole medicine cabinet full of pills he stockpiled when he arrived in this county and locked them away. I'm sure he wouldn't mind sorting you out.'

'I wish it were that simple.'

Kezia eyes her sidelong. 'Shit, are you pregnant?'

Rowena scowls.

'Dying?'

This time Rowena bites the inside of her lip, unsure how to reply.

'Here,' Agatha says as she joins them, 'this'll loosen you up a bit.' She kneels down next to them and hands Rowena a steaming china cup. 'Go on, try it,' she laughs, her dark eyes sparkling.

It looks like puddle water but Rowena does as she's told and sips the nutty liquid. 'What is it?'

''Shroom tea,' Agatha says, pouring cups for herself and Kezia. 'With a bit of nutmeg and a hint of ginger. Aggy's special recipe.'

'Trust me, it's really good,' Kezia says, drawing out the vowels for effect, their previous conversation seemingly forgotten.

'My boyfriend died last year, while he was tripping,' Rowena mutters as she runs her finger around the rim of the cup.

'Damn,' Kezia frowns. 'Don't worry though – this stuff gives a mellow high, eases you into it. Don't look into any mirrors though, that's the thing that always gets me. Fucking weird. We've drunk it a million times, haven't we, Ags?'

'Mm-hmm. It helps when you're with the right people too. You're safe with us.' She gathers Rowena and Kezia into a hug and holds them both next to her bosom.

She smells of moss and rosewater, thinks Rowena, enjoying the human contact, remembering the warm sensation of being held.

The three of them sit like that for a while, Agatha running her fingers through Rowena's hair as they drink their tea. Eventually Rowena relaxes, manages to think about things other than gaping jaws and matted fur. Her hands smell of geranium soap instead of mud and blood, and her hair is washed and brushed to a shine. At last she feels clean. On the outside at least.

'I saw something in my room last night,' Rowena says, her tongue loosened by the tea. The girls turn to look at her, their cheekbones iridescent with a dusting of colour. 'I saw my pa. He's been dead for almost three weeks. I have his ashes in my bag.'

Agatha lights a rollie, her scarlet-painted lips leaving a kiss mark on the cigarette paper. 'I've seen things here too,' she says. 'It's this place, it's got such a strong energy it practically pulls you to it, like everything that's happened here over hundreds of years has soaked into the walls and it wants you to know about it. Oscar's convinced Dingle House is haunted, bless him.'

'Do you think my pa was drawn here, then? That it's this place? Do you think he'll come again?'

'Maybe,' Agatha shrugs, the crocheted shawl slipping off her shoulder, revealing the purple lace of her bra strap. 'But maybe he only came here to give you his final goodbye.'

I hope not, thinks Rowena, I need him to forgive me. She gulps down the last of the tea, and almost chokes on the gritty dregs.

'Ooh, we could hold a seance,' Agatha continues, 'find out from the source!'

'NO!' The cup slips from Rowena's fingers and she catches it just in time. 'I mean, it might, you know, be too upsetting.' And it might open the door to something much darker, she thinks.

Agatha raises an eyebrow.

'Do you wanna know what I think?' Kezia doesn't wait for an answer. 'I think you leave behind a stronger imprint the longer you spend somewhere, you become part of the fabric of a place – like putting down roots, you kind of grow into it. But why stay in one place that long when there's so much world to see, am I right?'

'Preach,' agrees Agatha, using her cigarette as a pointer. 'There's nothing more sexy than a horizon line or a bend in the path. I like to think that Kez and I have left a little bit of our essence everywhere we've been, and if we leave something of us behind it doesn't matter – because the journey fills us up again.' She taps her breastbone. 'Sometimes I feel so full of the beauty we've seen I feel like I could burst.' Her expression shifts from thoughtful to serious as she tucks some hair behind Rowena's ear. 'You're packing a lot of daddy issues, Ro – you need to let some of that shit go or you'll age before your time. Frown lines, babe, nobody wants them.'

Time passes in a pleasant fug until Agatha jumps up, startling the other two. 'Come on, let's go for a moonlit walk,' she says, shooting indigo from her hands as they clap together. She runs out through the French doors.

When Rowena stands up it's as if the whole sky comes unstuck and swoops down to swaddle her, the stars rippling and bending so close she can almost see their swirling gas shells and the secrets that lie beneath ... She knocks over a cup and it smashes; is fascinated to watch the flexing fragments slither away like slugs across the parquet floor. When she bumps into Kezia as she's dragged out the door their limbs spark with gold wherever they touch. 'It's beautiful,' gasps Rowena, as they laugh in each other's faces, hold each other's cheeks and shed molten metal down their necks and chests.

As Kezia and Agatha brush across the grass ahead of her, Rowena imagines that she's moving like them: graceful as a dancer, acutely aware of her body as her limbs extend and contract, following the lines the other two leave behind, skimming their silvery wake.

'What do you think, Ro?' Agatha calls out over her shoulder. 'Look at the moon!' she howls.

Rowena looks up and watches with delight as the crescent shimmers and swells until it's full and round. She squints at the grey patches appearing, looks for the doughy eyes and lopsided smile; the face of an old friend. What she sees instead are two dark sockets, a skull that turns towards her and opens its jaws wide to scream ...

'Ro? Are you okay? Why are you screaming?'

'Shh! It's okay, babe, come here!' Agatha rushes over and wraps her arms around Rowena's stiffened body.

Rowena pushes her away and watches, aghast, as Agatha's arms lengthen and her fingers grow twig-like and ragged as a branch. 'No, not again. Why won't you leave me alone?' She turns to run, but Kezia rushes over and gently guides Rowena down to the cool grass.

'It's okay, it's just us. It's Kezia and Aggy. What are you running from?'

Rowena shakes her head and a too-loud laugh escapes her. 'That's just it, I don't know. Nothing.'

'That's right, it's just nothing. You can stop running now, Ro. Let's just sit and be still for a while.'

Rowena looks up into Kezia's face and sees love coming off her in waves, feels it pool around her like a mantle. 'Yeah,' she nods. 'You're right. I should stop running.'

Agatha joins them on the grass and takes Rowena's hand in hers. 'You're just where you need to be,' she whispers.

17

7 May

———

'WE'VE VERY MUCH ENJOYED your company these past two nights,' Oscar says over breakfast the next morning. 'I know things haven't quite gone to plan for you both, but you're more than welcome to stay on at Dingle House as long as you want. All we ask is that everyone pitches in with cooking, cleaning and general upkeep. Perhaps you could try hunting again?' He catches the look on Halim's face. 'Or not. That's fine. Vegetables are fine,' he smiles.

Halim watches him gloop even more syrup onto his mulch-thick porridge. Syrup – not honey. The good stuff, imported from Canada, no less.

Rowena chews on freshly baked bread as Kezia leans across the table towards her. 'We've got some friends stopping by next week, I'd love for you to meet them. They're musicians. One of them used to tour with this famous glam-noir band, I think you'd like him.' She winks.

'We have to set up another contract and get going,' Halim says, louder than intended.

Kezia fixes him with a stern look. 'Your ankle isn't healed yet. And besides, look at her – Ro's spent. You both need to take a break and rest up for a while, don't you think?'

Halim glances at Rowena, thinks that maybe she does look a bit paler than usual. He remembers her dig at him on Beltane Eve

– and wonders if he has lost the art of relaxing and having fun. 'I suppose we can afford a day or two here and still make Culcrith before the twenty-sixth,' he concedes.

When Rowena smiles at him she holds his gaze a little longer than usual, and something shifts in his chest.

'You know what you should do?' Oscar says, through a cheek-ful of porridge. 'Visit the lake. That cold water would do your foot the world of good. I often go wild-swimming there with my guests. In the summer it's the ideal picnic spot – in fact, I was thinking of building a summer house there this year, just a little ...'

Halim zones out, wonders why Rowena seems to love this place so much and hang on every word of these spoiled, vacuous people.

'Are you gonna keep staring at your phone? There's still no signal. Look at what you're missing.' Rowena twirls around, her arms spread, her dress billowing like a parachute.

'Yeah, sorry,' Halim pockets his phone and solar charger and draws a breath. She's right, this is beautiful. He limps down the meandering path as they head for the lake. It's overgrown, but that only adds to its dishevelled, clandestine charm. On either side of them lush, dappled greens are flecked with bluebells and scattered with other flowers he doesn't know the name of.

Rowena disappears into the trees and comes back a minute later dragging a large branch. She jumps on it to snap it and hands him the longer piece. 'A walking stick,' she says. 'Though you really could've left your slippers at home, Granddad.'

He looks down and sniffs. 'They're called loafers, and they're really comfy.'

As they continue on he notices Rowena looking up at the canopy and glancing behind as if searching for something. He looks up too and sees nothing but leaves, more leaves, and lemon-coloured clouds caught in the morning light. 'How far is it?' he asks. 'I should be resting my foot.'

A second later, the path opens out onto a grassy clearing next to a small lake, swollen from the recent rain. Halim's spine tingles – not from the breeze, but from the soft, effortless sweep of the hill behind the rippling water, the droop and sway of the weeping willows, the way the sun brings out Rowena's freckles as she turns to smile at him. It's a wonder that such a place exists in this bleak county, he thinks.

Rowena kicks off her boots, unpeels her socks and heads for the stony shoreline. She tucks the hem of her dress up into her knickers, steps into the water and squeaks from the cold.

Mindful of his foot, Halim folds himself down onto the grass nearby and tilts his face to catch the warmth of the sun. He closes his eyes and the world turns pink. Rowena's gentle splashing soon sends his mind floating off into a blissful nothing and unconsciousness soon slips over him like a blanket. His body gives way bit by bit, sinks into the ground for a few seconds, then emerges again at a flutter of wings nearby.

His face grows cool as a shadow falls over it.

'Come with me, Granddad, I wanna show you something.' Rowena is standing above him.

Halim groans, but she holds out her hand and waits. She helps him up and leads him to the water's edge. 'What's that?' she asks, pointing.

'A flower.'

She rolls her eyes. 'Try harder.'

'Clover?'

'It's water mint.' She picks a few leaves and hands him one. 'Try it.'

Halim hesitates, thinking it might be one of her tricks, but it actually tastes pleasantly sweet.

'I saw some wild strawberries back there too but they're not ripe yet,' Rowena says, rolling the leaf between her fingers and sniffing it. 'And pineapple weed. There's loads you can eat for free if you only look for it – main course and dessert!'

'I should keep you around for when my money runs out,' Halim sniffs.

They share a look and he's not sure what it means, but for the first time he pictures himself driving away, leaving Rowena at her grandmother's, sees her shrinking in the rear-view mirror as she watches him go.

Halim breaks eye contact first.

'Oscar asked me to stay on here at Dingle House,' Rowena says, twirling the mint leaf.

'Oh, yeah?'

'Yeah. I could live here, it could be good. I can hunt and forage and just sit it out until … It either gets me or It doesn't. Like you said – we all die some day.' Behind her, a swan skids across the water and lands with a few wheezing beats of its great white wings. 'I mean, just look at this place!'

Halim draws a hand down his stubbled chin and wonders if she was sent to test him. 'So you're giving up on being healed? What about this curse of yours?'

'It can't hurt anyone if I don't get close to anyone. Maybe it's time I stopped running and just accepted that I'll always be alone? Deep down, I'm not sure my gran can save me. Besides, it's not like I have any other plans.'

'But isn't it worth a shot? Especially after all the effort your mother made in sending you north?'

Rowena sniffs. 'So suddenly you're a believer? Gimme a break.'

'Do you trust that sleazy "Johnny-lord-of-the-manor" boho brat? What if he's just like that guy from the saltmarsh? What about all the other thugs and grunts in this county?'

'Oscar's not into women if that's what you're getting at.' She flicks the crumpled mint into the water. 'I told him I'd stay.'

A stab of heat rises to Halim's face and his jaw becomes so tight he has to push his next words out: 'So you just changed your plans without even talking to me first?'

'It's my life!'

'It's mine too!' he snaps. 'This job was my last chance. *Fuck!*' Halim grips his walking stick so tight the damp wood crumbles under his knuckles. The soft inner parts of his head press against his skull. He turns, kicks off his loafers and limps into the water, slipping a little on the age-worn pebbles.

'You've been paid half already, haven't you?' she calls out. 'Just take the money and leg it, that's what I'd do.'

He stops. Ripples grin up at him from below. 'I'm nothing like you.'

'At least you've got rich folks to bail you out – most people have nothing!'

Halim scolds himself for being so gullible, for expecting this selfish, impulsive girl to honour the contract. Instead, she's forcing him towards his parents, wresting his fate out of his hands, and what can he do about it? He focuses on the swirling sensation around his calves and pushes forward. His tracksuit bottoms suck up the lake water as it knocks his hips and moves him, urging him on, making him its puppet. His breath stutters from the chill.

'Halim?'

Deeper now.

Murky, soft hands tug at his clothes and rock him like a baby. His mind becomes as hollow as his chest. With a sigh, he gives in to the lake's embrace and sinks to the silty bed as the water strokes his hair and purrs in his ears. He keeps his eyes open, lets them sting, and it's like looking through the dregs of a whisky tumbler. He can hear his father's mocking laughter in the vibrations of the water, looks down at the stones under his feet as they become little round tablets that dissolve under the crush of his heels. The chalky effervescence makes him giddy – until he realises that the bubbles are from his own mouth and his lungs are screaming for air. Relenting, he kicks off and bursts up into the sky.

He's surprised to find Rowena right beside him, her hand on his arm, water lapping at her ribs.

'What the hell was that?' she yells. 'I thought you were trying to drown yourself or something!' She thumps him. When he doesn't respond she thumps him again, spraying the air with droplets.

Halim turns to face her. There's barely two inches between them as their dripping bodies sway like dancers. He gets a sudden, angry urge to kiss her – and almost does, but she spins around and wades back to the shore, muttering to herself.

He punches the water, and it retaliates by spitting in his face.

When he reaches the clearing he finds a pile of twigs and branches. Rowena emerges from the trees with an armful more. 'What are you doing?' he asks.

'What does it look like? I wanted to stay out here so I'm making a fire to stop me getting hypothermia.' She kneels and holds a lighter to the kindling. 'You can go back to the house if you want, nothing stopping you.'

He considers it, but an annoying tug in his gut tells him to stay, that this might be their last day together. Why can't I hate her? he broods, his body clenched against the shivers. He lifts off his jumper and T-shirt and wrings them out, catches Rowena's eye before she looks away. Even if I do find her moderately attractive, he thinks, it's a pointless investment of time and emotion: she's a complication, nothing more. He holds on to that thought, raises it up like a shield as Rowena strips to her underwear and hangs her wet dress on some sticks she's skewered into the ground near the fire.

'If you're staying, you'd best take those off too,' she nods towards Halim's sodden joggers.

He hesitates.

'Don't worry,' she sneers, 'I'll try and control myself at the sight of your rippling muscles.'

He sets his jaw, drags off his joggers and wrings them out – twisting them so tight that his biceps shake from the effort. He stabs some sticks into the dirt, hangs his clothes up next to hers and then thumps himself down on the blanket they brought.

Rowena throws some more wood on the fire and sits right next to him.

Halim pulls up his knees to cover his groin, aware that his boxers are wet and clinging.

He can feel their goose-bumped skin almost touching, can see the angles of Rowena's strong arms, the curve of her breasts and the folds in her belly as she—

'Eyes front,' she snaps, her own eyes doggedly fixed on the twisting plume of smoke. She makes a diamond shape with her fingers and blows on the flames, stirring them to life.

'What if I offered you a cut of my fee when we get to Culcrith, would you stay with me then?'

'You can't buy me! And anyway, I don't need your money, I need to do what's right for me and my instinct is to stay put. Oscar said you could stay too. You could give up this contract: you don't need money to live off-grid.'

'I do need money, though. I told you before, I'll lose the truck if I miss another payment.'

'Fuck the truck.'

'It's not just a truck, it's my way out, it's everything I've worked all this time for.' It's my freedom, he thinks.

Rowena sighs loudly. 'Have you heard the tale about the Cunning Woman and the fisherman?' she asks.

Halim doesn't respond.

'An ambitious young man went to see the old woman asking for help to make him the best fisherman in the county. She tells him to cut open the first fish he catches on Midsummer's Eve – inside he'll find a smaller fish, and if he cuts that open, inside he'll find a fly.'

Halim stifles a yawn.

Rowena ignores him and continues. 'She told him to use that fly to bait his hook and then he'll catch a bigger fish. Then, if he cuts that one open he'll find a smaller fish and inside that a fly – bait for an even bigger fish, and so on and so on ...' The fire pops, making her flinch.

'So the moral is, if you work hard you'll reap the rewards. Great story, thanks.'

Rowena shakes her head. 'No, the fisherman went missing. Days later, the locals found his body at the bottom of the river – his little boat had been broken and sunk by the weight of a giant fish he'd landed. Sometimes you've gotta know when to stop and let shit go, Halim, life's much shorter than you think. You need to fill yourself up on it,' her voice wobbles as she taps her breastbone and turns towards the lake.

He follows her faraway gaze, wondering if she's about to cry, and for some reason this only makes him angrier.

'Yeah? Well, we can't all be free spirits like 'Captain Vampire' and your new best friends,' he mutters, 'some of us have contracts to honour, responsibilities. Of course, you wouldn't understand that, since your only responsibility is for yourself.'

18

AS HALIM LIMPS DOWN THE HALL he's accosted by Kezia. The frills at the neck of her old-fashioned dress threaten to smother her face, but the rest of it fits like a second skin.

'How's the foot after your swim?' she asks.

'A bit better, thanks.' He wonders what Rowena told her about his meltdown at the lake.

She beams at him. 'Great! You can help me bring some more wine up from the cellar. It's just here.' She leads him to a small wood-panelled door tucked under the staircase.

Halim shuffles down the stone steps after her, following the golden light from her oil lamp.

'You're not scared of ghosts, are you? Oscar said he felt a hand on his shoulder down here once,' Kezia's eyes dance to the flame in her hands.

'I'm more scared of twisting my other ankle, to be honest.'

'Oh, you'll be fine, there's a handrail. Besides, I'll catch you if you stumble.' She twists her lip in a half-smile and starts scanning the bottles in the racks as they enter the cavernous cellar. The musk of rotting wood and brick dust is almost overpowering.

'It's amazing how much we get through, poor old Oscar.' Kezia hands Halim a bottle. The label reads 'Rote Flamme, Spätburgunder, 2014'.

'Isn't this wine really expensive?' Halim frowns.

Kezia shrugs. 'Wanna see something particularly creepy?' she asks. Without waiting for an answer she takes the light deeper into the cellar, forcing Halim to follow.

They reach a corner where the ceiling draws lower and each breath becomes amplified. Kezia swipes away some cobwebs and holds the lamp up to a part of the wall where the brickwork has cracked and crumbled, revealing a hole about a foot high. 'Look closer,' she nods. 'Go on!'

Unimpressed, Halim holds her gaze a moment before moving in.

He spots the balled-up claws first, sticking out from the hole, like an upturned spider. Attached to the paw is a stiff, mummified cat, its fur rotted away to ash-grey leather and its flesh dried tight to its bony body, pulling its face into a toothy grin. He recoils.

'Pretty gross, huh?' Kezia laughs. 'Oscar thinks it was hidden there to drive away witches and bad spirits.'

'Pass me the lamp,' Halim takes the light from her and holds it up to the hole. 'There are scratch marks in the cavity, it looks like the cat was alive when it was bricked in.'

'No way!' gasps Kezia. 'That's awful, the poor creature!'

Halim brings his eyes level with the cat's ragged sockets. I know how you must have felt, he thinks, staring into the empty holes.

'Okay, well, I'm ready to leave now. That's some macabre shit right there.' Kezia takes back the lamp and leads Halim through the cellar, grabbing a few random bottles on the way.

'There you are,' Rowena says, sitting up as Halim and Kezia enter the dining room, laden with wine. 'Oscar's offered to drive us to the butcher's in the village, he wants to cook you a farewell feast.' She scans Halim's face for any glimmer of reconciliation and finds none.

'Is there a pub or fuel station there?' he asks.

'I don't think so,' Kezia replies as she uncorks a bottle. 'It's just a pop-up butcher's run from someone's kitchen once a week.'

'Then there's no point going.'

Rowena rolls her eyes. 'You can stay mad at me for as long as you like, Halim, but is it worth ruining your time here, shutting out every nice experience?'

Halim clunks the wine bottles onto the table, creating a waterfall of dust.

'Ugh, suit yourself.'

Oscar comes in, waving his car keys. 'Ah, he's here, are you both ready?' He winks at Halim. 'The Mustang's primed and raring to go.'

With the breeze roaring in her ears, Rowena only catches snatches of the conversation between Halim and Oscar, who are sitting in the front of his bright-red convertible – something mundane about V8 engines and fuel costs. Everything still carries a woody smell from the recent rain, the sun has sunk lower since their visit to the lake and is skulking behind white streaks of cloud. Rowena wonders what life in Pendleshire might be like, and how she's going to tell her mother that she's staying put. She's pretty much cut me out of her life anyway, Rowena thinks, so what would it matter to her? Besides, I could stall for time and tell her once I hit eighteen, she won't have parental rights over me then.

The overhanging trees are untrimmed and crowding the road, and the fields either side are nothing but mud and dung, their smells mingling with the occasional hit of Oscar's cologne. Just as nausea threatens to creep in, the car pulls up in a small hamlet, near an old stone cottage. A queue snakes from its open door all the way to the ivy-choked postbox.

'I reserved us a leg of lamb and some black pudding,' Oscar says as he straightens his hair in the rear-view mirror.

'How much do we owe you?' Halim asks.

Rowena notices that he still includes her in his question and something jolts inside her.

Oscar waves his hand. 'Nothing at all, it's my treat.'

As they approach the line of people Rowena notices that not one of them is chatting, and the silence colours everything. A few skinny, dour-faced villagers leave the cottage carrying parcels wrapped in brown paper and jars of blood. Rowena catches Halim's eye and he frowns.

They shuffle forward.

Halim checks his phone again.

'No signal here either, I'm afraid,' Oscar whispers, close to Halim's cheek.

The sun flickers in and out of cloud cover, scrawling strange patterns on the road that Rowena tries to read, desperate for a sign, perhaps a message from her pa.

They shuffle forward.

A shriek from behind makes Rowena jump and press a hand to her chest. Two boys are playing in the road, fighting over a crudely made corn doll. She watches them bicker and tear at it, their dirt-smeared faces snarled up in the moment.

The line shuffles forward.

A moment later, the screams shoot towards her and she sees that the corn doll is on fire and the boy holding it is panicking. He drops it at Halim's feet and starts crying as he sucks his fingers. The boy's mother scoops up the bawling child and glares at Halim as he stamps on the doll again and again, crushing it into nothing but black strands of smoke.

Rowena smooths out the silk for her Tarot cards on the walnut writing desk in Oscar's study, a cluster of candles gilding her hands as she works. 'You sure, Halim? It's your last chance for me to read you. Aren't you even a tiny bit curious?'

'It took us ages to convince Rowena to get her cards out, but we've all done it,' smiles Agatha, stroking the long feather dangling from her earring. 'There's nothing to be scared of, she's really gifted.'

Halim frowns. 'I'm not scared. I just don't really believe in this stuff.'

'Well then, what's the harm in doing it?' Oscar says, one hand draped over Halim's shoulder, a glass of port in the other. 'Think of it like an elaborate game of patience.'

Kezia, perched cat-like on the window seat, watches him. The shocked faces of stuffed animals peer down at him from the walls. He's tired and doesn't have the energy to argue, so he takes the moth-eaten chair opposite Rowena as she shuffles the deck.

'How long will this take?' he sighs.

'Not long, we'll do a five-card spread. Now you shuffle, and as you do, think of a question you'd like guidance on. The cards help you find answers from within.'

He hesitates.

'Can we get some privacy, please?' Rowena eyes the others.

All three pout as they leave the room. The floorboards creak in the hallway and Halim imagines them pressing their ears against the door as he takes the cards and starts passing them between his hands. The edges are soft and worn, but their backs are a smooth glossy black decorated with gold.

He thinks of a question and asks it silently: Should I give up on this life?

On Rowena's instruction he chooses five cards and lays them face down on the silk.

She turns them over one by one. 'Knight of Swords: this represents the here and now,' she says, her voice strangely solemn. 'The Hermit: this is the past. The Tower: this indicates the future.'

That doesn't look promising, Halim thinks, looking down at an image of two people falling, gaping-mouthed, from a fiery tower that's been struck by lightning.

'Eight of Swords,' Rowena continues, 'represents your question and this ...' she turns over a picture of a young man and young woman exchanging golden cups. Her grey-green eyes flick up to meet his. 'The Two of Cups. This is a potential outcome, something that's just within reach.'

She's quiet for a moment as she scans the cross-shape she's made, her head tilted.

'That bad, huh?'

The candle next to her stutters and spews a line of smoke. 'This was you, of course – the lonely old Hermit, looking for something inside himself, turning away from the world. But this one's you too,' she points to the picture of a bound and blindfolded woman hemmed in by swords. 'I don't know what you asked, but the cards are saying that you need to save yourself. That you're the only one stopping you from getting what you want.' She looks up. 'What is it that you want?'

He struggles to hold her gaze. 'Not that,' he taps a finger on the Tower card to the right of the spread.

'The Tower isn't all bad, it represents a clearing out, liberation through destruction, so that you can rebuild.' Her mind seems to wander as she goes silent for a while. 'This one's me, you know,' she points to the Knight of Swords at the very centre of the spread, an illustration of wind-stretched clouds and trees, a mounted figure galloping into battle. 'I've charged into your life and fucked things up for you, haven't I?'

Halim doesn't know what to say. You've made it more interesting, he thinks. He pushes the chair away and tests his weight on his bad foot. 'Thanks for this but I'm tired and I've got an early start. Goodnight, Rowena.' He opens the door and the others tumble into the room, muttering their apologies.

'Remember,' Rowena calls after him, 'the future's not fixed, the path is always forking.'

He knows they're only pictures, but something about them has made him uneasy, is gnawing at his skull. As he climbs the creaking stairs it comes to him: both of the 'future' cards showed a man *and* a woman.

19

8 May

———

HALIM'S HEART CRACKS almost as much as the glass in the wind-screen of his truck. He stares at the fissures as they glint in the early-morning sun like rivers. He traces a finger over one and, for the first time in his adult life, he feels like crying. When he walks around the truck it gets worse – someone has spray-painted black letters across the side of it, the message simple but effective: 'FUCK OFF'. He rocks on his heels for a few seconds, taking it in, his brain processing everything at a hundred miles an hour but getting nowhere. And then he punches the O, sending a shock of pain through his wrist and scraping his knuckles. He watches as the white layer under his peeled brown skin starts pooling with red.

'Who would do such a thing?' Kezia asks as she bathes Halim's hand in salt water.

Rowena catches Halim's eye across the dining table. 'The two thugs we met the other day,' she says. 'They knew we were staying at Dingle House.' And it was my idea to run, she thinks: if we'd just given them the rabbits this wouldn't have happened, but I was too stubborn.

Halim draws a sharp breath as Kezia wraps a bandage around his knuckles.

Agatha stands in front of the mirror plaiting her thick black hair while Oscar sits next to her, his legs spread and his hands in the pockets of his immaculately creased trousers.

'Didn't any of you hear or see anything?' Halim asks. 'Don't you sleep on that side of the house?'

A shrug, a shake of the head, a twist of the lip.

'I'd offer to run you up the road to get some reception,' Oscar says, 'or take you all the way to Butsfield, if fuel allowed, but truth be told I've had a skinful so I'm not much use to anyone.'

'It's eight-thirty in the morning,' Halim says, glancing at the empty bottles on the table in front of him.

Kezia snorts down a laugh as she starts to roll a joint. 'Whoops! Time for bed!'

Agatha giggles.

Halim wipes a hand across his mouth and is scowling so hard it looks like his face might fold in on itself. He seems broken, Rowena thinks, casting her gaze down to the wine-spotted rug.

'Oh, come on, Halim,' Kezia yawns, 'it's a hunk of metal on wheels, it's not like they killed your kid or something. Why don't you have some wine? Wine fixes everything, especially this vintage – what was it you said about old things, Oscar ...?'

Rowena slams her hand on the table, making everyone jump. An empty glass tumbles and rolls towards her. 'This isn't a joke, this is his livelihood!' she snaps. 'Most folk don't get gifted mansions or sports cars from Mummy and Daddy, so when you *earn* something – like he has – it's *everything*, and you take care of it like it *is* your baby.' She glares at Oscar, whose Merlot-stained mouth is gaping open. 'You live in this piece-of-shit county full of thugs and vandals, yet you've got no wards, no hag stones, no alarm system, no ditches. You don't deserve a nice place like this if you don't know how to take care of it.'

The room goes still. A chiffchaff peeps its own alarm call outside the window.

Face flushed with anger, Rowena heads outside to see the damage for herself.

Halim eventually joins her as she stands by the truck with her arms folded, staring at the giant black letters.

'You know, I'm beginning to think you're right, Halim.'

'About what?'

'That most people are arseholes.' She chews the inside of her cheek. 'What will you do now?'

'Drive to Buttfield or Butthole, whatever that place is called.'

'Can you drive with the windscreen like that?'

He shrugs. 'It's only bad on the driver's side, I suppose I could lean out of the window.'

'I'm so sorry, Halim. This is my fault, I should've just given them the bloody rabbits, I should learn to keep my head down and my mouth shut.'

'No.'

Rowena frowns.

Halim presses on his bandaged knuckles. 'You should never let yourself be silenced by a bully. You should take up space, show them you have the right to be there.'

'I feel like shit though! You've done nothing but look out for me and this is what you get for it.'

He nods at the graffiti. 'See that? "FUCK OFF". This isn't about rabbits, it's about me. A foreigner. A trespasser.' He heaves a deep sigh. 'Perhaps it's another one of your signs, telling me I should give up.'

Her mind goes to the Two of Cups, the Tower ... She shakes her head. 'The future's not fixed,' she mutters. 'Signs are flags, warnings, it's what you do with them that counts.' She turns and strides back into the house to fetch a bucket of soapy water and some scrubbing brushes.

Twenty minutes later they've got the worst of it off.

'That'll do, I need to get going.' Halim drops the brush into the dirty grey water, reaches into the back pocket of his jeans and holds out Rowena's passport. 'Here, you'll need this.'

'Thanks.' She takes it, turns it over. It's bent from where he must have been sitting on it.

Halim opens the truck door, and almost without thinking her hand is on his arm, holding him back.

He looks at her, confused.

'I'd like to go with you,' she says.

'Sure, I can give you a lift into town.'

'No, I mean, stay with you. For good this time. See this thing through.'

'Is this your hangover talking?'

She shakes her head. 'I got this all wrong, I treated this trip like a joyride, but I can tell how much it means to you. Besides, life at Dingle would be too ... small, too suffocating, just like Pickbury. I need to believe there's still hope for me in Culcrith. I need to be the knife and not the lamb.'

Halim frowns and crosses his arms.

She widens her eyes, but he gives nothing away. 'We've come pretty far already, haven't we, it'd be a shame to stop now?'

He seems to think for a minute, rubs the back of his neck.

She can sense she's losing him. 'Look – you have a contract with my mother,' she says, 'so I'll make a contract with you.' She swipes her thumb across a jagged line on the windscreen, draws blood, and crosses her heart with it, leaving a smear on her white T-shirt. 'I promise to stick with you all the way to Culcrith. I'll get you your payment in full. I swear it on my mother's life.'

The corner of his mouth twitches.

Blood drips onto her boot.

He sighs. 'I don't want you bleeding all over my cab, and you should wash that cut before it gets infected.'

Rowena smiles. 'Yeah, I should.'

Oscar and the girls have given them a guilt package of cheese, wine, apples, fresh bread, underripe tomatoes and home-made relish. They say their thank-yous and air-kiss goodbyes under a sprinkling of rain as the sun pulls itself higher. Halim's heart sinks as he sits in the driver's seat behind the broken screen and he stares through the cracks.

'We'll get it fixed,' Rowena says.

With what money? he thinks, turning the key. With his head out of the driver's window, he takes them along the winding drive and back towards the main road, heading north to Butsfield, a town near the border of Langtonshire. 'Keep checking my phone for a signal,' he tells Rowena, who's peering through the spiderwebbed glass on the passenger side where it's not so bad.

When they reach the junction he pumps his foot on the brake but it's slack. 'What the fuck?' He steers them onto the road.

'What's wrong?' Rowena asks.

'The brake's gone!'

'What?'

The road starts curving downwards through a tunnel of trees – it's a gentle slope but the weight of the truck is propelling them on, faster and faster, giving him less time to think.

He guides them around the bends, scans the roadside for any safe place to swerve onto.

'Halim?'

The truck's speed has picked up faster than he expected and up ahead he can see the road narrowing as it bends across a small stone bridge. They won't make it, he thinks, palms springing with sweat.

'Halim, can't you do something?'

Leaves blur outside the windows, a wall of green.

'Look out!' Rowena screams.

'HOLD ON!' He cranks the handbrake and jerks the steering wheel as he finally spots a gap in the trees. The truck skids on the road and careens through the hedge – narrowly missing a tree trunk. It bounces into a weed-choked field, grinds its suspension across something hard and slams to a stop against a rusted trough.

Silence.

Slivers of the shattered windscreen trickle to the floor of the cab.

Halim's heart is pounding so hard it hurts. 'Are you okay?' he whispers, trying to process what just happened, his hands still strangling the steering wheel.

Rowena groans.

He unclips his seat belt and slides over to her. Her forehead is bleeding from where it must have caught the dashboard when the airbags failed. 'Look at me – Rowena, can you look at me?'

Her eyes shift around before finding his face. 'Told you I'm cursed,' she smiles, touching her fingers to her head. 'Everything I love dies,' she slurs as her eyelids drift shut.

20

—

ROWENA'S NOSE TICKLES. She opens her eyes to find a large spider dangling above her face, twitching its legs towards her. She opens her mouth to scream, but it's snapped away in a blur of feather. A grey crow lands on the windowsill above, its third eyelid blinking white as the spider's legs flex and curl in its beak. Rowena can tell this isn't her usual nightmare and her skin prickles – alert for meaning in this strange bedroom that feels both unfamiliar and somehow like she's been here before. When she sits up her head lolls as if a screw in her neck has come loose, and it takes a while to turn towards the thump-squeak thump-squeak in the corner. A dapple-grey rocking horse with a red saddle and patchy mane gallops on the spot, perhaps buffeted by the crow? It slows to a trot, nodding gently, its square teeth bared in a manic grin, the bit drilled right into its smile. Something about it chills Rowena, and reminds her of a story Tessa used to tell about growing up in Culcrith ...

The crow starts to chip at the windowpane: tap-tap, tap-tap, tap-tap.

Rowena tries to raise herself up to shoo the bird out, but her legs are leaden, and the effort makes her gut rumble and cramp. She presses a hand there – and finds her belly swollen and round. 'No!' she gasps. 'No way!'

The crow starts beating its wings, it scratches and screeches so loudly that the sound slices through Rowena's skull and she can't think straight.

'Shut up!' she screams. '*Shut up!*'

The bird slams its head into the glass and breaks through, spilling diamonds into Rowena's lap. It's gone in a flicker – leaving behind a jagged hole etched in blood and snagged with grey feathers. An icy breeze snakes its way around the room now, plucking at all the cobwebs as sunlight bursts through the broken window, bleaching the walls.

She grits her teeth. 'Either get up or wake up, Rowena.' She reaches over her bulbous middle to try and unstick her legs – but they're not lying on a mattress any more, they're sunken into the trunk of a tree that's somehow grown up around her, its bark cracking and creeping over her skin as it ages and moulders before her eyes. It's crushing me, she thinks, panicking that she won't wake up before then. Her frantic fingers catch on something as they scrabble over the bark – letters carved fresh into the wood, white lines like scars, two words: 'LET GO'.

There's a drip.

Another.

She realises it's coming from her: blood is filling the grooves of the carving as her hand hovers above, clasping a shard of glass.

She lets it go …

Rowena blinks, takes a deep breath, touches her stinging head and finds a square of plaster. Above her is the grey roof of the truck. A cool breeze slides through the holes in the windscreen, tickling her face with strands of hair. She puts a hand to her belly and is relieved to find it flat.

'Here,' Halim passes her a bottle of water.

She kicks off the blanket and winds the seat up. 'How long was I out?' she asks between gulps.

'Only a few minutes, but you had me worried. I still don't have a signal here and I didn't want to leave you.'

She finds herself smiling at him, comforted by his words.

'Someone tampered with the brakes,' he says.

Her smile fades.

'How many fingers am I holding up?'

'You're swearing at me.'

'How many?'

'Two.'

'And now?'

'Four.'

Seemingly satisfied, he leans over and checks her forehead.

He smells of sweat and grass. She notices a large mole on his neck that she's not seen before. 'Stop fussing. I'm okay, Halim, it's just a bump.'

'It's a concussion. You need to keep still and rest. I'm going to head up the road to try and get a signal and call a tow-truck.'

'I'm coming with you.'

'No, you're staying here.'

'No, I'm coming with you. I don't want to be left alone.'

'You'll be fine, this place is deserted and you can't see the truck from the road.'

She frowns, scratches at the plaster pinching her skin. 'It's not people I'm worried about, it's ... the other thing.'

He looks at her with something like pity and she hates it.

'This place is a black-spot,' he mutters, 'it could be a long walk to find a signal.' He empties the glove compartment and puts the rest of his things in the small metal locker behind the seats.

Rowena opens her backpack and pulls out her clothes and the library book on *Lochs and Mountains of the Highland Borders* that her pa gave her years ago, and starts repacking it with the food they were given.

'You taking that?' Halim asks, pointing to the urn that's nestled between the wrapped cheese and a cob loaf.

She looks at the tear-stained sticker listing her pa's name and date of cremation. 'I'm not leaving him alone either.'

Outside the truck, Rowena waits for Halim as he stands in front of the old metal trough that they ploughed into. It lies on its side, wrenched from the mud and dented from the impact. She waits as he just stares at the hunk of rusted metal, his shoulders slumped, defeated. He takes a few steps and kicks the trough with his good foot, sending out a dull metallic gong. He kicks it harder, then picks up a rock and slams it down – except the rock is more chalk than stone and it crumbles into powdery white pieces, enraging him even more, and that's when he starts with his fists ... Rowena knows to stand back and let him have this, knows that it's the lava inside him splitting open and catching fire.

They make their way back across the field, its lush grass stippled yellow with the pom-poms of dandelions and pentacles of butter-cups. The temperature drops as soon as they enter the huddle of trees lining a hollow beside the road.

'Bloody hell – is that what I think it is?' Halim scowls.

Rowena follows his finger to an ancient-looking elm, its thick upturned branches resembling a tarnished candelabrum. Nestled into one of the nooks is a milk-white human skull. A collarbone and shoulder blade are also wedged into the trunk, as if the whole body was consumed by the tree: Rowena's vision made real. A chill passes through her, leaching her strength for a moment.

Ignoring Halim's protestations she climbs down the slippery bank to get a better look – gripping roots and saplings to steady herself – and peers into the gnarly grey folds. The skull is female by the size and shape of it, most likely a young woman. Moss and bark have crept over the skeleton like a shroud and, as a final macabre touch, droplets from the leaves above are sliding past her empty eye sockets like mock tears. Rowena imagines her own skin stretched over those bones and reaches out to touch the woman's dirt-filmed teeth. 'Who did this to you?' she whispers. 'What does it feel like where you are? Will it hurt when it's my time?'

A sudden flutter of wings catches Rowena off-balance and a second later Halim has her in a rough grip and is half-dragging her back up the slope. 'That's enough,' he snaps. 'I want to get out of this armpit of a county. We can report the body when we get to Butsfield.'

'No point,' Rowena sighs, filling her nose with the scent of a million living and dying things. 'No one cared about her for decades, why'd they care now? Well, no one except whoever tied that scrap of white silk to the branch over there.'

They walk on in silence for a while, Halim's brooding anger filling the air like lightning straining for a place to strike.

'I'm sure your truck can be fixed,' Rowena says.

'I don't want to talk about it,' Halim's voice is more like a rumble than actual speech.

Shafts of midday sun cut through the light drizzle, reminding Rowena of the glass fragments falling into her lap – and then she remembers the swell of her belly and how it made her feel like she wanted to be that crow at the window, making a desperate escape.

'You okay?' Halim asks as she stumbles. 'Let me carry your pack.'

'No, I'm fine.'

'You don't look it. Let's rest here for a bit and get some food in you.'

They sit next to each other on a stile at the edge of the road and unwrap the bread and cheese. The public-footpath sign points to another overgrown field, left fallow for so long that saplings are sprouting amongst the cornflowers and poppies, and the air is filled with the soft hum of bees and the zip of dragonflies.

'Right before you passed out you said, "Everything I love dies,"' Halim says, spitting out an apple pip.

Rowena touches the lump on her forehead. 'Did I?'

He nods. 'You're a smart girl – woman – Rowena, do you really think you caused your boyfriend to fall down a hill and your dad to have a stroke? Don't you realise how dumb that sounds?'

She wrinkles her nose. 'After what just happened with the truck you still don't believe that I'm cursed? We could've died back there and it was my fault! I'm marked, touched by Death: anyone I get close to I drag towards It.'

'We're hardly close, Rowena, I'm just your "ride" – isn't that how you described me back at Dingle? I overheard you that night, my room was above the garden.'

She looks away. 'I was cursed since I was born,' she says. 'My mother says that on the day she had me, two hundred and fifty starlings dropped out of the sky and hit the main road. If that's not a bad omen I don't know what is.'

'It was probably just the glare from the concrete – had it been raining?'

'How would I know, I was a newborn.' Rowena grabs her pack and stands up. 'I'm done resting.' She heads off up the road, as Halim's phone beeps with a flurry of delayed messages.

'That'll be four quid.' The barman places the pint of ale on the counter.

Halim fishes some coins out of his pocket. 'I don't suppose you know anywhere cheap to stay around here, do you? We need a couple of rooms.'

The barman glances over at Rowena sat in the corner, eating crisps while scratching something into a white candle. 'You mean one room?'

'Sure, fine, if that's all you have.'

'Nah, nothing round here.' The barman continues serving a hairy ox of a man with arms the size of logs. 'That'll be three quid, please, Gabe.'

Halim looks at the identical pint of ale placed on the bar next to his. 'Sorry, I thought you said it was four pounds a pint?'

The barman squeaks a dirty-looking cloth around a glass. 'Locals get a discount.'

Halim glares at him, bristling. He grips his pint and turns away.

'You're drinking – that means bad news.' Rowena puts down the candle as Halim joins her.

'The garage won't have the truck ready until this coming Wednesday,' he says, ale slopping over his hand. 'They said it can take up to four working days to get parts in.'

'So that means we're stuck here for like, six nights ...' She counts on her fingers. 'So that would make it the fourteenth of May!'

'*We're* stuck here? So you'll wait here with me? Even if it means we might not make it to Culcrith in time for your birthday?'

'I made a contract with you, didn't I? Besides, there's still time if we can fast-track some jobs. We'll figure this out.' She frowns and chews the inside of her cheek. 'We have to.'

Halim picks at the beer mat under his glass and then fishes out his phone and rereads the half-composed text to his mother.

'Must be a relief to know your truck's not a write-off,' Rowena says, taking a sip of his untouched pint.

He snorts and buries his phone in his pocket. 'The call-out fee itself was a hundred and eighty-five, brakes were a patch-up job, and the chassis was only scratched, but a replacement windscreen could cost between four and eight hundred pounds.'

'So, you've got insurance, don't you?'

'Of course, but I can't afford the excess so I'll have to default on my truck payments again, and I won't get any slack if I'm late a second time. That means repossession.'

'Can't you pay the repairs in instalments?'

He shakes his head. 'Bad credit rating. That's what happens when you work erratic contracts and don't have a steady income. And they won't release the truck until full payment's been made, so basically I'm fucked whichever way you look at it.' He clings to his glass and stares at the dartboard on the wall opposite. Something large obscures his view and he refocuses on the ox-like man from earlier, who's now standing in front of their table.

'Name's Gabriel,' the man says with a smile, his three-quid pint in his meaty hand. 'I'm the local blacksmith. I own the forge down the road. Mind if I join you?'

'I'm Rowena, and this is Halim,' she says, pushing out a stool with her foot before Halim can object.

Gabriel sits and turns to Halim. 'I couldn't help overhearing at the bar – you still looking for a place to stay?'

Halim knows by now that everyone has an ulterior motive and everything comes at a cost, but he's tired to the bones and has nothing left to lose. 'Yeah, for six nights, as cheap as possible.'

'Great, well, I've got a barn near my forge, kitted out with beds and electrics. My kids use it when they come and stay, but they've grown up now and don't visit so often. That's what happens when—'

'How much?' Halim asks.

'You can have it for free if you agree to help me out at the forge a bit – May's a busy time of year, see, and with my arthritis and that I can't go full pelt like I did in my younger days.'

Rowena nudges Halim under the table and raises her eyebrows at him.

'Sounds interesting, thank you. We'll think about it and get back to you,' Halim says.

Gabriel looks at each of them in turn. 'Ah, right. Well then, I'll be over at the bar.'

As Gabriel gets up Rowena kicks Halim.

'Ow!'

'What's wrong with you?' she hisses.

'How can we trust him? What if he's part of a mob? What if he's another racist prick?'

Rowena rolls her eyes. 'Look at him, he's practically an old man, a lonely old man who's offering us a place to stay. *For free.*' She places a hand on Halim's arm and leaves it there. 'I know we've had a shit time of it with strangers, but I've spent my whole life reading signs, so I also developed a knack for reading people. I'm pretty sure he's one of the good ones, Halim. And you can't spend your whole life avoiding everyone.'

The warmth from her hand seems to spread up his arm and across his chest. 'Fine,' he sighs. 'But if I get bludgeoned to death in my sleep I'm coming back to haunt you.'

21

9 May

——

ROWENA NARROWS HER EYES AGAINST the bright, butterscotch light and yawns as Halim comes into the barn. He's shaved off his stubble, is dressed in tailored navy trousers and a crisp white shirt unbuttoned at the neck. He looks ... different, she thinks, sitting up. 'Whose funeral is it?'

'Probably mine. I've got a meeting at the bank to see about a loan. Gabe says there's coffee and breakfast in the cottage if you want it.'

'Oh, it's "Gabe" now, is it?' she grins.

'How's the head?'

'Throbbing a little.' She touches the bump, acutely aware that the skin around it has turned a putrid purple.

Halim frowns as he taps furiously into his phone.

'So, I had an idea about the money,' Rowena says, wrapping the blanket around her. 'I know you don't want to ask your parents for help, but there's no reason I can't ask mine—' she catches herself, 'my mother.'

He looks up. 'Why would Tessa help? If anything she'd be mad that I had an accident and put you in danger. No, I can't risk her cancelling this contract. Not now. This job's hanging by a thread as it is.'

It irks Rowena that he still refers to her as a 'job', but she brushes it off. 'You didn't put me in danger, it was all my fault.'

He pinches the bridge of his nose. 'Not this again.'

'No, no curse – just the reckless behaviour of a seventeen-year-old who drank too much and decided to take a joyride and crashed your truck into a tree.' She tilts her head and watches her words register. 'I take the blame. You phone Tessa and explain that there'll be an amount added to your fee, for the excess or whatever, or you'll ditch me here and terminate the contract. Call her bluff. She'll believe it, coming from you.'

Halim seems to think about it for a minute, then shakes his head. 'I need more money than that anyway – I have to try the bank, even if it is a long shot.' He spits on his hand and starts polishing his mud-flecked boots. 'I wish I hadn't pawned my brogues,' he mumbles.

'You sleep okay?' Gabe asks as Rowena sits at a wonky little table in his kitchen eating black-edged toast. 'I know it's a bit cramped for the two of you, but my boys used to tell me the mattresses were comfy enough.'

She smiles. 'Slept like a log, thanks.'

'Speaking of which, do you know how to chop wood?'

She nods.

'Good, you can start in the yard today, I need to get my stores up before more of this blasted rain comes. Then Lucy – that's my horse – could do with mucking out and a brush down. That sound okay?'

'Sure. I like horses. My pa taught me to ride when I was five.' She waves her fingers through the light that's sneaking in under the net curtain.

'Smart man,' Gabe says, 'a good skill to have these days, what with cars costing the earth.'

'I suppose he was a smart man,' Rowena mutters. 'Though my mother always used to say that the man might think he's the head of a household, but the woman is the neck – and where the neck turns the head follows.'

Gabe chuckles, his eyes barely visible between the wrinkles. 'Where are your folks now?'

'One's in my backpack and the other's in Pickbury, Dunfordshire. Halim and I are on our way to my gran's farm in Culcrith.'

Unsure how to respond, Gabe scratches his chin. 'There's the

Flora Dance in town tomorrow afternoon, where everyone gets dressed up in their finest. Halim scrubs up well – you two would make a right handsome pair.'

Rowena feels her cheeks redden. 'We're just friends.'

'Right, well, there's more coffee on the stove.' The table shakes as Gabe gets up. 'I'd best get on and stoke up the forge.'

As he leaves, Rowena spots a neat line of dried blood across the doorstep. If his protective wards have held, she wonders, how did they let a cursed girl cross the threshold?

'Are you checking out my arse again?' Rowena doesn't turn around but can feel Halim's eyes on her as she brushes the flank of Gabe's horse in the yard, her free hand following each stroke of the brush.

'No, I was just thinking I'd never seen you work so hard before,' he replies. 'But now that you've drawn attention to your arse ...'

Rowena wipes her forehead with the back of her arm. 'How'd it go at the bank?'

Halim slumps down on a nearby hay bale, his tie bunched up in one hand. 'As expected. They said no. As did your mother.'

'You spoke to her?'

'For all of thirty seconds.'

'So what now?'

Halim stares at his hands and shrugs. 'Sell my soul?'

'You could call your parents.'

'Same thing,' he says. 'I can't do it. I just can't.'

'Your pride'll screw you over, you know that, don't you? That's *your* curse.'

When he raises his head he has a strange look on his face like he's thinking so hard he doesn't even see her. 'My family's money is blood money,' he says, rubbing the back of his neck. 'My father owns a pharmaceutical company and years ago he withheld essential medical supplies to artificially inflate stock prices. That's how he got to where he is. Countless people have died because of him, children included. My mother feigns ignorance, and it's never mentioned, but I can't ignore it. He wants me to follow in his footsteps, thinks I'm the same as him because we share a few genes, but I'm not. I'm nothing like him.' Halim twists the tie around his knuckle like a boxing wrap. 'Being a good guy in this world, though, following the rules – it all feels like a disadvantage.'

Lucy pushes her soft nose into Rowena's shoulder and flicks her mane. Rowena takes the hint and goes over. 'It's okay,' she says, sitting next to Halim. 'We can get more jobs, or stay on here with Gabe and save up so that the garage releases your truck. I've got some money I can put towards it – I was saving to rent my own place in Pickbury one day so it's not like I need it now. And I can sell more charms, Gabe says it's the Flora Dance tomorrow, so the whole town'll be out.'

'We don't have time though – my contract was to get to Culcrith before your birthday, and I only have five weeks before ...' He shakes his head, looks uncomfortable.

She watches him toy with the dog tag around his neck. 'What is that?' she asks. It looks like real gold and she wonders why he hasn't pawned it already.

He tucks it under his shirt. 'A reminder that other people let you down. When I was little my parents promised me a dog if I aced my exams; they even bought me the gold tag for its collar, said they'd engrave it with whatever name I chose.'

'So you failed your exams?'

He shakes his head. 'Got straight A's.'

'So what happened to the dog?'

'Exactly.'

He gets up and disappears into the gloom of the barn.

A moment later, Rowena's phone rings. 'Hello, Mother,' she says.

'Is it true? Did you crash the truck?'

'I'm fine, thanks, how are you?'

'Don't play with me, girl – did you damage Halim's truck?'

Even through radio-waves across a vast distance Tessa's voice has the ability to make Rowena's pulse quicken, and when it's her turn to speak she genuinely stutters: 'It was an accident. I didn't realise how drunk I was. I was thinking about Pa again and ... I guess I sort of lost control. I'm sorry.'

'Sorry won't pay for the damage, will it? You know I'm not made of money!' Tessa's voice is so loud it distorts through the earpiece. 'I've already forked out too much in sending you north, don't you dare ruin this—' She breaks off. 'This curse isn't a joke, Rowena. I can't help you if you don't help yourself.'

'I know.'

'That was an omen, mark my words, next time you might not be so lucky to get away with just scrapes. I need you in Culcrith in one piece, you hear? You have to stay safe.'

'But I won't get there if we can't fix the truck, and if I don't make it there before my birthday you said that my curse will settle.' Saying the words out loud makes the reality hit home, and Rowena's mouth turns chalky. 'Maybe I'd have been better off staying at Dingle House, away from everyone. I guess I could hitch a ride back and—'

'No! You can't just hide and wait this thing out, Rowena, there'll never be a distance far enough or walls thick enough to stop It finding you and hurting everyone you love. You should've realised by now what we're dealing with. Culcrith is the only place for you.'

'So ... does that mean you'll help us?'

Tessa lowers her voice. 'Promise you'll keep yourself safe? Swear it on the soul of your pa.'

Taken aback, Rowena clears her throat. 'I swear I'll keep myself safe.'

'You should also bear in mind that Culcrith is in Laithness, and that's an Iron County, so you can't set a foot outside the law. And that includes poaching.'

'An *Iron County*? Are you serious? Of all the counties in the Kingdom you're sending me to one of the few that took up the death penalty?' Rowena barely stifles a laugh. 'Well, I suppose if this curse doesn't get me the small-minded locals will.'

'Not if you're careful and do everything your gran tells you. She's a hard woman, but she means well.' Tessa softens. 'I've not seen her for many years, so when you meet her you'll need to make a good impression for the both of us, okay? Do me and your pa proud – you owe him that much.'

It's a cheap shot and Rowena winces.

The line goes quiet. She can almost hear Tessa thinking of something to say.

'Are you eating well?'

'Yes, Mother.'

'Tell Halim I'll transfer the extra when he emails me the bill from the garage.'

'Okay. Thank you.'

'And Rowena?'

'Yes.'

'Has he touched you?'

'No!'

'Good, keep it that way. Go well.' Tessa hangs up.

With Gabe's permission, Rowena saddles up Lucy and takes her out at sunset to gather herbs and flowers for her crowns. As they clop along the steep track towards the glade, Rowena counts the hoof-beats in an attempt to clear her head and dampen the panic brought on by her mother's warnings. I really don't have much time, she realises. Is it the curse that's delaying us? Does It not want me to reach Culcrith now that I've set my mind to it?

She picks up a lily-like scent in the air, shakes herself and climbs down to snip at the flowering clouds of a wayfaring tree, envying those it's said to guide home. Shrill peeps turn her head to the dimming sky and she follows the stuttering wings of the swallows until they fade into nothing at the horizon. 'Seems like everyone else knows where they need to be,' she sighs.

Lucy has loped off and is heading for a gap in the hedge, so Rowena jogs after her. The tangle of broken hazel opens out into a darkening field, choked with the yellow and green sprays of wild parsnip. As Rowena grabs Lucy's noseband, a movement catches her eye and she sees a slim woman in a pale dress standing in the field, facing away from the lane, dark-brown hair falling loose down her back. Pollen rises like smoke around her, lifted by a breeze that for some reason Rowena can't feel. She narrows her eyes and tenses, expecting the worst, but the woman doesn't move, and she looks more solid than shadow.

'Come on, Lucy,' Rowena whispers as she swings herself into the saddle, ignoring the shake in her legs.

From up high she sees the real reason for the woman's stillness: her wrists and ankles are bound and tied to stakes in the ground, and she's stood in a perfect circle of flattened stems.

128

Lucy jerks as Rowena gasps and calls out: 'Hello? Should I get help?'

The woman stirs, then slowly turns her head. Her mouth is gagged with a cloth, a crust of old blood rouges her cheek, and the shaft of a black feather protrudes from the charred socket where her left eye should be.

Rowena chokes out a panicked whimper and yanks on the reins, desperate to get a skittish Lucy to turn, but they end up coming full circle – and as they face the field again the woman is gone.

The wooden stakes remain, however, and there's a rust-coloured stain on the flattened fronds.

Rowena urges Lucy into a gallop, and doesn't dare look behind her as night chases them all the way back to the forge.

22

10 May

———

'YOU LOOK NICE,' HALIM SAYS as Rowena walks into the barn in a blue embroidered dress, shaking droplets from her damp hair.

'Nice? That's what people say when they *pretend* to like something.'

'Fine. You look beautiful, then.' She does, he thinks, putting his book down.

'You not wearing your suit for the Flora Dance?' she asks, hands on hips, unintentionally showing off her curves.

'I've got to get online at the pub and secure some contracts, so I'll come into town with you.'

'Come on, Halim, this aloof, moody thing is really wearing thin.'

'My future's crumbling around me, so forgive me if I don't want to dance around holding a bunch of daisies or whatever it is you do at a Flora Dance.'

She picks up his shirt and tosses it at his face. 'Well then, let's celebrate getting the money from my mother instead.'

'What?'

'She called me after you disappeared yesterday afternoon. I wanted to tell you when I got back from my ride but you were already asleep by the sound of it.'

'She agreed? How?'

'It's not so hard to convince her I'm a liability, especially now that she can't keep a close eye on me.'

'Don't you feel even a little bit bad about lying to her?'

'What's the problem? You want to complete this contract, and I want to be rid of this curse, one way or another.'

'What do you mean "one way or another"?' Halim sits up. 'You're not planning on doing anything stupid, are you?'

Rowena curls her lip. 'Stop calling me dumb and stupid! Just because I didn't go to college doesn't mean you're better than me. Fucking hell, the arrogance on you!'

'You know I didn't mean it like that.'

She stuffs her hand-made charms and flower crowns into a basket and bangs out of the door.

Halim throws his shirt on over his jeans and jogs down the lane to catch up.

oFolk line the cobbled high street, dressed in gaudy evening gowns, big hats and creased suits, it's like stumbling upon a giant outdoor wedding, thinks Halim. He takes a brief mental note of his surroundings, of possible escape routes – just like Rowena taught him. A few drab-clothed men and women weave in and out of the throng, their cupped hands awaiting food or coin. One of the beggars tugs two children along behind her, past shopfronts festooned with spring flowers – a kaleidoscope of colour, laminated photos of food and faceless mannequins in fussy knitwear.

Halim and Rowena find a spot on the pavement as five young girls walk past in white dresses, their little faces blurred behind veils. They hold up plump doll-shaped loaves on sticks as a man in a conical hat of woven grass plays a flute behind them.

'I will never understand this Kingdom,' Halim mutters.

'The girls are wearing lily of the valley, a flower of purity,' Rowena explains, taking it upon herself to educate him. 'Then there's gorse, see? And laurel, marjoram, mallow, bluebells … local flowers, each with their own meaning.'

Seeing the flush of delight on Rowena's face, Halim softens and takes his hands from his pockets. A woman in a frothy pink dress comes up to him, tucks a sprig of something behind his ear and then swishes off down the line.

'Hawthorn,' Rowena whispers with a wicked smile. 'For fertility.'

Halim shakes the flowers off.

'I'm gonna do the rounds with my charms and that,' she laughs. 'By the way, you're chosen now – so if that lady comes back and asks you to dance you can't refuse her, it'd be a huge insult. Like, *hex*-worthy. We'd be chased out of town for sure.'

Halim narrows his eyes, suspecting another of her jests. 'I'll wait here for a bit. Don't go too far.'

From what he can tell, the Flora Dance involves people throwing petals, twirling and skipping about and then barging into a few of the shops and houses, like genteel looters who forget to take anything. A thick, heady perfume tickles his nose, and when the crowd becomes too boisterous, he escapes and sits on the churchyard wall. A shadow falls across the pavement before him and he follows it to the source: two young children stare up at him, dressed like twins – she in a pale dress with a yellow ribbon in her hair, he in a matching yellow necktie and knee socks. Their chubby berry-stained fingers are entwined, but the girl is clutching something in her other hand; a chunk of rubber, or meat perhaps, glistening with pins.

Halim frowns and waits for them to move along, but their round faces remain fixed on him, unblinking. He wonders if it's the colour of his skin they're fascinated by.

He offers them a vague smile.

The girl lifts up the moist lump in her hand and holds it out towards him.

'Halim! Good to see you here.' Gabe claps him on the back as he joins him at the wall.

When Halim looks back the twins are gone, and a crushed punnet of strawberries smears the pavement red.

'You enjoying yourself?' Gabe asks.

Halim blinks, tries to rearrange his face into something more convivial. 'Um, I really don't dance, so I'm hanging back,' he says.

'Oh, no need to worry about that, you have to be born here to join the Flora Dance, and you need an invite from the pastor. It's a very special honour.'

Of course it is, thinks Halim. 'What does this dance mean?'

'It's to rejoice in the fullness of spring. The noise and dancing drive out bad spirits left over from winter,' Gabe says, lighting a cigarette rolled from liquorice papers. 'They go from Church Street all the way through town, across the bridge and back again.'

'Everyone's so convinced they're surrounded by bad spirits, it seems like a constant battle. Do you believe in spirits, Gabe?'

The old blacksmith expels a wedge of smoke and fixes his dark eyes on the dancing. 'Got no proof either way whether they're real or not, but if I can do anything to protect myself then it makes sense to do it, eh? You could think of it like insurance. I do believe there are ways to make your time on this Earth easier, though, to make the hammer fall harder and truer.'

The music gets loud as the band passes by.

'Tell you what though ...' Gabe leans over, but Halim can't hear what he's saying over the booming drum. And then the moment's gone.

Back at the barn, Halim stirs the pot of fresh mint tea as Rowena counts her notes and coins. 'The secret is lots of sugar,' he says, adding lumps to the glass tumblers borrowed from Gabe's kitchen. 'I used to drink this when I was younger, before I got packed off to boarding school.'

He watches Rowena wrap up her money and stuff it into the urn.

'When will you release your dad's ashes?' he asks.

She tenses for a moment, before screwing the lid back on. 'When I'm ready,' she says.

'How will you know when you're ready? Isn't it better to just let him go?'

'When you lose someone you love you might begin to understand how hard this is – until then I don't need your pep talk.'

He raises his hands. 'I do understand. I lost geddeti – my gran – a few years ago. And I didn't get to say goodbye because I was thousands of miles away, obsessed with driving pigs around in a tin can. I don't carry her ashes, but she's still with me.'

He follows Rowena's gaze out the window, where sunset is in full blaze above the lane.

'Let's take our tea outside,' he says. 'I think I saw a way up to the roof.'

Halim helps Rowena climb the fence and lift herself up. He

133

passes her their steaming glasses and follows. The view is something else: the trees seem to be dangling droplets of gold instead of leaves; a gossamer cloud of birds sweeps past; chimney smoke draws grey vertical lines across the pink, windless sky.

'This tastes great,' Rowena says, licking her lips.

'Geddeti taught me how to make it,' Halim says. 'I remember sitting on her little balcony above the sea in Alexandria, where the light was so hard and clean. I've not seen that kind of light since.' He inhales the mint aroma before letting the sweet tea slide down his throat.

'You know, I saw my pa's ghost when we were at Dingle House,' Rowena says, watching the erratic flutter of a passing moth. 'I guess that's partly why I wanted to stay there – I thought he might come back and visit me.'

'I only met him a couple of times,' Halim says, 'but he seemed decent.'

'Yeah, he was. He was one of the good ones. Like you.'

Halim snorts. 'I think that's the first compliment you've ever paid me.'

Rowena puts down her glass and pulls something green out of her cardigan pocket. She reaches towards Halim's head, making him flinch.

'Hold still!' She leans in and tucks something into the dark folds of his hair.

'What is it?'

'A sprig of rowan. My namesake. The rowan tree symbolises courage, wisdom and protection. Some folk carry rowan twigs bound with thread to guard against enchantment, or sew them into their coats, close to their heart.'

He doesn't really hear the words because he's watching her mouth make different shapes, so close to his own. 'Do you think I need protection from enchantment?' he asks, his voice rough.

She smiles, her eyes sparkling. 'I don't know, do you?'

All sounds seem to fade as he leans forward, hesitates, and then takes her face in his hands. When their lips touch it sends a velvet shiver through his skin, jolting his heart as if it had been flatlining until now. He's never had this reaction to a kiss before. It's just a kiss, he tells himself, but as their tongues find each other, and her fingers brush his jaw, he draws her closer – kisses her harder in case it ends too soon. He loses himself in the moment utterly and completely, like a naive fool, like a love-struck schoolboy. Like someone under a spell.

23

———

ROWENA PULLS AWAY. 'No, I can't do this. Not with you.'

Confusion and anger flicker across Halim's face, and before she can take the words back and explain he's kicked his tea-glass off the roof in his haste to get away from her.

He climbs down and disappears into the barn beneath.

Let him hate me, she thinks – the curse won't let me get close to anyone and I don't want him to get hurt. Touching a finger to her lips she tells herself that it was just a kiss, a brief touch of skin, nothing more, nothing real. Yet, perhaps it's too late and the damage is done? Is It watching her every move?

She picks up the sprig of rowan that slipped from Halim's hair and startles as it pricks her fingers: instead of soft green leaves a strip of barbed wire lies in her palm, tarnished by old blood. Attached to one of the barbs is a scrap of pale skin with a red underside, a sliver of flesh. Drew's flesh. Rowena gags, her mouth bitter as ash. She tries to shake the thing off, but the barbs dig deeper.

A loud fluttering makes her look up to a huge vortex of starlings, swerving and tilting, breaking apart and coming together, disturbed by something. They start circling above Rowena's head, swinging lower and lower.

'It didn't mean anything,' she calls out, but many wings beat her voice away and the starlings ripple closer, an amorphous beast of feather and air.

The barbs bite harder as she picks and claws at them. 'It was nothing!' Rowena scrunches her eyes shut, counts nine breaths: in-hold-out; in-hold-out ...

Finally, she forces herself to look again. The sky is empty. Her palms are dotted with splinters and pink lines from where she's been scratching them, and in her hand is a crumpled sprig of rowan, its green leaves fanning out from the stem like a feather.

'What is it, what's wrong?' Halim sits up in his bed and watches Rowena dart about the barn throwing on clothes.

'Take a look out the window,' she says, hopping on one leg to get into her jeans.

Halim rubs his eyes and throws off the blanket.

It's almost midnight but the full moon lights up the lane and picks out every puddle, weed and stone. Lucy, Gabe's horse, is standing outside the cottage, a feathered headdress attached to her bridle and her white nose-stripe painted black. Her saddlebags are laden and her hooves have been wrapped in straw to muffle them.

'I couldn't sleep, and I saw that,' Rowena says, joining him at the window.

'More weird fancy dress,' Halim yawns.

Lucy paws the ground as Gabe comes out of the cottage, dressed in black with two bull horns attached to his head by thick leather straps. He places a soothing hand on Lucy's muscular neck and whispers something in her ear as her tail flicks away midges.

'This I have *never* seen,' Rowena whispers, a spark of delight in her voice. 'I dunno what's going on, but I sure as hell intend to find out.'

'Don't you get enough nightmares without filling your head with this stuff?'

Rowena scowls. 'If you're scared you don't have to come with me. In fact, I don't remember asking you to come with me.'

Halim thinks about letting her go, but knows she has a habit of finding trouble, so he slips into his trainers and reaches for his jumper.

'Remember what I taught you?' she asks.

'Dark clothes,' he sighs.

*

The humid night air clings to Halim as he and Rowena tuck them-selves into the fir trees at the side of the lane, keeping a good distance between themselves and Gabe as he rides past the outlying houses. The lane switches back and forth between the crook of two steep hills, beholden to the route of an ancient riverbed. They follow the quiet, hulking shapes of bull-man and horse, a conspicuous silence hanging between them like a clock that's just stopped ticking.

'You know, I'm kind of glad you came,' Rowena whispers. 'I think I saw a ghost-woman the other day, tied up in a field, and then I saw all these starlings—'

'Don't tell me: they were a sign, warning you off me?' mocks Halim. He can feel Rowena bristle next to him, but he doesn't care.

'Look, I'm sorry about what happened on the roof ...'

'So am I,' he mutters as they round a bend. 'Wait, where are they? Have we gone too far?'

'There.' Rowena points to a field that has opened out to the left, across which Gabe and Lucy are loping, heading towards the pale, pointed ruins of an abbey. Light is flickering through what's left of the windows and spilling out from the roofless nave, giving the building a shimmering halo against a dark wall of trees.

'What's all this silvery fuzz?' he asks as they creep through a fine mist, heading towards the tree-line for cover.

'Thistledown,' she whispers, suddenly close to him.

It's magical, he thinks, brushing his hand through the air. It's like moving through the dim haze of a dream.

They slow their steps and tuck in beneath the trees for cover. Three men dressed in black are waiting for Gabe at the abbey entrance. Halim squints to watch as Gabe raises his index finger and seems to place it between his teeth like a horse's bit. The other men do the same and then unhook Lucy's saddlebags and follow Gabe inside.

Halim touches Rowena's arm as she moves off again to get closer to the ruins. 'Are you sure we should be here? What if they see us? Perhaps we should go back?'

When she jerks away from him it's like a punch to the gut.

'You can go back if you want,' she says, 'but if you were serious about a life outside the city I suggest you stop being such a pussy and actually see what you've signed up for.'

Halim used to be taken aback when she spoke to him like this, but he realises that at some point along the way he must have become accustomed to it.

They keep low and circle the abbey to stay on the darkest side, where branches bump up against the stone and tease their way through it, reclaiming the place for Mother Nature. A whiff of stale urine hits Halim's nostrils as he folds back the ivy to peer in through the narrow glass-less window. Stacks of fat white candles are honeycombed into corners, turning the damp-streaked walls apricot. The fungus-covered pews have been pushed aside and in the middle of the aisle kneels a blindfolded boy of about fifteen, naked from the waist up, the word 'Cain' painted onto his bony chest. Gabe stands behind him, throwing a quivering, horned shadow across the broken floor tiles.

Halim glances at Rowena but her face is rigid with focus.

'This doesn't feel right,' he whispers, his mouth near her ear. 'Maybe Gabe wasn't one of the good ones after all?'

She darts him a look to silence him.

Gabe draws a long gold dagger from a lambskin sheath, and as the light flashes across the blade Halim's jaw falls slack.

He watches in horror as the boy's head is pulled back. His Adam's apple bobs up and down as Gabe raises the dagger.

Halim's about to leap up, but Rowena catches his arm and holds him still.

A second later, the boy's blindfold falls to the floor, cut through, and Gabe moves off towards a wooden chair raised up on what was once the chancel.

'Rise, foal, and shake the hand of the High Horseman,' says one of the men dressed in black.

The boy blinks, stands up and follows Gabe.

Every movement seems to whisper around the building's carcass to find Halim's ears, drawing him in, making him feel exposed and vulnerable. He's distantly aware that he's sweating, and that Rowena's hand lingers on his arm as they crane their necks to watch.

Gabe picks something up from the floor – a branch wrapped in fur with a goat's hoof tied to the end of it. The foal-boy takes the hoof in his hand.

'Heed the Horseman's Word,' Gabe says, his voice unusually hard and clipped. 'To hold, conceal and never reveal. Neither write nor dite nor recite. Nor cut nor carve. Nor draw in sand nor snow, nor mud nor blood.'

The foal nods. 'I heed.' He shakes the hoof three times.

Gabe then turns to the other men, who have crept up behind the boy to block the aisle, hands clasped in front of their bellies. 'What shall we teach this foal?' Gabe asks them.

The men reply in unison, a solemn rumble of baritone, a twisted canticle:

'*To walk, to trot, to canter, to run.*
To break, to tame, to master.'

The trio come forward and lay their hands on the foal's shoulders and spine and guide him backwards down the steps. They lower him to his knees again and press him there.

Gabe picks up a half-filled wine glass and turns a small iron skewer in a brazier at his feet, warming it in the flames.

Halim searches the foal's face for any flicker of fear, but sees only a calm reverence.

The resonance of Gabe's deep voice sends a shiver up Halim's spine. 'Then moon-shod and fleet-footed he'll be, with unbridled dominion over beast and man. Verdant be the grasses he feasts on, bountiful be the seed he sows, and wild and unbroken be the heart he carries.'

One of the men offers the foal a piece of wood to bite down on as Gabe rises and comes towards him with the glowing brand.

Halim shifts his weight. A shard of glass makes a loud crack under his foot, drawing the attention of one of the men, who flicks his head towards the window.

Halim and Rowena duck down. He nods for them to run.

She bites her lip and shakes her head.

A moment later there's a hissing sound from within the walls, a grunt, a clatter of wood and a gasp.

Rowena tentatively raises her head again and peers through the ivy.

Overwhelmed by curiosity, Halim does the same.

Gabe whispers something to the foal and then raises his voice. 'Now, drink the hippomane and seal the Word within.'

Rowena must have noticed the disgust on Halim's face.

'What's a hippomane?' she mouths.

'The mucus-like substance on the head of a new foal,' he whispers.

'Looks like red wine to me,' she shrugs.

'Now that you have the Horseman's Word,' Gabe continues, taking back the glass, 'I must know that you're aware of its true power and that you've fully understood. Show me, in the dirt there. Prove to us that you've heard, so that we may witness the change in you.'

The boy reaches out his arm to write something but is pulled up short by a sharp CRACK of a riding crop next to his ear, making him flinch and tumble over.

Gabe narrows his dark eyes and looks down at him. 'Neither write nor dite nor recite!' he yells, spit flying from his mouth, his words echoing around the ribcage of stone.

The boy looks askance at the others. *Now* his face is filled with fear, thinks Halim, tensing, readying to grab Rowena and run.

A sudden burst of laughter glances off the walls.

'Here's to the horse with the four white feet,' the men chant, 'the chestnut tail and mane, a star on his face and a spot on his breast, and his master's name was Cain.'

The boy grins from ear to ear as he joins the cheering and laughter. The men clap him about his shoulders, lift him to his feet and brush the dirt from his knees. Out of Lucy's saddlebags they produce loaves, cold meats and a bottle of something that looks like whisky.

'Pff, okay,' Rowena sighs, 'this is getting lame now, let's go.'

Halim nods and wipes a sweaty palm down his face.

They sneak off under the low embrace of the trees, tripping over roots and kicking up mulch in the darkness.

'What the hell kind of cult was that?' Halim asks Rowena as his heart finds a steady rhythm again.

'They'd never call it a cult, they'd call it a society or guild. That one looked pretty harmless, but you get all sorts across the Kingdom – ancient ones set up to share knowledge and craft that have mutated over the years into something more sinister. I think there used to be one up at Culcrith, Tessa seemed pretty proud of it.'

'After the weird shit I've seen so far, I was expecting the worst. I still don't understand the need for all these rites and rituals.'

'It's all about claiming a sense of power and destiny,' Rowena says as they reach the road. 'You know, in Celtic times they would strike a man between the shoulder blades with a sword, and divine from his death struggles.' She pauses to pluck bell-shaped flowers from the hedgerow, at pains to avoid Halim's gaze.

'Are you warning me to watch my back?'

She ignores him.

He remembers the feel of her hand on his arm as Gabe's words float to the surface – haunting him much more than the brand or dagger: '*Wild and unbroken be the heart he carries.*'

'I heard you shouting on the roof,' Halim says. 'That the kiss meant nothing, and to leave you alone.'

'I wasn't talking to you when I said those things.' Rowena turns her back on him and continues up the road.

He catches up with her. 'Well, I want to assure you that I feel the same, that it meant absolutely nothing.'

'Sure, whatever.' She rolls a white flower between forefinger and thumb, only vaguely listening.

'I don't usually do things like that and it won't happen again, so – will you *look at me* when I'm talking to you?' He spins her around, heat rising to his face.

'Don't worry, I won't report you to my mother if that's why you're freaking out,' she snarls, jerking her wrist away. 'And if you ever grab me like that ag—'

He doesn't let her finish: before his brain can talk him out of it he's kissing her.

She shoves him away – so hard that he almost falls into the road. She wipes her mouth with the back of her hand, her chest heaving, her eyes sparking. 'Don't you get it? Everyone I get close to *dies!*'

'I'll take my chances,' he says through clenched teeth, matching her glare.

She seems to think about it, and he wonders if she's going to shove him again when she strides over, but instead she takes his face in her hands and kisses him. The force of it pushes them through a gap in the brittle hedge and into the open grassland at the foot of a barrow.

They stumble and Rowena breaks away long enough to say 'You're a fucking idiot,' before pulling him down to the ground and pressing her mouth to his again.

Halim tries to take his weight on his hands, not wanting to crush her, but she pulls him closer until every inch of their bodies is touching and it feels as if the friction between them might actually start a fire. Her urgent hands unbuckle his belt, making something flutter inside him and he knows he's approaching the point of no return: he drags off her hoodie and lifts her from the damp grass to gather and throw off her T-shirt. Burying his face in her neck, he breathes her in, can taste the salt and smoke on her skin as his nimble fingers slip the hooks from her bra and he teases the fabric free from her breasts. She bites his shoulder, scratches her nails down his jeans as she claws them away and her hips rise to meet his. Soon they become a messy tangle of limbs and thistledown and dew as their bodies writhe in the dirt. When he finds the wetness between her legs she shudders like a rockfall. He briefly raises his head to the darkness surrounding them: 'Fuck the curse,' he whispers.

24

11 May

——

'WHAT HAVE WE DONE?' Rowena mutters as she steps back into her grass-stained jeans. Her foot catches on a tear and makes it bigger. 'Fuck! These are my only jeans! Everything's falling apart!'

'Are you okay?' Halim asks as he lifts his T-shirt from the mud.

'Yes. No! Why did you do that?' she glares at him, her fingers fumbling the laces on her boot.

'Me?'

'Yes. Why didn't you stay away? I warned you. It's not safe. I need to bathe, remove you from my skin, burn some sage, sleep with it under my pillow – something to trick It.' She tries to catch her breath, unsure whether her body's on fire from the sex or the panic.

Halim runs a hand through his hair and looks up to the sky. Thin clouds are streaked across the stars like scratches. 'I really hope your gran can cure you of this curse because it's making you unbearable.'

'Good,' she snaps, ''cause my curse seems quite picky and seeing as we barely like each other perhaps you'll be spared, because It will know that this was just hormones or some shit.'

'Or some shit,' mutters Halim, lifting a snail from his jumper.

She can't even look at him on the way back to the barn, certain that if she did it would bring back the feel of them together, remind her how different his touch was to the messy, greedy fumbling of

Drew when they used to fuck behind the charnel house. She sighs, pushes everything down deep inside – everything except her fury at Halim for complicating things.

She tumbles into bed in the early hours and spends a long and restless night trying not to think about all the ways her curse might kill Halim.

Rowena and Halim spend the morning sweeping, scrubbing rust off tools and cleaning the forge, heads down, in silence.

'I'll be sad to see you two go,' Gabe says as he scratches his chest and inspects their work. 'It's been nice having extra help around here.' He eyes the two of them in turn, picking up on the atmosphere. 'Well ... you should both take the afternoon off. You can clean up in the cottage while I make the tea. I've saved some cold cuts and bread for you, might even have a spot of beer if you've got a thirst on?'

Rowena suppresses a smile. 'Don't suppose you have some whisky or red wine, do you?'

Gabe mumbles something about those drinks being too rich for the likes of him and shuffles away.

'It's so weird seeing him in normal clothes,' Rowena grins. 'I can't unsee those giant horns.'

Halim leans his chin on the broom handle and looks at her as if she's a puzzle he needs to solve.

Her smile fades. 'You've got charcoal on your nose,' she says, heading out.

He calls after her. 'I don't regret what happened last night, Rowena.'

Rowena's surprised to find herself outside St Christopher's Church in Butsfield, wondering why her feet led her up the winding path between the headstones. She gazes up at the square, stocky tower, at the dove-shaped weathervane that's straining to fly. Probably Gabe's handiwork, she thinks. An image of her pa sat on a wooden pew floats into her mind, a memory of one of his secret Sunday visits. Something stirs inside her – she pegs it as curiosity and approaches the church entrance. In the porch is a corkboard stuck through with service notices and leaflets, including one promising 'Tea, Cake and Sex: A discussion on the complexities of sexuality from a Biblical perspective'. Rowena scowls and pulls the door open.

Stained-glass windows surround her on all sides, filtering the light a strange, pale green as she steps inside. Sunday services are over and the pews are empty, prayer books and cushions all neatly tucked away, but there's a mossy scent of stale flower-water hanging in the air. She half-expected to see her pa sat next to one of the stone pillars, staring at the cross on the altar, sending his private prayers into the ether. She wonders what he might have been praying for: a new life? His old life, before Tessa … before her? Rowena was never sure her pa was happy with how things turned out, but, unlike Tessa, he refused to speak of Culcrith. Perhaps he was praying for the salvation of his cursed daughter? Perhaps *she* should pray? Rowena runs her fingers along the back of a pew and takes a seat. She finds it oddly comforting sitting straight-backed in silence, surrounded by the solemn ghosts of other people's thoughts and petitions. The power of their belief seems to linger; coursing through the old stone, refracting in the coloured glass, billowing high into the rafters to drift back down and settle like a fine powder of snow on everything below.

Rowena absently strokes the fur on her rabbit's foot as she studies the intricate designs in the windows: a stony-faced procession of cup bearers; a lamb carrying a flag in its mouth across a green field; a crucified Jesus with ruby droplets pouring from his head, his eyes, down his neck and ribs … So much blood.

A voice behind makes her flinch.

'Worthy is the Lamb who was slain, to receive power and wealth and wisdom and might, and honour and glory and blessing.' The pastor, a grey-haired man with a wide forehead and glasses, smiles as he approaches. 'I see you're admiring our stained glass,' he nods.

Rowena swallows and slips the rabbit's foot back into her pocket as she gets up to leave. 'Yeah, it's, um, striking.'

'Please – don't let me disturb you. I can sit and pray with you if you'd like?'

'No, thanks, I'm, like, late for this thing. I should go. Thanks though.' She shuffles along to the aisle and heads for the door.

'Well, my blessings go with you,' the pastor calls after her.

I hope so, she thinks, I'm gonna need all the prayers and blessings you can muster to keep me and Halim safe.

When Wednesday morning comes around, Rowena and Halim wake early, strip their beds, slide a thank-you note and a pressed flower under the door to Gabe's cottage and head off to collect the truck. They walk in silence down the lane, under a glaze of sickly pastel clouds. Rowena listens for messages in the chaotic morning chorus. Perhaps they got away with it after all? she thinks.

At the garage, the mechanic checks his records to make sure the money's cleared, and for a few tense minutes Rowena wonders if Tessa came through or if she's changed her mind and given up on saving her daughter. Thankfully the bill is paid, and as they climb into the cab Halim takes out those turquoise beads and wraps them back around the headrest. They're his version of a rabbit's foot, Rowena realises with a smile.

The radio fills some of the space between them but it's still not enough, and Rowena breaks first. 'So,' she says, 'you reckon three days max until we hit Culcrith?'

'Yes.'

With a sudden lurch of her gut she realises that their journey is almost over. This is good – she's closer to being healed and will be further away from him. So why does she feel empty? She draws her knees up, perches her feet on the glove compartment and starts painting her toenails. She can tell Halim isn't happy about it but he doesn't complain – he'll be rid of her soon anyway, what's the point? The thought scratches at her ribcage.

'I was thinking,' she says, 'I might book myself into a hotel tonight, it could be my last bit of comfort before whatever the healing ritual is, and Culcrith doesn't exactly sound that welcoming from what my mother told me.'

Halim's eyes dart back and forth even though there are only two cars on the road, and they're a fair distance away.

'I know you like taking the more scenic route,' she continues, 'but are we passing any towns on the way?'

'We hit the border soon, then we'll cut across this county and

147

into the next where we'll spend the night. Brackwell's convenient, I suppose. I've got a job early tomorrow in West Watling, so you'll have to stay put for the day.'

'I can help with the job if you need me.'

'I don't need you.'

She raises her eyebrows at the sharpness of his reply. 'Right. Well, I can book a twin room if you want, treat you to a proper bed before you hit the road again? As a thank-you and that.'

'It's fine, I'm used to sleeping in the truck.'

'Whatever, I just, you know ... got used to having you near.'

'I'm not your babysitter, Rowena, I'm not going to smooth your damp brow every time you have a nightmare or think you see something in the shadows.'

She swallows, scrapes off the nail polish where her hand slipped, embarrassed that he's seen right through her.

'You need to stop treating people like things you can pick up and discard whenever the fancy takes you,' he continues.

'Says the man who literally made a contract to deliver a person for money.'

The radio is playing a classic love song so Halim hits the scan button.

It stops at another local station and a man's thick northern accent pounds out of the speakers: '*Behold, I will corrupt your seed, and spread dung upon your faces, even the dung of your sacrificial animals, waste from your solemn feasts; and one shall take you away with it—*'

Halim hits the button again.

Rowena lowers her feet and watches her toe-prints fade from the plastic.

25

14 May

————

AS THEY APPROACH THE BORDER the truck pulls up in a rare traffic queue. Vans, trucks and cars choke the lay-bys to either side, with only horse riders and motorbikes being cleared to cross.

'What's this about?' Rowena asks, sitting up.

Halim turns off the engine, the cab trembles and becomes still. 'Not sure,' he says, 'the northern counties escaped most of the floods and there was nothing on the news about quarantine orders.'

The engine ticks as it cools. People are hanging out of car doors or pacing, stretching, smoking, chatting. Rowena notices that there are only two white faces among them.

'I'll go and see what the hold-up is,' Halim says, unclipping his seat belt.

A loud bang and a yell makes him freeze – there's a fight breaking out near the Border Guard's office.

'Are those guns?' Rowena's jaw drops as a couple of patrolmen in navy uniforms arrive, rifles looped over their shoulders and what looks like tasers at their belts.

Halim frowns. 'Surely only plastic bullets?'

A small crowd is gathering up ahead. Another shot is fired, making all the bodies jerk back as if they were standing on a fault line. The patrolmen shout at the crowd to clear the area and return to their vehicles. A defiant hand thrusts into the air clutching a camera-phone.

'These things can flare up quickly,' Halim says. 'We might need to turn the truck around and get out of here.' He lowers his window and leans out. Angry curses tangle with music from truck stereos. He calls out to a man standing in front of a red builder's van. 'What's going on? How long are they holding people?'

The man, black-skinned with a bushy, white-streaked beard, tosses his spent cigarette and comes over. 'Some of us have been here for six hours,' he says. 'Border Guards say the system went down, but that's just an excuse for the searches they're doing. They're confiscating goods under by-laws or some shit.' He sucks his teeth. 'And when they let this chromed-up two-seater driven by a white boy through it all kicked off again. Fuckin' vultures.' The man spits on the tarmac and then notices Rowena in the passenger seat. 'Pardon my French,' he smiles.

'They can't do that,' she says. 'We'll report those pricks to the police.'

The man laughs. 'They can do whatever they like,' he jiggles his fingers in the air, 'they're the ones pushing the little buttons to make the red lights go green. Police probably know about it and let it slide, as long as no one gets hurt. But that might be about to change ...'

Halim leans further out of the window to be heard above the din. 'We can't wait six hours, is there an alternative route? What's the traffic like in these parts?'

The man considers Halim's truck and scratches his chin, his fingertips disappearing into his beard. Up ahead, a patrolman hammers his fist on the bonnet of a van and quickly finds himself surrounded. As Rowena watches, one of the crowd stiffens and then turns to look right at her, his brow knitted, his eyes wide.

'Bit risky, but you could hit the North Circular, take Greenfield Lane and then when you see the "Pick your own fruit" sign at Rowland's Farm head on up that track, keep going, going, going right to the end, yeah?' The bearded man grits his teeth. 'Not sure how safe it is these days as I can't try it myself, what with four points on my licence.'

Another man turns his head in Rowena's direction, then another, and soon the whole crowd is stood silently staring at her. She stares back, dumbstruck, as one by one the skin and flesh on their faces starts slipping like melting wax, slackening and sliding over cheek-bones and jaws, exposing the bright pink jelly of their eye sockets. Horrified, Rowena recoils and blinks: the crowd have their backs to her once again – their bodies sparking with anger, their voices raised ...

'We'll risk it, thanks,' Halim nods, oblivious to Rowena's distress in the seat beside him.

The bearded man reaches up to clasp hands with him. 'Good luck, man. Go well.'

The canals outside the passenger window seem to be in a state of torpor, tired of dragging themselves through the countryside with so many boats on their back. Clusters of barges bump against the banks, festooned with painted flags and bunting and pots of bright geraniums. Rowena sees families sitting on decks, laughing and toasting things over small grills, knocking bottles of beer together to congratulate themselves over their lifestyle choices. She thinks about where she might end up if the healing goes well, and pictures the vast valleys and skies of the Wilderness, wonders if she'll ever make it that far.

The track next to Rowland's Farm is stony and unforgiving and as it begins to narrow the truck slows to a crawl. Brambles scratch and whine across its metal flank.

'I didn't think you'd have it in you to attempt an illegal border crossing,' Rowena says with a hint of admiration. Even though it's for the best, she hates that Halim is pissed off with her, and finds herself trying to appease him by making small talk crumbed with compliments.

'Yeah, well, this trip is full of firsts,' he says, checking his wing mirrors. 'Keep a lookout for anyone. If we're spotted we'll just say we're lost.'

He brakes. 'There –' he points to a wide ditch at the end of the lane. Someone has laid a couple of old barn doors across the gap and cut a jagged line through the chain-link fence behind it. He gets out to inspect the wood, testing it with his weight before folding the fence right back and pinning it with heavy rocks. 'I need you to get out and guide me as I drive over that ditch,' he says, jumping back into his seat, 'we can't afford any more accidents, and we wouldn't be able to explain this away if we got stuck here.'

A mould-stink hits her as Rowena approaches the ditch, its brown water, dimpled by bugs, hiding whatever man-made deterrent might lie beneath. That familiar tingle up her spine tells her something's not right as she steps onto the wood, keeping one eye on the water. The feeling gets so strong that she considers going back to convince Halim to try another way when something dark breaks the surface – a dead thing with matted fur, a muzzle bloated and alive with maggots. Don't look, she tells herself, but she can't not look as a head emerges and rolls on its side. The dog's grey eye stares up at her as its rough white tongue starts lapping at the water through a jaw that's more sinew than flesh.

Rowena's foot slips, sending her crashing down onto her hands and knees. 'Fuck!' she yelps, as pain shoots through her arms and thighs.

A mist starts to rise, like it did in the saltmarsh, and her insides crackle with fear ...

'Are you okay?' Halim's voice pulls her back into herself.

The water is empty again – filled only with her trembling reflection as she slowly rises. 'I'm fine,' she manages, angry at herself for falling for these constant tricks.

'Hurry up, there's a mist coming in.'

'You can see it too?'

'Of course I can!'

She shudders with relief and makes it to the other side of the ditch. The truck's headlights flick on and she guides Halim slowly over the makeshift bridge, one agonising inch at a time until the wheels reach solid earth.

'I can't believe we're lost again,' Halim tuts. He's done his best to get them away from the illegal crossing but there were no road signs, no GPS signal and now the truck's choked by fog.

'At least we're in Langtonshire now and that bit closer to Culcrith,' Rowena says.

He pulls over. 'I can't drive through this. We might need to spend the night here.'

'You sure you can handle being in this small space with me?' Rowena sighs, barely loud enough for him to hear.

He notices an empty can in the footwell, crisp packets stuffed into the door cavity next to him, and wonders when he stopped caring.

'I'm going outside for a smoke,' Rowena says.

When the passenger door doesn't open he looks over and catches her eye.

'Will you come with me?' she asks, biting her lip. 'I don't like fog, it ... hides too many things.'

He nods, his own thoughts returning to the saltmarsh.

She smiles weakly, opens the door and steps out into the swirling grey.

'Is that a joint you're rolling?' he asks as he joins her in front of the truck.

'Only a little one, just ends.'

'Are you crazy? You can't keep that stuff in my truck! Do you know how often I get stopped and searched? What if we got searched at that checkpoint earlier? The one with the guns!'

She hesitates, her thumb folded over the soft paper cylinder. She shows him the silvery insides of the tin. 'It's okay, it was the last bit.' The fog muffles her voice, making everything she says sound secret. 'I need things like this to take the edge off, help me forget ... stuff.'

Rowena takes his silence as permission to spark up. Her face, and the cocoon of milky air around it, turns orange as the lighter flashes. 'You know, I read that human eyes only see a certain light spectrum,' she says on the exhale, shivering a little. 'What we actually see is just a tiny portion of all that there is. Have you ever wondered what we're missing, what's going on out there – in all the in-between bits?'

Halim leans back on the truck and gazes into the pale nothingness. 'I guess I've never really thought about it.'

'I have,' she says. 'I had a lot of time to think as a kid. I was left alone a lot.'

'Are you okay?' he asks, not expecting a straight answer.

'Not really,' she sighs. 'I'm worried my gran won't be able to heal me, and my weird visions are getting stronger.'

'Have you thought that maybe the visions, your nightmares, all the "signs", might be your brain trying to deal with real life and work things through?' he asks. 'Like your dad dying, your boy-friend's accident.'

She shakes her head. 'You can't explain away all the stuff before then – I grew up with my mother pointing out everything I'd broken and ruined, and now that I'm nearly eighteen it's not just curdled milk and rot and vermin, it's *Death* that's following me.'

She pulls on the joint and offers it to Halim.

He hesitates, then takes it, watches her move a few steps forward, stretching out her arms to grasp fistfuls of ether.

'Maybe all those things your mother pointed out were just bad luck? Shit happens, Rowena.'

'Not this much. This isn't normal. I'm not normal.'

No, he thinks, you're not. You're unlike any other girl I've met.

Far off, two owls call to each other as dusk beds in.

She walks back to him, takes the joint and has one last drag before stamping it out. 'What about you? Are you okay?'

Halim's not been asked that in a long time. He crosses his arms over his chest to keep them from wanting to hold her and tell her everything will be all right. 'I don't know. I thought I wanted this life, but maybe I'm too soft for it.' I'll need to decide soon, he thinks, because in four weeks' time the choice won't be mine any more.

'I don't think you're soft – you've picked up a lot of great habits from me.' Rowena waits for him to look at her, and when he does a smile teases her lips. 'After Culcrith, if all goes well, I plan on heading further north, into the Wilderness. You could join me if you want? There are more sheep than people there, you'd love it.'

He drinks in her mad, bright-eyed beauty and for one wonder-ful heartbeat he actually considers it. 'Isn't the Wilderness called that for a reason? Isn't it abandoned by the government, full of vagrants, criminals and mass graves?'

'Maybe those are just rumours spread to keep everyone else out?' Rowena sighs. 'Aren't you sick of following other people's rules and being put into boxes like the animals you cart around? We live in boxes, die in boxes, divide our land into boxes and call them coun-ties – let's make another fucking shape for once.'

Halim sniffs. 'Easy for you to say – you can settle anywhere in the Kingdom and just immediately belong. That's a privilege I don't think you seem to appreciate.'

'Maybe I don't want to settle.'

'You can't keep running for ever,' he mutters, his words clinging to him – held and dampened by the fog.

The windows are steamed up with stale breath when Rowena wakes. She opens the door to a blast of fresh air and a beautiful, glimmering dawn, swings her legs out of the cab and sits there for a minute, blanket-clad and yawning. The fog has cleared to reveal a wind-ruffled heath tufted with bread-brown heather – it's as if the Wilderness has come to her, or at least what she imagines it to look like. She gets up and walks around the truck, clicking her neck and spine, watches an arrowhead of noisy geese strike across the brightening expanse of sky.

And then she looks down.

26

15 May

———

'WHAT IS IT, IS MY ALARM going off?' Halim stutters.

'Come and see!' Rowena practically drags him out of his seat and leads him to the front of the truck.

His face says it all.

Just a few feet from where they're standing is a sheer drop – a curving cliff that plummets into what must have been a quarry once, its depths still untouched by the morning sun. Rocks and grasses cling to the banks, snagging threads of mist, adding a sublime beauty to the gaping chasm below. It's nothing but a deep wound in the land, gouged by man and left to scab over, yet something about the air-filled space pulls Rowena towards it and makes her want to fill it with her body.

Halim rubs his stubbled jaw and mutters something in Arabic. Looking down, with his head bowed, it seems as though he's praying.

Rowena shivers. 'Look how close we came to death last night. If you hadn't stopped the truck where you did, if I'd just walked a few more steps in the fog … Do you *still* doubt my curse?'

'Well, we're not dead, are we?'

It's no good, Rowena thinks, he'll never listen, he's always so sure he's right.

'Maybe this *is* one of your signs,' he continues, 'a sign that you've been saved, protected – that someone or something's looking out for you. Have you considered that?'

Her face softens. If only that were true, she thinks.

When Halim places a comforting hand on her shoulder before turning back it's all she can do not to clasp it in hers and cry.

'Wait, slow down!' Rowena points to a brown tourism sign at the side of the road that announces 'The Brack Well & Waterfall Trail'. 'Can we stop for a few minutes? Your pick-up isn't until ten-thirty, and they might have somewhere we can freshen up.'

Halim slows the truck and flicks the indicator.

The parking area is empty aside from a toilet cabin and a large information board explaining the birds and mammals you might come across on the trail. Stuck to it is an orange sticker that reads 'OF NO SCRAP VALUE'.

Towel in hand, Rowena heads down the leaf-softened path towards the well, a large pool fed by multiple springs pushing their way between the rocks. Coloured ribbons decorate the branches near the water's edge, and she can hear the distant swooshing of a waterfall, a balm to her ears after the persistent drone of the engine.

'Are you actually going in?' Halim asks as Rowena unlaces her trainers and peels off her socks, tossing them aside.

'You should never pass up the opportunity to bathe in a holy well. Especially if you're cursed.' Deep down, though, she knows the water's blessing won't nearly be enough.

Halim stands there, hands in his pockets, scuffing his boot next to the rusted tea lights and candle stubs left by dozens of hopeful visitors.

'You know, I wasn't gonna mention it,' Rowena says as she unbuttons her ripped jeans and lets them fall, 'but you stink. If you wanna make a good impression at your job today you should probably have a wash too.'

He looks away as she lifts off her vest and steps out of her knickers.

'Suit yourself,' she says, running naked into the pool, relishing the shock to her senses and the coiled knots it makes of her muscles as the cold rises up her calves, thighs, stomach and ribs. Closing her eyes, Rowena places her dripping hands over her heart and silently mouths thanks for their miraculous escape and then, sucking in the woody air, she slips her whole body under. Emerging beneath a veil of droplets, she brings her silt-thick fingers to her forehead and paints a line down her face, willing it to draw out her impurities and remove the taint of death. She stands there for a while, her back to the shore, her hands nudged by the gentle flow, the silt squishing between her toes. When a blackbird trills nearby it's as if her heart rises up to meet it. Remember this place, she tells herself, capture this moment to look back on, like a snapshot to hang on the wall when you find your home at last.

A splashing behind makes Rowena smile.

Halim swims past, his arms slick and shining. He ducks under and comes up bubbling curses from the cold.

'Feels amazing, doesn't it?' she asks, bumping through the ripples in his wake.

'I'd avoid this warm patch if I were you,' he says, swiping the hair out of his eyes.

'What the hell, Halim – you can't piss in a holy well!'

'It was just a joke!' He flashes his teeth in a grin. 'Or was it?'

She splashes him and laughs.

'It's nice to see you laughing,' he says, sinking lower so that their heads are level.

Annoyed at the flush he's coaxed from her skin, she changes the subject. 'I bet the Wilderness has tons of places like this. Places yet to be discovered and made sacred.' Without realising it, she's drifted closer to him, marshalled by the current. She looks into Halim's deep-brown eyes – alive with a dozen reflections, framed by long lashes that dangle droplets like pearls – and becomes acutely aware of his naked body below. For a heady moment she imagines that the water sliding between her thighs is his hand, and wonders if he feels it too – this carnal energy buzzing between them like the teeth of a zip being drawn together.

Before her urges take control of her limbs she dives under and kicks herself through the gloom, far away from him, slipping through the pool like an eel.

They dry off and dress in silence. Rowena's mind swirls as she's torn between harvesting the magic and memory of the well, of *him*, and tamping everything down, defying her feelings to protect them both. She feels like elastic stretched to breaking.

On their way up the path she stops in front of a fallen ash tree, its trunk soft with age and decay, frilled with fungi and stuck through with silver and copper coins. She takes one from her pocket, wedges it in amongst the others and makes a wish for this all to be over. She's surprised when Halim appears next to her, reaches down and presses his own coin into the bark.

He looks at it for a moment, and then heads off without a word.

Halim leans his elbows on the hotel bar as he waits for Rowena, staring at the half-composed text to his mother. It's a white flag, a truce – as close as he'll get to begging for more time. In four weeks he turns twenty-one and that's when his name will be struck from his parents' lives, and the door to that secure future will be firmly closed. An embarrassment to the Hosny name, he'll be erased line by line, clause by clause, picture by picture. Yet what hurts more than losing my inheritance, he thinks, is knowing that their opinion of me is so low that they considered me a failure before I'd even started down my own path. He pockets his phone and swirls the whisky in his tumbler before swallowing it in one.

'It's late but there's a Chinese takeaway up the road,' Rowena says as she joins him, a brightness to her face at last. She notices the empty whisky glasses on the bar but doesn't say anything.

'Sounds good.'

He follows her past the hotel stables, a neon-drenched casino and a row of boarded-up shopfronts, some scratched with the shapes of animals and birds, some pasted with food-bank appeals. A homeless man sits by the door of the Lucky Dragon, small bundles of what looks like sage spread out on a blanket before him, labelled as 'smudge sticks'. Rowena buys one and then heads inside. They order and take a seat on the plastic chairs by the steamed-up window. The TV in the corner shows some period drama where a flaxen-haired woman with heaving breasts is embracing a soldier in a sun-dappled grove, but Halim's eyes are drawn to the grinning cat on the counter, whose paw rises and falls as it grasps imaginary coins from the air.

A young man with an earring and a buzz cut blusters through

the door. 'Picking up some spring rolls and prawn crackers,' he says to the woman. She heads out back. The young man turns to Halim and Rowena and he offers her a nod as his fingers drum the counter. Halim looks at his mangled trainers, the hole at the knee of his too-tight branded jeans, and wonders why the wealthy ones try so hard to look poor.

'Busy night?' the young man directs his question at Rowena.

She shrugs.

'Wanna come to a Chargers' moot? There's one tonight if you fancy it, I can get you in.'

Rowena perks up. 'Yeah? Him too?' She touches Halim's arm.

'Sure.'

The woman returns with their food order, and hands the young man a paper bag with grease stains.

'Halim, you have to come with me,' Rowena whispers. 'I'll never get the chance to go to one of these again. You'll love it, I know you will.'

'I'm not sure it's a good idea.'

'Come on, live a little, Granddad!'

'I'm only twenty.'

'Exactly! Haven't our recent brushes with death made you even more hungry to live?' She looks up at him, her eyebrows raised, eyes wide and lips parted.

Before he can draw a breath to reply, she's jumped up and is following the young man out of the shop.

'Shit,' Halim mutters, running a hand through his stubble.

'What's a "Charger"?' Halim asks as he finds himself sitting next to Rowena in the back of a blue family saloon, his knees bumping a plastic toy stuffed into the seat pocket, the hot takeaway bag on his lap.

'Chargers,' she whispers with relish, 'are rich kids who have their own cars. Since the government lowered the driving age Charging's kinda become a youth sport: they meet up at secret locations to bomb around, hang out with their mates and lose their L-plates.' The corner of her mouth twists. 'I guess the smell of burning rubber's a turn on.'

Finishing his phone call, the young man gets into the driver's seat and swivels around to face them. 'I'm Grouper,' he says.

'Rowena,' she smiles. 'And this is Halim.'

'Grouper's an interesting name,' notes Halim.

'We don't do real names on nights like this. Just a precaution.'

'Why?'

Grouper smiles in the rear-view as he starts the engine. 'Well, the moot's not exactly legal and there might be some substances knocking about.' As if to prove his point, he taps out a line of coke on the dashboard and snorts it. 'Sure you don't want to sit up front, Rowena?' He pats the passenger seat.

'I like it back here,' she smiles. 'It's cosy.'

Grouper switches on some ironically mediocre R&B and turns it up before jolting the car into motion.

When the windows become fogged up Rowena draws an eye on the glass.

Halim sighs as the street lights strobe past, not wanting to acknowledge that he only tagged along to have more time with her before they go their separate ways.

Grouper drives them to a section of wide country road, far from any county border, with an unfenced field running parallel to it. He turns the car into the field, bumps it across the grass and parks with a jerk under a sprawling beech tree, alongside a handful of other cars and three horses. The more impressive vehicles – those with shining alloys, spoilers and shouty colours – are parked in a semi-circle facing the road with their headlights on and a stereo blasting.

A young man with a backpack taps on the window and looks them over. His white T-shirt has the words 'GOOD TIMES' emblazoned across the chest in block letters and his forehead has a sprinkling of acne.

Grouper opens the door and shows him a text. 'All right? These two are legit, they're with me.'

'Yeah, that's cool. Want some hooch?'

'Two, please,' Rowena says, getting out of the car.

He hands two jars of honey-coloured liquid to her as she pays him. 'Engines off, no photos or recording on your phones and keep to the left-hand side of the road,' he explains. 'Have a good night, folks.'

She hands a jar to Halim and hooks her arm through his. 'Thanks so much for the lift, Grouper,' she says with a smile. 'So we'll meet back here after, yeah?'

Grouper looks gutted. He scratches his neck. 'Er, yeah. Sure.'

Rowena leads Halim towards the flashy cars. The sweet smoke of barbecued food and bitter tang of weed hang in the air. He surveys the crowd: red lips; whites of eyes stark against black liner; T-shirts cropped just under the bra; shirtsleeves rolled up over biceps and jeans slung low to reveal the waistbands of expensive boxers.

'Why are you frowning?' Rowena asks.

'Just feeling a bit old and under-dressed.'

Rowena laughs. 'Don't worry, you and your designer sweatshirt, gold chain and fancy phone fit right in here. These,' she points with the jar she's holding, 'are your people.'

'If these were my people we'd have been charged an entry fee, with extra for parking and a printed programme.'

They share a grin that strikes him in the breastbone.

A girl in a fluffy cardigan appears between them holding a tray: 'We made too many mushroom burgers. They're vegan. Go on, dig in!'

'No, thanks,' Halim says, holding up the takeaway bag.

The girl winks at him before bouncing off towards another couple.

As he and Rowena sit cross-legged on the daisy-studded grass tucking into their chicken noodles, he wonders if they look like a real couple, and he doesn't find the thought entirely unpleasant.

'You've got something on your chin,' Rowena says.

He wipes his sleeve across his face.

'Over there – no – the other side. Up a bit.'

Halim rubs his fingers around his mouth. 'Has it gone?'

She squints at him, her cheeks full of prawn toast. 'Yeah, I think that frown's gone now, you're golden.'

He rolls his eyes as she laughs.

Around them, people are chatting, giggling, eyeing each other up. The air is bristling with desire. It reminds him of that moment at the well this morning. It reminds him of a lot of moments around

Rowena. Then he remembers the half-finished text in his pocket. He takes another swig of the pungent hooch and it seems to blend with the single-malt whisky to loosen his tongue. 'I expected to be better at this life,' he sniffs. 'In my arrogance I thought that – being an educated man – I could do anything, be anyone, and that it'd be easy. But something wants to steer me down certain roads, and I feel like I'm losing control.'

'None of us have control over our lives,' Rowena says. 'We think we do, but really we're only making small choices that nudge our direction. You believe in gut instinct, don't you?'

He nods.

'Well, that's kind of the same thing as signs and omens – they're like a hand on your back, guiding you. A feeling. My pa always used to say, "Go with your gut. Unless you're hungry – in which case eat first."'

Halim smiles.

'You know, you might find things a bit easier if you opened yourself up and tried to tune into the world. Go with the flow.'

He gazes out across the field. The bursts of music and laughter, pops of colour and haze of headlights through the blue-grey smoke make everything feel like a carnival. Orange orbs are strung across the horizon: even the town looks beautiful from here, he thinks, and for a moment he marvels at how people are able to find joy in the small things, in some field in the middle of nowhere.

'Here.' Rowena sticks something in his face. A fortune cookie.

He wrinkles his nose but takes it anyway, splits the red wrapper, breaks the biscuit and unfurls the thin strip of paper.

'Well, what does it say?'

'It says, "*Don't let your heart close like a fist.*"'

She snorts a laugh and he can't help but join in.

'Go on,' he sighs, 'what does yours say?'

Her fingers hesitate before ripping it open. "*Be the ripples, not the stone.*" What? That doesn't even make sense.'

'Yes, it does.'

She rummages again, spilling more fortune cookies onto the grass.

'Did you steal those?'

'I've got a sweet tooth,' she shrugs. 'Besides, I figured we both needed some good advice.' She rips open the next wrapper and cracks it. 'Ugh!' She tosses the paper away and grabs another.

'How many are you going to open?'

'As many as it takes.'

Eventually she gives up and lies back on the grass.

Halim joins her, their eyes to the sky and its myriad stars and not another word passes between them. Though they aren't touching, he can sense the press and heat of her body next to him, becomes aware of the rise and fall of her breasts and remembers the feel of them with a stirring in his groin.

A loud bang from an exhaust makes them both jump. Engines are starting up and people seem to be gathering their things, kicking dirt over barbecues and taking one final piss in the bushes. Halim helps Rowena up and they follow the crowd to the roadside. Claps and whistles bounce off into the darkness like excited puppies. He stops the hooch-man as he's walking up and down the line and gets a refill for them both.

'To tuning in,' Rowena smiles, clinking her jar against his.

Halim takes a deep gulp, grateful for the cool breeze against his booze-flushed cheeks.

The lead car's wheels spin as it screeches off, leaving behind an acrid mist and a crescendo of cheers. Taking it as a signal, the other cars fall in and speed off down the road, exhausts roaring into the thick black night.

'Now what happens?' Halim asks, watching the red tail lights fade.

Rowena shrugs. 'They drive back, I guess?'

A horn sounds. Seconds later, one car after another zooms past at what must be pushing 80 mph, blasting the audience with a backdraught, making a few people leap away from the tarmac and click their fingers in the air, laughing. Rowena touches the sleeve of Halim's sweater as she jumps up and down, hollering and whooping.

By the third time the cars flash past Halim gets swept up in it too, imagining himself behind the wheel: foot to the floor, spine pressed into leather as the world melts either side of him – the almost sexual rush of being in command of so much power. He adds his voice to the throng and feels a weight lift from his shoulders.

The lead car slows as it nears the crowd and performs a tight U-turn in one fluid motion, its hazard lights flashing in time with the bass thumping from its speakers. Another car pulls alongside and the drivers high-five each other through their windows, sending the crowd into a frenzy. A third, misjudging his speed, swerves left to avoid them, then swerves right again and spins into the middle of the road, screeching to a sudden stop. The cheering stutters and fades to an eerie silence.

Halim cranes his head to look.

Through the windscreen, the driver's mouth is agape, his eyes round and staring, the road striped black from his skid. The driver of the lead car jumps out and waves her arms in the air at the other approaching cars, bringing them to a stop before the bottleneck. The bass in her car continues to pulsate – only now it's joined by gasps and screams.

People bash into Halim as they stream past, others linger, hands over their mouths, staring at something on the verge up ahead.

'What is it?' Rowena asks a passing girl.

'Oh my God!' is all she says, her eyes shining with tears as she flees into the field.

———

27

HALIM TRIES TO HOLD HER BACK as they near the body, but Rowena shrugs him off.

The hooch-man is lying in the grass, his arms and legs flung out at his sides, staring up at the wind-whipped sky, unblinking. His 'GOOD TIMES' T-shirt is pinking with blood at the collar where a piece of bone has punctured the skin. Brown liquid from his back-pack snakes onto the road and runs towards her.

'Holy shit!' Rowena mutters. She instinctively turns to find Halim and comes face to face with the shadow-man, Its branch-like arms almost touching her. She yelps and leaps back, and in that hideous moment the shadow becomes nothing but the scrawl of the hedgerow as headlights swing through it and disappear.

'Has anyone called an ambulance?' Halim shouts, but no one's listening because they've scattered and the road is red with tail lights. He curses something in Arabic, gets out his mobile and dials.

Rowena cups her hands over her nose and mouth and tries to slow her breathing.

'Where are we?' Halim asks her, his phone to his ear.

She shakes her head, transfixed by the hooch-man's face, frozen in surprise.

Halim waves his hand in front of her. 'Find Grouper, ask him. GO.'

Rowena runs up the road as the murmur of engines fades. The

field is empty, churned up by tyres and littered with cigarette butts and empty jars. 'Wanker!' she yells into the darkness.

She returns to Halim, out of breath. 'He's gone. They all are, and we should be gone too.'

'We don't know exactly where we are,' he tells the person on the phone, 'and Maps still isn't loading. Right, yes … okay.' He hangs up. 'The lady said she can trace our call to the nearest mast, so we should wait here and not move him.'

Rowena trails Halim as he paces up and down the road. 'We can't wait here. We can't be here when they come.'

'What? Why?'

'You know what happened at St Cross, you've seen what people are like. They'll blame us for this – they'll blame me.' Her voice breaks.

Halim looks up at the sky and pinches the bridge of his nose. 'For fuck's sake, he was hit by a car, Rowena!'

'There's nothing we can do for him anyway, and help's on the way. Do you wanna get pulled into the police station to explain all this? What if this county has the death penalty? What if they find out we used an illegal border crossing?'

'What do you suggest then?'

'I suggest we leave. *Now.*'

Halim shifts from foot to foot, runs his hand through his hair. 'I don't know, it seems wrong.'

'All of this is wrong, but you can stop this kind of thing happening again by getting me to my gran. Please, Halim.' There's a thin whine of a siren in the distance. She grips his arm. 'Please, I don't want to be here. Please.'

He relents, quickly turns off his phone and she leads him away from the road at a run across the flat, open fields, heading in the vague direction that Grouper had driven them.

Sirens wail behind them now. She needs to catch her breath but knows if they stop they might be exposed by the white slice of a torch.

A vehicle door slams, sounding like a cannon in the stillness. She imagines them bent over the body now – checking for a pulse, shaking their heads.

'I think there's a building over there,' she gasps, 'let's head for that and wait it out.' She shunts her screaming legs onwards as they blindly stumble over stones and turf, a stop-start run that seems to take for ever.

At the edge of the field, nestled in a stand of beech trees as if grown there like a fungus, is what looks like a stone shed. Rowena rips the ivy from the door – showering them both in cobwebs and dirt – and presses down on the rusted handle. It gives, and the door opens with a judder.

A slant of moonlight from the window reveals the disgust on Halim's face. 'What the hell is this place?'

'A charnel house,' pants Rowena. 'It's where they stuff all the bodies of the poor bastards who get dug up because the wealthy bastards think graveyards are a blemish on their precious land. That, or they're old plague victims, gathered from local pits.'

They squeeze their way past stacks of human leg bones and sprigs of smaller bones.

'It's like a grisly jigsaw puzzle,' Halim mutters, looking up at the skulls jumbled high on the shelves, one carelessly on top of the other.

Mindful not to knock any of the crumbling wooden units that fill the space, Rowena sits on the floor, her back to the cold stone wall. 'There was one of these in Pickbury. I'd hide there when I was poaching on the Northwood estate, sit with my candles, waiting for dawn so I could check the traps.' She tries not to think about the times that Drew was with her.

Halim's not listening though – his whole body has turned rigid. He rushes to the far corner where he doubles over and vomits.

Rowena tries to tune out the sound of heaving and spitting as she reaches into the lace of her bra and digs out a pre-rolled cigarette – bent now, and damp from sweat. She lights it, watches the smoke form Stygian mists around the summits of yellowing bone, and kneads her hands to stop them shaking.

'Sorry,' Halim says sheepishly as he sits nearby. 'I've never seen a dead body before.'

Rowena sniffs. 'I've seen plenty, and it doesn't get any easier.' Remembering the smudge stick she bought from the man outside the Chinese takeaway, she fishes it out and lights it with her cigarette. The dried sage catches and glows red. 'When my pa collapsed in front of me I just stood there, freaking out about my curse and what Tessa would say, knowing she'd blame me.' She circles her head with the smoking bundle and breathes it in. 'I should've done something, gone for help straight away – curse or not, I killed him.'

Something scurries across the floor in front of Rowena's feet, making her jump and press her spine so hard to the wall it clicks.

'It's okay,' Halim says. 'I'm right here, Ro.'

The hairs rise on her arms. 'That's what my pa used to say to me,' she whispers.

Hours creep by before Rowena suggests they get going again. With a throbbing head, Halim follows her across the fields until they hit electrified fences and have to take to the road. Eventually they reach the wood at the edge of town and pick their way around the trees, their bodies breaking through the silvery pools of moonlight that penetrate the canopy. Rowena keeps close to his side, her hand almost brushing his, and when they reach the hotel car park she seems reluctant to leave him.

'Goodnight, Rowena,' he says.

'Night, Halim.' She half-turns back to him before changing her mind.

He watches her pass between the box-hedges that rise up like tombstones in front of the automatic doors, and then she's gone.

Hoping for a few hours' sleep, Halim unlocks the truck, flicks on the overhead light and groans at the crumbs, chocolate wrappers, crushed petals and tobacco scattered around the cab. He gathers up the mess, and after he's dumped the rubbish he sticks his hand into one of his clean socks and polishes the dashboard, dusts down the seats and wipes the door handles. Sitting back to admire his work, Halim realises he's just removed every trace of Rowena and satisfaction turns to a gut-scraping emptiness. The solitary life he planned veered way off course when he accepted this contract, yet he can't say he's hated it. He realises, with some reluctance, that Rowena's taught him more in the past few weeks than he's learned the past few years, led him into things he'd never have discovered without her hedonistic impulses and insatiable curiosity ... And seeing the broken body of a man not much younger than himself has thrown his own life into sharp relief.

Halim's phone rings and in a moment of madness he answers it before checking the name. 'Hello?'

'Halim!' His mother sounds surprised to be speaking with him. 'Habibi, it's so nice to hear your voice!'

Shit, he thinks, I can't hang up now.

'How are you?' she asks in Arabic. 'Are you still crawling about in that ugly truck?'

'Well—'

'You know, the board are starting to ask questions, Halim.'

He thunks his forehead on the steering wheel and listens to her heel clicks echo down what sounds like a corridor.

'They wanted to know when your studies in Paris were ending and when you'll be joining Messis – they're particularly keen on this father–son partnership; it would help establish a more wholesome, family image, don't you think? We've been discussing a re-brand, actually, and I expect your father would love to talk to you about it.'

Halim snorts and scrunches his eyes shut.

'Don't you feel the slightest guilt at squandering this opportunity, tossing it away to someone who's not even blood? Because that's what will happen; you must realise that there are plenty of talented young men who would die for a senior position at Messis International.'

'I'm sure plenty of young men have already died for Messis,' he mumbles.

'What was that?' A lift pings, followed by a mechanical swoosh.

'Nothing.'

'Your father's doing all he can to placate the board but they are getting skittish, and if those doubts turn into fears the shares might suffer.'

'Well,' Halim sighs, 'I have been thinking about my future actually.'

'Oh, that's wonderful! I told your father this was all a whim and that you'd come round, given time.'

'That's just it – I need more time.' He despises asking for things, especially from his parents.

'You've had over two years since boarding school, Halim.'

'Yes, but it takes time to build up a business, as well you know, and this could really work for me. I only want the chance to make him proud.' He despises lying, too. 'Can't you speak to him?'

He hears another ping, the swoosh, the heels.

'Mother?'

'Yes, I'm still here,' she says, her voice hard. 'You know I can't do that. You have until the seventeenth of June, Halim. That's about four weeks. I pray in that time you'll have come to your senses and realised that this coarse peasant life isn't for you.'

He hears his mother light a cigarette and take a drag. She only smokes when she's drunk or when his father's out of town – it must be around 10 a.m. in Singapore so he hopes it's the latter. Halim pictures her stood on the balcony of the apartment he's only ever seen once, skyscrapers glinting across the harbour like standing stones erected for a different kind of worship.

'You know your father and I made an investment in you, Halim, in your education, your upbringing. We're willing to write off the fact that you turned your back on university, but you can't turn your back on your father and I. Don't let us down.'

Without Halim realising it, his fingertips graze the gold dog tag at his neck.

'Of course you won't let us down: you're a good boy, and you love and respect your parents. We'll speak soon, habibi.'

She hangs up.

Halim eventually lowers the phone from his ear and tosses it onto the passenger seat, next to an arrowhead that Gabe gave him and a fortune-cookie paper he'd saved.

Rowena frowns at the painting on the wall above the bed she's hardly slept in – the hotel's attempt at injecting colour into the characterless room looks like blood-soiled washing fallen from the line. She goes to the sink and splashes cold water on her face in a half-hearted attempt to wash off the part of the night where it got bad. Up until the accident she'd been loving it. If it even *was* an accident: the hooch-man walked past her a few moments before, was just a dozen or so steps from where she'd been standing. If Death was aiming for her, perhaps It was getting sloppy?

The TV that she'd kept on all night for comfort goes from a silent satellite feed of the weather to the citrus-drenched breakfast news: rainproof make-up tips, followed by a temporary-housing scandal that caused the death of three families. Rowena flicks it off, claws through her hair and pulls it back, tying it extra tight in the hope that it might keep her eyes open. She throws all the hotel biscuits into her backpack, zips it up, drops down onto the bed and stares at the phone in her hand. Her bones, her muscles – everything feels too heavy, as if she might sink through the floor.

After four rings her mother picks up. 'Rowena? Is everything okay?'

'Will Gran really be able to fix me?'

'Why, what's happened now?'

Rowena pinches the bridge of her nose and closes her eyes. 'I don't know, curse stuff I guess. It's everywhere I look and ... I'm so tired. I just want someone to tell me it'll all be okay.'

There's a rattle and shucking sound of curtains being drawn. 'I know it must be hard being on the road this long, but stick with it and stay strong, okay? Where are you now, you must be close to Culcrith?'

'I guess.'

'Well, it's ten days until your birthday and the solstice is a way off – there's still time to set things straight. Have you tried putting a clove of garlic in your pocket?'

'Nothing works.'

Tessa stifles a yawn. 'Don't be daft! Didn't I look out for you all these years, show you the herbs and the ways? Was I just wasting my time?'

Rowena wishes her pa was here to talk to instead. She opens the window to lean out and speckle her face with rain, but the safety lock will only allow her a small slice of air.

'Have faith in your gran and in Culcrith, it's a special place. When you're there you'll feel it, like a vibration in the air, a humming in your bones that tells you anything's possible.' Tessa's voice slips into a warm timbre that's alien to Rowena's ear. 'Even the sun's clearer up there, and it's so taken with the place it hangs around longer – you'll see. And that land produced the finest horses in the county, beautiful they were – I'd spend hours grooming them, gazing at them, watching them thunder across the field whenever the mood took them.'

'If you loved Culcrith so much why did you leave?'

She can hear Tessa breathing, her mind ticking over. 'Your pa and I did something stupid and we had to leave. These things happen ... Anyway, look at the time, I have to get on. Send me a message to say you've arrived, okay?' She hangs up before Rowena can reply, and the room feels somehow colder than before.

28

16 May

'YOU LOOK LIKE SHIT,' ROWENA says as she sneaks Halim into the hotel breakfast buffet. They appraise each other in the mirrored wall behind the hotplates.

'I didn't sleep much,' he replies, dripping two slippery eggs onto his plate.

'Me neither.'

'More nightmares?'

Rowena narrows her eyes at him. 'No. Just crushing guilt at being unable to stop people dying around me.'

She takes her tray to a table. He follows.

Halim stayed up too long searching for his own signs; in the brushstrokes of cloud through the windscreen, or in the pixels of his phone – scrolling through what little information there was about the Wilderness. Most of it was local folklore claiming that the land was set aside for the devil himself, or stories of haunted heaths and a mountain hag called Liath who stalks unwitting travellers by stepping into the footprints they leave behind.

'Why are you so sure that the Wilderness is the place for you?' he asks.

Surprise flickers across Rowena's face as she looks up, and he catches a sparkle in her eyes.

'There's a reason that land's not farmed or policed,' he continues.

'How will you live, survive, make money? It doesn't sound like some bucolic Arcadia.'

'I know it's hard for you to believe, but not everything revolves around money, Halim. Opportunity and smarts is what it's about. I know the land's unfamiliar but I'm sure I can figure out its potential, its quirks: it won't be easy, but nothing worth having ever is. At least in the Wilderness I'll have the freedom to try, the freedom to make mistakes and start over.'

He looks down at his plate and pushes the food around, annoyed at how much braver she is than him.

Rowena reaches into her backpack and clinks her dinosaur tin onto the table. 'I made you something. Open it.'

Halim slides the tin towards him, lifts the lid and gets a hit of tobacco and marijuana. It's empty except for a teardrop-shaped stone with a slender green ribbon wrapped around its middle. He lifts it out. As he holds it, warmth seems to soak through his fingers.

'It's a hag stone I found on the beach back in Wellshire – a stone with a hole right through it. I rolled up some rowan leaves, placed them in the hole and then bound it with the ribbon. It's for luck. And before you kick off about charms or whatever, take a look at that dog tag hanging around your neck and those beads in your truck – you're not so different from me.'

He touches the chain at his neck. 'This was the last proper gift I ever got. Until now.'

She shrugs, picks up some salt grains from the table and throws them over her shoulder. 'It's not much, but I wanted to give you something. A reminder, I guess.'

'Thank you,' he smiles, 'though I doubt I'll ever forget you.'

Rowena goes back to her food, breaking the moment with a sharp scrape of her fork.

They cross the county border into Northinverland with minimal fuss, and then sleep consumes Rowena as she nods along with the motion of the truck. Her dreams are distant, too smothered in exhaustion to reveal themselves. She wakes up when they come to a stop. 'Where are we?' she mumbles through a sticky mouth.

'Still in Northinverland, only a mile or so past the border.' Halim sighs. 'We've been flagged down by a volunteer patrol.'

A middle-aged man and woman in high-vis jackets and wellington boots head over. They remind Rowena of plump garden gnomes.

'Welcome to Northinverland,' the man says as Halim lowers his window. 'Can I ask what brings you to our beautiful county?'

'We've just been through all the official checks, so you could ask the Border Guards, Mr, er, Tanner,' Halim says, reading the lanyard around the man's neck.

Tanner rubs the ruddy apple of his chin. 'Don't worry, this is a routine check on behalf of the mayor. Only a random stop, shan't keep you long.'

In the wing mirror Rowena spots the woman holding a clipboard in one hand and what looks like a selfie-stick in the other. She thrusts the stick under the truck and sweeps it around.

'I'm a registered livestock driver and this is my assistant,' Halim says. 'We're travelling on to Laithness, contracted to arrive in Culcrith today, so if you would oblige us, we really should get going to make up lost time.'

'*Oblige* you?' Tanner raises an eyebrow. 'Where are you from?'

'Look, if I show you my passport will that be the end of it?'

'Well, that'd be the start of it – we also need to know what stock you're carrying and see in the back of your truck. Could you *oblige* me and pop it open?'

Halim curses under his breath and swings his door wide, making Tanner leap back or be struck.

As soon as they're gone, the woman taps on the window beside Rowena, startling her.

'Hello. Is this your truck?' she asks.

'No, it's his. Oh – you thought because I'm the white one it must be mine?' Rowena scowls.

The woman smooths her floral neck scarf and continues. 'So how many people have you killed now?'

Rowena pales. 'What?'

The woman smiles as her nails dig into her clipboard and make a clawing sound that sets Rowena's teeth on edge. 'I said, how many have you killed? Everything you touch turns to shit.'

Rowena shakes her head. 'I, I don't understand ...'

The woman speaks louder. 'Could I just check inside, where you're sat?'

'Oh.' Shaken, Rowena jumps out and stands in the mud next to the truck, staring at the back of the woman as she rummages around the cab.

The woman takes out the dinosaur tin, pops it open, sniffs and pulls a face. 'What's this?' she asks, holding up the hag stone bound in ribbon.

'A good-luck charm. I made it.'

'Are you hiding drugs in it?' the woman asks, picking away at the ribbon. 'It smells like you are.'

'No, it's a rowan leaf. Stop putting your fingers all over it!'

The woman's head springs up. Something that looks like a flame-flicker catches her eyes. 'No, *you* stop!'

'Everything all right here, Marge?' Tanner appears beside them.

Rowena gapes at the woman, who ignores her.

'Well, I'm not sure, this tin smells funny,' Marge hands it to him.

'Does indeed,' Tanner replies, scratching at the ribbon to reveal the green leaves tucked beneath. 'Did you find anything else?'

Marge shakes her head.

'Hmm. Well, we'll have to confiscate this – you shouldn't have brought foreign vegetation into the county without prior consent.'

'Oh, come on, it's a rowan leaf!' Rowena yells. 'What gives you the right to take our stuff? Where I'm from, that's called stealing.'

'Look, Mr Tanner, if that's everything we really should be on our way,' Halim says.

Tanner nods and bares his teeth in what could loosely be described as a smile. 'Watch your speed and travel safely.' He and Marge step back onto the verge and wave them on.

Back in the truck, Rowena grips the leather seat, still trying to process what happened.

Halim nods to the wing mirror next to her. 'Watch,' he says.

In the reflection she sees Tanner and Marge scribbling down notes.

Halim presses his foot on the accelerator. As the back wheels spin they spray wet mud over the two fluorescent shapes, making them fling their arms up and cry out. He releases the handbrake and, as a parting gift, reaches a hand out the window and gives them the middle finger as they speed off.

'I am so proud of you right now!' Rowena laughs so much she gets tears in her eyes.

It starts to rain almost the second the truck's tyres cross the Laithness county border. Rowena teases a thread of chewing gum from her mouth and winds it around her forefinger as she gazes out at the steep hills rising either side of them – a muddle of myrtle green and sedge yellow. A mountain stands proud in the distance, crying thin white streams.

'I'd always thought the north must be the most beautiful part of the Kingdom,' she says. 'I wasn't wrong.'

Halim grunts an affirmative.

Rowena presses her shins against her backpack and sighs. Look how far we've come, Pa, she thinks, I've brought you back to your home county. Not that you talked about it much, Tessa did most of that for you. Rowena knows all about her mother's fondness for running across the heath, or riding bareback as a child with her feet dangling 'miles from the ground'; getting the wooden spoon for it, but doing it again the following week.

Halim brings the truck to a standstill as a drover in a wax jacket and wide-brimmed hat ushers a herd of shaggy-furred cattle across the road, their thick bodies moving like a muddy river.

'You must be relieved this is almost over,' Halim says, his eyes fixed on the road.

Rowena counts the squeak of the wipers. 'I just hope my gran can fix me.'

'You don't need *fixing*, Rowena, you're not a thing, you're not broken. Perhaps all you need is family around you, someone to talk to? That's healing in itself.'

'Sure.' She lowers the window and leans out to let the droplets prick her face. She wills the rain to strip the doubt from her skin so that her gran won't sense it.

'You're getting the seat wet,' Halim says.

*

178

The rain clouds have emptied and turned sepia as they reach the lane that winds all the way up to Culcrith Farm.

'When was my gran expecting us?' Rowena asks, checking the clock on the dashboard.

'I didn't specify when I texted her as I knew we might be held up at border crossings. Hopefully we're in time for dinner though, I'm starving.'

'*Starvin', starvin' – Cator Gate, Cator Gate – dead 'oss, dead 'oss,*' Rowena mutters.

Halim raises an eyebrow. 'What was that?'

She shakes herself. 'Some old rhyme about a family of hogs roaming the moor for food.'

'Well, I could eat a horse right now.'

'Don't say that in front of my gran, Culcrith used to be a stud farm.'

'Look at that,' Halim points to a blackened tree in the middle of the field, lacerated by a lightning strike. 'It looks like a flayed man.'

Rowena shoves another stick of gum in her mouth, keeps her thumb pressed against the rabbit's paw in her pocket and focuses on a crack in the clouds that's letting the light through.

It's the light that's a sign, she tells herself, it's the light that's a sign.

29

A SMALL CAIRN, GREEN WITH MOSS, perches next to the road, above which sits a freshly painted sign that reads 'CULCRITH: NO TRESPASSING'. The truck rumbles over a cattle grid and passes through a metal gate onto a stony lane, its potholes packed with rubble. A rag-tag collection of buildings with flaking iron roofs lies beyond, some with no doors, their insides laid bare and at the mercy of the weather. After a few more bends the lane opens out into a wide yard with wooden stables down one side and a sturdy two-storey farmhouse opposite, dappled grey and oatmeal from the local stone, with a chimney at each end of a slate-tiled roof.

'What happened to the horses?' Halim asks, as he parks up next to a dented, rust-pocked ATV.

'My mother never really spoke of it, just said that business went bad and they had to change things up. I think that was around the time she left Culcrith.' Rowena keeps chewing her gum, hoping it will stop her stomach from roiling.

'How long do you think this healing will take?'

Rowena notices that Halim emphasises the word 'healing', as only a sceptic would. She shrugs, watches the pine trees flinch from the wind. 'Depends how strong my gran's nerve is, I suppose, or how deep my curse goes.'

'I've managed to book a couple of extra deliveries in Laithness from tomorrow,' Halim says, hesitation in his voice. 'I could – maybe – swing by in a couple of days and see how you're doing … Only if you want?'

'I'd like that,' she smiles.

Halim reaches over and puts his hand on hers. She twists her palm and curls her fingers through his. With the engine off they sit there for a minute, listening to the ticking as it cools. A countdown to goodbye.

'So this is it,' Rowena sighs. 'Maybe once I'm healed we could go for a drive for old times' sake, head further north and explore a little?'

Halim shifts in his seat as he searches for a reply.

Forget it, Rowena thinks, I'm not begging you. She unhooks her fingers and flings open the door. 'Let's get this over with then.'

The wind lifts her hair as she turns to face the farmhouse. In the door, stood beneath an upturned horseshoe, is a short woman in her fifties, draped in a colourful crocheted blanket.

She beckons them over. 'Dunna be blate,' she tuts, in a thick Highland accent, 'the longer I stand here the colder my house gets.'

Rowena recognises Morag Murray from the photo her mother has on her dressing table in a delicate filigree frame. Nothing about this woman looks delicate though. She was probably very pretty once, Rowena thinks, noting Morag's high cheekbones and sparkling blue eyes as she crosses the yard.

Morag reaches over to grasp her granddaughter's shoulders but pulls up short, cups her hand under Rowena's face and holds it there.

Rowena frowns, then realises she means for her to spit out the chewing gum. Blushing, she opens her mouth and lets the mangled lump fall into her gran's palm.

Morag tosses the gum into the ivy. 'Now, let me get a good look at my beautiful wee granddaughter in the flesh!' She takes Rowena's chin and urges her head this way and that, her eyes narrowed and searching. She nods, mutters something about 'good stock', and pulls Rowena into a tight hug. Morag's body is bony but strong, hardened by years of labour and infused with the smell of peat and woodsmoke. Rowena hesitates, then bends her arm across Morag's back and gazes down at the Norwegian slipper-socks on her gran's feet.

'I've waited so long to meet you, but I knew I would one day!' Morag waggles a finger at her. 'I knew you'd come to us.' She moves

Rowena into the house and then turns her attention to Halim. 'And you must be young Halim, the one my daughter trusted with her only child?'

'Pleased to meet you, Mrs Murray,' he nods. His hand twitches as if he were about to hold it out, but Morag spins to the side.

'Brush your boots and come on in,' she says.

He bows his head to get under the low frame of the porch.

Morag waves her hand at the yard. 'By dint of sickle, horseshoe and hollow flint,' she whispers before closing the door.

The house is a knot of wood and stone, its ceiling lined with thick beams and its floor a mosaic of flagstones – everything fixed tight and in its place. Herb bouquets hang from the pan rack in the kitchen and Rowena notices a cluster of cinnamon sticks dangling above the window, a ward against bad spirits.

Morag directs them to the dining room opposite, where a few red logs lie brooding in a fireplace. 'Take a seat and put your bag down,' she says, indicating the water-stained table and mismatched chairs. 'You too, Halim, supper'll be ready soon and you'll be staying for that.'

She reminds Rowena of Tessa – the way she directs people but makes it seem as though it's the habitual order of things, and to go against it would be to defy nature itself.

The second Rowena's backpack hits the flagstones Morag swipes it up and starts rifling around. 'This is heavy!' she huffs. 'What on earth have you got in here, a dead body?' Her fingers find the plastic urn and draw it out. 'Oh.'

'Please don't touch that.'

'Why did you bring him here?'

Rowena frowns. 'I brought Pa home. I thought I might release his ashes somewhere in Culcrith.'

The look Morag gives Rowena stops the air in her throat for a second.

'This is not your father's home,' she says. 'It never was and never shall be.'

'But the Muir family were from nearby, weren't they, before they moved away?'

'You'll not be spreading his ashes anywhere near Culcrith: you promise me that or you leave right now.'

Rowena's taken aback by the sharpness of Morag's words, but has no choice – she must be healed. She nods.

'Say it.'

'I promise.'

'Sorry, but I'll not have him in my house.' Morag takes the urn away.

Rowena digs her nails deep into the grain of her chair as she resists the urge to leap up. When she hears the front door open and close she catches Halim's eye and a flicker of pity crosses his face.

Morag returns and glances between the two of them. She softens and rests a hand on Rowena's shoulder. 'Forgive me; I'm not used to visitors in these remote parts so I'm very particular about the company I keep and who I let into my home.' Morag continues rummaging around the backpack: she pulls out the hotel biscuits, Rowena's Tarot cards and hunting knife and shoves them into the deep pocket of her apron, then she lifts out a bottle of wine and clunks it in front of Halim. 'You'll take that back with you, young man, she'll not be needing it here on her strict diet.' Seemingly satisfied with the rest of the bag's contents, she closes it and hands it back to Rowena. 'Now then, I'll get us some tea and check the oven. Rowena love, will you come and help me?'

Rowena bites her lip and follows her gran into the kitchen. 'What did Pa do to make you hate him?' she asks.

Morag ignores the question and bustles about the space, making Rowena step around her like two boxers in the ring. 'Fetch that tray there from the sink and pop these cups on it,' she says. 'Now I don't expect a pretty lass like you to be a virgin, but I do need to know if you've any conditions, afflictions, rashes, infections or the like.'

Rowena almost drops the little milk jug in her hand.

Morag must have seen the look on her face and laughs. 'We're family, you can tell me anything – I won't judge, I've seen and heard it all before, trust me. Your cleansing's quite specific though, so I must know what I'm working with.'

Rowena takes a breath. 'I'm fine, healthy I guess.'

'And you're not with child?'

'No!' Rowena remembers her vision – the shock of her round belly and how it had felt like a burden, a trap.

'Good. Now take that through and I'll follow with the tea.'

'She seems nice,' Halim says, drumming his fingers on the table as Rowena enters the dining room and clatters the tray down.

'You heard all that, didn't you?'

He nods.

'Kill me now,' Rowena mutters. Checking over her shoulder, she hurries to the front door, quietly clicks it open and finds the urn under the ivy by the doorstep. She rushes it back inside and stuffs it into her pack.

'All good?' Halim asks, his eyebrow raised.

'Sure,' she says with a twist of her mouth. 'Let the healing begin.' When she rubs the top of her arms to fend off a shiver Halim gets up, chucks a couple of logs onto the fire and stokes it to flame. Rowena's heart sinks a little, touched by his attentiveness and already mourning his departure.

When Morag returns and sees Halim by the fire she freezes, and Rowena notices her knuckles whiten around the teapot handle.

With a slight shake of her head Morag sets the teapot down and lays out the cups. 'Let it mull for a bit.' A chink of late-day sun casts the room in gold as she takes a seat at the head of the table and places one veiny hand on top of the other in front of her. 'Now, how was your journey – no trouble, I hope?'

30

HALIM MOPS UP THE LAST of his lamb stew with a wad of spongy sourdough. 'That was delicious, Morag, thank you very much.' It feels strange that they're on first-name terms already – he'd known Rowena's mother for a couple of years and she was always just 'Mrs Murray'.

Morag tilts her bowl to slurp the meat gravy. 'Such a well-spoken young man, with impeccable manners,' she smiles. 'Your parents must be very proud. They're in Singapore you say, but you were brought up in the Kingdom?'

It takes him a while to work through her accent and follow the quickness of her words. 'Yes. They're actually Egyptian but lived here for many years. When the economy crashed after the Split they followed the money. I was left in boarding school to continue my education here and join them after.'

'And yet here you still are,' she says, wrapping her lips around a sprig of rosemary before dropping it into the bowl.

He darts a look at Rowena. His heart jolts when she looks up. 'Yes. I wanted to earn my own money and live by my own rules, out on the road.'

Morag nods. 'But now ...'

He frowns. 'Now ... what?'

'Exactly. Now what? You seem restless, like you have stable fever and are about to kick the doors down and fly across the field, tearing up the turf. Do you know where you'd like to run to next, Halim?'

'Well, I … I am thinking about returning to my parents soon.'

He can feel Rowena's eyes on him.

'Following the money,' Morag nods. 'Well, I'm sure your folks would be glad to have you back under their wing, safe and sound.'

Halim swallows, disturbed by the way Morag seems to find and needle his weak spots. 'Well, I haven't really discussed it with them in detail – we don't really speak that often.'

'Oh? Do they not follow your exploits and keep track of where you are?'

He shakes his head.

Rowena scrapes her spoon across her bowl and clumsily changes the subject. 'Did you know that the ears and eyes of domesticated animals became smaller because they didn't need to hunt any more? They're basically lazier and needier than their wild cousins, it's like they went backwards in evolution or something.' She glances at Halim. 'I read that in one of my books.' She drops her spoon and turns to Morag. 'So when do we start the healing?'

Morag places her elbows on the table. 'Well, look at you pawing at the ground: impatient, just like your mother.'

'Wouldn't you be if you had a curse on your back?'

Morag doesn't rise to it, she watches her granddaughter as if trying to peel away the skin to see what's beneath.

Halim's chair becomes uncomfortable and creaks underneath him. 'It's a nice place you have here, Morag,' he ventures, 'how much land is it?'

She replies without taking her eyes off Rowena: 'We had to sell some off, so we only have thirty-six acres arable and twenty-eight pasture. Breaks my heart to see it reduced to this.'

A log falls in the grate. Halim clears his throat. 'A lot of farms up here were ravaged by Storm Jonah, weren't they? Makes sense to diversify in this difficult climate.'

'Much as I find this conversation thrilling, I'd like to go to bed, so I'll have to leave it on a cliffhanger,' Rowena says flatly.

'Of course, child. I'll show you where it is after—'

'Please don't call me child, I'm seventeen.'

'Of course you are,' Morag smiles, 'a woman grown.' She turns to Halim. 'Now I trust you'll be staying the night too? I've a spare room prepared as I thought you'd be arriving late.'

Halim's shoulders crunch as he rolls them back, stiff from the long drive. It would be nice to have a bed, he thinks. 'That's very kind, thank you. I actually have a local job tomorrow so I'll be out of your way at first light.'

'Oh, it's no bother,' Morag says. 'You and I will have a dram by the fire and a nice chat. And don't worry – I haven't forgotten your payment, I'll fetch the envelope for you now.'

He doesn't want to stay up and chat but he can't bear to be rude, so he smiles and nods.

'Rowena dear, will you help me clear the plates?'

Halim can tell Rowena's pissed off by the way she bangs around, but wonders if her mood was sparked by Morag or by what he'd said about returning to his parents.

Later that night, as Halim's yawning and climbing into bed, there's a whisper under the door and a creaking of footsteps down the landing. A map is lying on the floorboards. Rowena's map. He unfolds it and sees that she's drawn a circle around the word 'Wilderness', the rugged expanse in the Highlands that she's mentioned so often. His gut twists as he reads the words she's written: *Change your mind?*

He badly wants to follow Rowena down the passage, knock on her door and say a proper goodbye away from Morag's watchful eyes. He imagines holding her, peeling her clothes from her skin and exploring every inch of flesh with his fingers and lips ...

No, he thinks, I have to let her go, she needs this time to heal without me complicating things. Perhaps Morag's straight-talking will make Rowena see sense and realise that she's not cursed after all? Maybe then she'll be free, and things will be different for her? He sighs, slides back under the scratchy blankets and presses his spine against the headboard. His finger traces the contour lines of the map as he thinks about how Rowena is an outlier, and he's a mere follower. In the blank space surrounding her words he notices a small watery smudge, a droplet of rain perhaps?

Halim gets dressed as dawn bleeds into the room. He considers leaving the map, and then slips it into the pocket of his jeans before creeping down the stairs, past all the pencil portraits of horses. He imagines Rowena asleep upstairs – the way she places her hands under her cheek in a prayer position when she's lying on her side – and smiles. A creak from the landing turns his head, but he can't see anything up there in the gloom and his heart sinks back down again.

Outside the front door he's greeted by a mouse with its tiny eye caved in and its body split. A black cat, tail spiked high, darts past his legs into the house. Halim kicks the mouse into the roots of the ivy and closes the door. The sun's rays skim the roof of the stables and get caught in a net of mist, promising a fine day ahead, and as he crosses the yard he keeps a hopeful eye on the downstairs window, unsure if he saw movement there.

The truck feels empty without Rowena beside him. He sits there for a while, scrolling through their time together like the flicker of a film negative – circling the best bits in his mind. He shakes himself and starts the engine and soon he's crunching along the winding lane that leads out of Culcrith as the day is pinking in.

When he rounds a corner he slams on the brakes: a stag is lying on its side, blocking the lane. He sighs, checks the time and unclips his seat belt.

As he approaches the carcass he realises that there's no impact damage. Bending closer he spots a small, round puncture wound between the beast's ribs, surrounded by petals of dried blood. He looks up as shadows shift beside him.

Two men emerge from the trees, striding forward, and before Halim can even utter a word, the first – a burly older man with a thick grey-and-ginger beard – knocks him to the ground with a sharp blow to the side of his head. Birds burst out into the sky, clapping their wings in alarm. Stunned, Halim scrabbles to raise himself up – except now it's the younger man's turn and he jumps on him, pinning him with his weight. A signet ring cuts into the skin of Halim's lip as a salty-tasting hand smothers his mouth. Halim bites the flesh of the palm and it withdraws for only a second before crashing down on his face again, mashing his cheek into the jagged stones of the lane with a gut-wrenching thud.

'Check his pockets, then we'll try his truck,' the older one says as he kicks Halim in the ribs.

Something gives. Intense pain spikes through Halim's body,

making it impossible to curl up and protect himself. His lungs pull at the air in short bursts as the nerves of his wracked body fire useless warnings all over the place.

Rowena's map flutters free as his pockets are emptied and soon the men find what they were looking for – the envelope of cash that Morag gave Halim last night. 'Got it,' the young man says. 'Fuck you and your rich parents. Spoiled brat.' He spits into Halim's face and the sticky saliva makes its way across the bridge of his nose and into his eye.

'Stop playing with him and finish it, son,' the older man growls.

Halim manages to wrench an arm free and tear at the man's shirt, trying to unbalance him, but another kick from the older one sends an explosive grunt from Halim's lips.

'Ugh, fuck!' The young man jerks back. 'He spat blood on me!'

The pine trees tilt as Halim's torso is dragged up and his head lolls in mid-air. Then the ground comes rushing towards his skull.

It might have happened a few times – but by then everything has turned black.

31

17 May

———

AS SHE'S CROSSING THE LANDING Rowena sees a door ajar up ahead and a finger of buttery early-morning sun beckons her in. She pushes it open to reveal a bedroom with dusty floorboards, shelves bare as bones picked clean and a little alcoved window on one side. Her breath skitters as she recognises the worn dapple-grey rocking horse in the corner and spots a rectangle of unbleached wood where a bed once stood. She's seen all this before, in a vision – and realises with a shiver that this was Tessa's room and it must have been a glimpse of her mother's past, from when she had Rowena in her belly ... It's just as sparse and unloved as in her vision, and a strange sadness floods her as she pulls the door to again.

Reeling, she hesitates at the top of the stairs as two male voices drift up from the dining room, and is disappointed that neither is Halim's.

'There you are,' Morag says as she emerges from the kitchen holding a basket of bread and oatcakes. 'Did you sleep well? I see you found the slippers I left out.'

Rowena glances down at her toes, clad in slipper-socks with black pine trees knitted into them. 'Yes, thank you.'

When she enters the dining room the two men sat at the table look up: a stocky older man with a bushy red-grey beard and a younger one, perhaps her mother's age, his flannel shirt torn at the pocket. There's purpose behind their looks, as if they're appraising Rowena, and it makes the hairs on the back of her neck prickle.

'This is Tessa's girl,' Morag announces. 'Rowena, this is Bernie Kerr and his oldest boy Gus. Without Bernie and his three sons Culcrith would be a ruin – the Kerrs have truly been a blessing since my husband passed five years ago, I'm not sure what I'd have done without them.' She rests a hand on Bernie's thick arm as she leans over to place the bread basket on the table.

The men nod at Rowena as she hovers in the doorway.

'Well, Morag,' Bernie says in a voice crackled by age and alcohol, 'we'll leave you both to your breakfast, I'm sure you've a lot to catch up on.'

'Oh, I was going to boil some eggs for you both,' she tuts.

Bernie shakes his head. 'We have to seed the clover now the oats have taken, and we've had some late lambs that are causing us bother.'

'Aye, well, next time then,' Morag smiles. 'I'll make sure to have some beef squares for you.'

The two men nod at Rowena as they leave, and she's glad to see the back of them.

'You'll be on a strict diet now,' Morag smiles, her skin smoothing out over her cheekbones, 'so don't touch anything on the table until I return with your special tea.'

Rowena goes over to the window. Halim's truck is gone – he must have left very early, no written message, no proper goodbye. What did I expect? she scolds herself. I was only a contract. He was just slumming it with a country girl for a while, that's all. Rowena pinches the tops of her arms to distract herself from the feeling of betrayal that's rising like acid in her gullet.

'You're looking wan, child, are you feeling ill?' Morag asks as she returns with a teapot and strainer.

Rowena doesn't bother correcting her this time and accepts that she'll always be a child in Morag's eyes. 'I'm great,' she smiles, clenching her fists. 'Actually, could I get my Tarot cards back?'

'No. You'll have no distractions while you're in my care, and that includes that handsome young driver of yours, so I'll be taking your phone today too.'

Rowena's cheeks flush at the mention of Halim.

'Did you text your mother to tell her you arrived safely?'

'Yes.'

'Good, then we must focus your mind for the next five weeks, we have a lot to do.'

Rowena's eyes widen. 'Five weeks? Is that how long the healing ritual takes? It's my eighteenth birthday in just over a week's time, and my curse will be fixed by midsummer – it'll be too late by then!'

The teacup in Morag's hand clatters onto the saucer and spills. 'Damn you, silly old hands!' She dabs the tea with a wad of tissues produced from her sleeve. 'What did Tessa tell you about the ritual?'

'Nothing at all – just that you're to heal me and rid me of my curse, so that I can't hurt anyone else. And so that Death doesn't come for me next.'

Morag seems to think on it as she sits back in her chair and narrows her eyes to flinty-blue slits.

Panic starts to rise as Rowena wonders if her gran can actually do it. 'You can heal me, can't you?'

Morag tilts her head the way people do when they pity something. 'Of course I can, I'm the best healer from Greatmede to Upper Fremble, but this thing's had seventeen years to take root so digging it out will take time, and I can only do it if you open yourself up to the process wholeheartedly and do everything I say. Without question. And I mean everything, do you understand?'

Rowena chews her cheek. I can do this, she thinks, I *have* to do this. Five weeks of a special diet, no phone. Whatever. She nods.

'Good.' Morag pours the tea, puffing a steam of fennel and something woody into Rowena's face. She places three round oatcakes on Rowena's plate and points to the other little china dishes. 'You'll find sheep's cheese and my home-made blaeberry jelly a pleasant combination.'

'What about those eggs and beef squares you mentioned?'

Morag grabs a chunk of bread from the basket and starts slapping butter onto it. 'From now on, you'll only be eating the food Culcrith offers up – our sheep, our eggs and oats, local berries and the like. That tea you have there is full of nutrients from our precious soil. It's my own special recipe.'

Rowena sniffs at the dirt-brown liquid in her cup, puckered with sediment. She takes a sip and pulls a face.

Morag laughs, a smoky, pleasant sort of sound. 'You'll soon get used to the taste. It's all part of your cleansing.'

They eat in silence for a while.

Rowena tries to clear her head by counting the white-painted bricks in the wall and reading the spines of the books jumbled up on the shelves – most of them about horses or herb lore, others too worn to read. On the highest shelf, next to the window, she notices a jar stuffed with nails and broken glass and for some reason her thoughts drift to that woodworking book Halim always used to have his nose in. She shakes herself and focuses instead on a small, faded picture of a little girl – Tessa, smiling at the camera from atop a white horse. 'Why did my mother leave Culcrith?' she asks. 'She never actually told me, and it sounded like she really loved this place.'

Morag stares up at a moth circling the fabric lampshade as she chews. She gets up slowly, then in the blink of an eye her hands have snapped together, flattening the moth in her palms. 'Your mother made a bad choice that threatened our farm and brought ill luck on the Murray name,' she says. 'So she did the only thing she could – the noble thing – and left here at fifteen taking her full belly and her shame with her.'

Rowena almost chokes as a piece of dry oatcake grinds its way down her throat. 'What was the bad choice? Having me?'

'The bad choice was choosing to lay with your father, the son of the local Laird.'

'He was a Lord's son?' Rowena gapes.

'Aye. I expect your mother thought he'd put her up in a fine house down south.' Morag shakes her head, her white ponytail licking her shoulders. 'But Laird Muir cut him off and instead she got a crumbling bungalow in the arse-crack of nowhere, on somebody else's land.'

'Why was Pa cut off?'

'The Muir family were never kind to us Murrays. They envied our success and reputation with the horses, but they also looked down on us and our simple "un-Christian" beliefs; thought us no better than the muck on their boots. Tessa and your father were never a match. What happened brought anger and shame on both families, it was wrong. Even the land told us so.'

'What do you mean?'

Morag licks her fingers and starts picking up crumbs from her plate. 'As soon as Tessa and her foolish girlie head got turned and your father ploughed where he shouldn't, that's when the Strangles came and we had to start putting our animals down. Word soon spread across the whole county, and no one wanted hide nor hair of our beautiful fillies or colts. We couldn't afford to keep them so we buried them all in the top field, hoping they'd nourish our new crops and give something back to the land that had fed them. But that was also the year the drought took most everything we planted. And as we sold parcels of land it felt as though we were carving off pieces of me. It tore my heart to see what became of Culcrith.'

'So you blame Tessa for what happened here? Are we both cursed? Did I inherit it?'

Morag reaches out and places her hand on top of Rowena's. 'I'm not looking to point the finger, child, I'm only telling you what happened. Whether it was a wicked word from the Muirs or the twisted threads of fate, fact is Culcrith has struggled ever since. It's not the same place your ma knew as a bairn.' Morag's bottom lip trembles. She rubs a hand across it. 'Don't worry yourself: what's been has been. It's not healthy to dwell, so let's focus on the future, eh?' She squeezes Rowena's hand, a bit too firmly, her nails pressing in. 'Tessa's letter brought you to me and now it's a bright new chapter!'

'Why didn't my parents ever tell me any of this?'

'Because shame and pride are sins not easily admitted, and you – being a headstrong filly yourself – might not have learned from their mistakes.'

Rowena draws her hand away and places it in her lap. 'It's not a mistake to fall in love and have a child.'

Morag raises an eyebrow. 'You think they were in love, do you?'

'Yeah,' Rowena frowns. 'They both gave up their families and Pa gave up his title and wealth so they could run away together. It's kind of romantic if you think about it ...' Realisation washes over Rowena. 'Or did you kick Tessa out? Is that why you haven't seen or spoken to her all these years?'

'Your ma made a sacrifice in keeping both you and him, so I don't doubt that she loved that man once.'

'He has a name, you know.' Rowena gets up, knocking the table and rattling the dishes.

'Wait! Your phone.' Morag holds out her palm.

Rowena scowls, fishes out her old mobile and checks it in vain one last time before switching it off and handing it to Morag. 'I'm going for a walk.'

'That's a good idea, get some of our fresh Culcrith air in those stale lungs of yours. Don't go far, mind, and stay out of the stables, I don't want you tramping muck in there. I'll run you a nice herbal bath when you get back.'

It's a fine morning as Rowena crosses the courtyard and heads for the regiment of pines that lines the lane. She pauses atop a soft mattress of needles to draw a breath. Her fingers itch for her tobacco tin. Pinching the bridge of her nose, she closes her eyes, scrunching them tight enough to see constellations behind her lids. Tessa was banished because of me, she thinks – is it any wonder she resented having me around and kept me at a distance all these years? It doesn't matter any more: Rowena knows it's too late to build bridges because she doesn't plan on returning to Pickbury, and has promised to take her pa into the Wilderness once this is all over. Halim sneaks unbidden into her thoughts again – how, like her pa, he turned his back on his wealth and family. Only, Halim's resolve clearly wasn't as strong, since he told Morag he was slinking back to them. So much for morals, she sniffs.

Rowena follows the curve of the lane until something white catches her eye in a scrubby patch of heather. She goes over, picks up her map and turns it in her hands, searching every inch for a scribble, a reply, anything. Halim didn't mark it at all – he simply tossed it away like a piece of trash. Fingers trembling with rage, she folds the map, slips it into the pocket of her cardigan and spits on the ground. Something hardens and grinds inside her. 'Fuck you, Halim. Piss off back to your parents and die there for all I care.' She hopes the breeze will carry her words to him, wherever he is.

Feeling bruised, Rowena runs through the trees, veers off up the slope and stumbles into a field of green oats, their stalks thinly spread, some limp and broken. She runs hard and fast along the furrows until her legs wobble and lungs burn and sweat slides over her lip. She pushes on, up into the next field – empty but for a few black-faced sheep with their heads bowed to the grass. The trees that fringe the field look gnarled and ragged, their leaves an unnatural brown, their branches stuck out like pleading fingers. This must be the 'top field' that Morag mentioned, she thinks, looking back down over the scattering of farm buildings and the lane that snakes out of Culcrith like a chalky river.

The wind lifts the sweat from her cheeks and cools her. She lies down, between the dainty white bairnswort and nuggets of sheep shit, and presses her skull into the soil. Staring up at the featureless blue, she tries to clear her head and let Halim leech out of her body: take him, she thinks, *purge* him.

After a while she feels a slight tremble in her spine and shifts her weight. The trembling becomes more pronounced, an irritation. Soon she's sure she can hear a soft thudding of hooves. Rowena holds her breath and presses her ear to the grass. There's definitely a low drumming. Sitting bolt upright, she looks around and sees nothing but the shimmer of spiderwebs between the blades and fronds yet to be clipped by sheep's teeth. Digging her fingers into the dirt, she holds them there, can feel the undeniable vibration of a herd galloping closer, straining at the earth. The moment she hears snorts and whickers on the breeze she scrambles up and urges her tired legs on again, back across the empty field. As she hurries down the slope the drumming follows, getting louder, urging her on, building to a thunder roll of hooves: the restless dead know she's there. The culled ones whose only mistake, like hers, was being born.

32

────

THERE'S A LOUD, INSISTENT THUDDING, a rolling rumble like hooves. Halim wonders if it's in his head, if it's the blood pulsing behind his ears trying to push itself out of his skin – plenty already has. He's lying on his side, his cheek pressed into something wet and cold. It's good that I can feel the cold, he thinks, it means I'm not dead. He swallows a clot, feels around with his tongue and finds the jagged tip of a tooth where a chunk must be missing. When he tries to lift his head towards what feels like 'up' his skull can't take the pressure; he whimpers, turns back and attempts to keep his swollen lips above water. That's what he's lying in: cold, stinking water. Ditch water. I must be alive, he thinks, otherwise I wouldn't be feeling this shit – like my body is broken and there are parts of me on the outside that should be on the inside.

One of his eyes is partly submerged and gummed shut so he prises the other one open ... sees a murk of green, a haze of midges around his face. What leaves he can see, dangling from overhanging branches, look curled and brown. He wonders how long he's been lying there, if the season has turned. His bladder loosens, warmth creeps across his thighs and he tries to sob, but his ribs jab and scold him. I'm so fucked up I can't even cry, he thinks. He tells himself there's plenty of time for self-pity, and that if he survives this he can survive anything. That soft city boy dies right here in this ditch. You will emerge from this a man, he thinks. If you emerge at all.

More time passes. Halim can sense that parts of his body have already seized up and become weighty lumps of flesh – food for the bugs and worms that must be crawling all over him by now. He flexes his fingers and toes, tries to push himself up on one arm only to splash back down with a yelp of pain. All my efforts, all these years of work and what do I have to show for it? he wonders.

A cool breeze smooths his lank hair as lofty nettles and white-bearded grasses nod their encouragement. He tries to raise himself again and crumples, sinking further into his silty bed. His thoughts turn to Rowena and he conjures that last night they were sat together at Morag's table, the ephemeral magic of firelight dancing through her hair – first gold, then red, then gold again. Then he remembers that night under the barrow mound, and the way the moonlight turned her naked body to porcelain under his touch. Perhaps she was right about her curse after all? Perhaps she really did care for me and that's what did this? If I ever make it out of here, he grimaces, I'll try not to doubt her.

His empty stomach groans. The air becomes heavy again. A soft border closes in around his vision and he knows he's on the brink of passing out. Strange how he hasn't once thought about his parents until now ...

He's awoken by a jolt and a sucking sound as his head, neck and shoulders are lifted upwards. He moans, annoyed at being torn from a deep slumber. Hands appear under his armpits – their grip hard enough to draw bruises – and he hears a grunting, a huffing of breath. His body becomes light and he wonders if, when he opens his eyes, he'll be looking down at himself, if this is it ... No – searing pain shoots through his ribs again as he's dragged over the lip of the ditch and laid on the grass, a hand cradling his head to lower it last.

Halim coughs – regrets it – and coughs again. His good eye looks up at a dark-blue sky, a refreshing change from the brown and green he's been staring at for however many hours, maybe days, he can't tell. He puts fingers to his throbbing cheek and finds it bloated and wet like spoiled fruit. A shadow crosses his face and he reaches up to stop it coming any nearer.

'Easy now,' a woman's voice says. 'You're all fankled and beat up so you need to stay still while I make you a frame, okay?'

Halim lowers his hand.

A narrow sweat-beaded face topped by curly silver hair appears above. 'Those mares and colts had almost claimed you and carried you under,' the woman says as she dribbles water from a leather flask into Halim's parched mouth. 'You're lucky I was up here foraging – no one usually sets foot in this haunted place, let alone on Murray land.'

Halim hears the cracking of branches as the stranger whistles through her teeth, tutting and muttering as she makes a crude stretcher.

'Thank you,' Halim rasps.

The woman leans over and shakes her head. 'Don't thank me yet, you've a very long way to go.'

33

21 May

———

'IT'S BEEN FOUR DAYS NOW, when will you start the healing?' Rowena asks, using the spoon to cleave a line through the remnants of her salted porridge sprinkled with pine pollen.

'It's already begun,' Morag tuts. 'This is cleansing, Rowena, you must be purged of all the taint and poison you put into yourself over the past few weeks. It takes time for your body to come right and be ready to receive.'

'But why haven't you asked me anything about my curse? I see It sometimes – It appears to me, stalks me like a shadow.'

'You shouldn't be out looking for Death, child, that's practically inviting It in! You know, there's a reason why meat from stressed animals tastes sour – the mind can taint the flesh. So don't you let it.'

'Well, I hope you're not planning on eating me,' Rowena sighs as she pushes her bowl away. Morag's right, she thinks, I've spent so long freaking out and expecting bad things to happen, I might have willed them into existence.

'How about instead of moping around here stirring up the dust, you go for a walk today?' Morag says as she gathers up the breakfast things. 'You could pick me some flowers for drying and weaving. Take my quilted jacket though, that flimsy one of yours is no good for the winds we get on the ridges and gullies. You're not to leave the boundary of Culcrith, mind.'

'Sure,' Rowena mutters, even though Morag's already left the room.

In the narrow hallway she lifts the grey jacket off the hook and twists herself into it. It smells of Morag – a heady, spicy scent like the oil she must use on her skin. In the pocket her fingers skim something dry and wiry and she pulls out a concertinaed oat stem, tied and bound with horsehair.

As she crosses the yard, Rowena scolds herself for still looking over at the spot where Halim's truck was once parked. It's Wednesday now, she thinks, he said he'd come back to check on me on Monday ... She rolls her shoulders and quickens the pace, determined to find the very edges of Culcrith and explore all its nooks and folds.

Following the lane as it curves away from the farmhouse, Rowena pauses to admire the showy spears of foxgloves, the flower with a thousand names. They're bad luck to have indoors, so she heads towards a modest clump of primrose and cow parsley to pick those instead. She notices a splash of brown on the lane. It looks like old blood, she thinks, and wonders what poor animal was brought down there.

She ambles on, stopping to snip wild flowers and identify the chirrups of different birds – careful to enjoy their song without listening for messages. Although Rowena was expecting more from Morag, she has to admit that this does feel something like healing.

Far across the pastures pale lilac hills rise like the curves and angles of a reclining body. Somewhere out there is the Wilderness, she thinks, perhaps soon I'll see it for real. Perhaps Pa was preparing me for this all along – to be strong and skilled enough to strike out on my own, not having to rely on a Lord's land, a mother's charity, or a lover's whim.

Laughter and drumming carries on the breeze, rousing Rowena from her languid steps, and she realises that she's strayed across the burn that marks the edge of Culcrith. When she turns onto the road she sees a group of people marching towards her, some carrying hand drums, the children carrying willow wands. As they stop at a stone way-marker, an old woman steps forward and flicks water from a silver bowl that catches the sun.

One of the children breaks away from the group and runs up

to Rowena, carrying a little wicker basket. 'Hello!' he says, a gap-toothed grin on his face. 'Would you like a spiced bun? I helped make them.'

Rowena catches the eye of a woman who must be the child's mother, who smiles in encouragement.

'Thank you, I'd love one. That's really kind.' Rowena takes it from his sticky hand and bites into it, knowing that Morag would disapprove but unable to resist. 'Mmm! This is the best bun I've ever had.'

The boy beams at her.

'What's everyone doing here?' Rowena asks, her cheeks full. 'Is this some kind of festival?'

'We're beating the bounds. In the olden days they used to beat children with willow too, but that's not allowed any more.'

'Oh. Well, that's a relief,' Rowena says, sucking the cinnamon sugar from her fingers.

The boy swings the basket in his hands. 'Are you from here?'

'No, but I'm staying up at Culcrith.'

'Oh.' His face turns serious for a moment, as if he knows the place and what he knows isn't good. 'Okay, bye!' His feet clatter down the road as he runs back to the others.

The villagers wave at Rowena as they move on, back the way they came, singing something about wood-deep ways, sky-clad ways and the arrow path of a crow.

As Rowena raises her hand to wave back, a wasp zips into her face, making her jerk away and drop the bun. To her dismay it rolls down the road and disappears amongst the nettles.

Following a steep, old track that leads vaguely in the direction of Culcrith, Rowena passes the tree flayed by lightning, its limbs still imploring the sky for mercy. Further along, a late-flowering black-thorn draws her eye, a riot of white against the darker greens of its hedge fellows. Tucked away behind it is an abandoned barn, served by a wider dirt road that disappears down the slope, probably leading back to the farmhouse. She decides to follow it. As she passes the barn door – nothing but a patchwork of split planks – something glints from inside. A large windscreen. Rowena falters as she peers through and realises it's Halim's truck. Her body runs cold and her fingers prickle at the wrongness of it being there: she knows he'd never abandon it like this ... She yanks the door until it gives, the swollen wood scraping and juddering across the ground.

'What the hell?' It's definitely Halim's truck, raised up on jacks and stripped of its headlights and number plate. As she shuffles down the narrow gap between the truck and the side of the barn her foot scuffs something soft. She picks up Halim's woodworking book and sees that he's used the photo of his parents as a bookmark. She slips the book into the pocket of her gran's jacket. Through the passenger window the glovebox is gaping open, scraps of Halim's passport litter the cab and his beloved turquoise beads are scattered around the footwell like teardrops.

'Can I use your phone?' Rowena asks, panting, as she finds Morag on her knees in the herb garden behind the farmhouse.

'What for?'

'I just found Halim's truck stuffed into a barn at the edge of Culcrith, near the lightning tree, I think something bad must have happened to him.'

Morag sticks the trowel into the ground, stands up and clicks her neck. 'Are you sure it was his truck? We store a lot of scraps and parts in the old barns here, it could be one of Gus's many projects, he's always tinkering away at something.'

Rowena shakes her head. 'It was definitely Halim's truck. We need to call the police.'

'Steady, child. I'll send one of Bernie's boys to go and check on it. Now, why don't I run you a nice hot bath?'

'I don't want another stupid bath!' Rowena snaps. 'Can I have my mobile instead then? I'll make a call and give it right back, I promise.'

Morag rubs her forehead, smearing it with dirt. 'No. It would undo everything we've been working towards. This is a cleansing, Rowena, not a bloody spa break.'

'Something's wrong though, something must have happened to him.'

'Wheesht!' Morag shouts, spiking Rowena's nerves. 'That's *enough*, Rowena! If you're going to get into hysterics about every wee thing you see – or think you see – around Culcrith I'll have to confine you to the house.'

'What? No way!'

'You're not well, child, you need to settle your mind, it's too jumbled and suggestible – and to do that you're to stay indoors for the rest of your cleansing.' Morag's pale eyes narrow as Rowena opens her mouth to protest. 'Or do you not want to be healed? I'll not lie, Rowena, I've seen that shadow you mentioned, the one that haunts you, and it's all I can do to keep It in check each day, do you understand? If you're to break the back of this curse what you need is discipline, structure and purpose, and I doubt you've had much of that before now.'

Rowena gapes at Morag, unsure what's happening and how things got turned around so fast.

'Now get inside, I'll not tell you twice. I'll cast the stones tonight and see if I can find your driver.'

'He's not my driver, he's my friend.' Rowena drops the basket of wild flowers at Morag's feet and deliberately scuffs her boot through the protective line of salt beneath the back door on her way into the kitchen. Once inside, she touches the pocket of Morag's quilted jacket: the woodworking book lies nestled next to her body, proof that what she saw was real.

From her bedroom window Rowena sees Morag bent over the herb garden again, so she creeps down the landing, trying each unfamiliar door: the green-tiled bathroom; an airing cupboard full of crocheted blankets and bushels of dried lavender; another sparsely decorated guest room. She pauses here – considers the neatly folded woollen blanket and the dent in the pillow where Halim's head once lay.

The last door must be Morag's room – the phone has to be in there. Rowena's hand snags on the door handle, she rattles it back and forth but it's locked. 'Shit,' she mutters, wondering what to do next. She could sneak out now and head for Kinmuir, the village she and Halim passed on the way in, but Morag might follow, or send Bernie after her, and who knows what the consequences might be? She decides to wait it out until nightfall, sneak out to find a phone box or a pub, report what's happened and then be back before Morag even notices she's gone.

A grey shadow catches Rowena's eye and she flicks her head around. Something crosses the end of the passage and disappears into Tessa's old room. Heart in her throat, Rowena follows. Maybe I don't need Morag to protect me, she thinks, maybe I can face It on my own? She grits her teeth, raises her chin and nudges the door, inch by excruciating inch ...

She startles as a black cat appears in front of her. It stretches out its sleek body and drags its claws across the floorboards before sauntering past Rowena's legs. Rowena stands there, gripping the door frame, checking that the room is empty – that the rocking horse is still just a rocking horse and that there are no spiders or crows at the window to torment her. Then she looks down at the fresh claw marks – they cross the black horizontal gap of the floorboards, forming a perfect letter 'H'.

34

THE FLY DRONES ITS WAY from the open window to the lamp-shade and draws lazy circles beneath it. Rowena's eyes follow it to the picture frame above the chest of drawers where it sits for a while, rubbing its forelegs, before returning to its worship of the bulb. Rowena sighs and rolls candle wax between her fingers over and over, smoothing it into a poppet, its purpose not yet clear. She's been sitting on the bedroom floor for what feels like hours, her brain ticking over what might have happened to Halim, mould-ing horrific scenarios before smashing them to raise another, uglier creation – each one the product of her curse.

Her water bottle is filled and her map lies ready; she wants nothing more than to be cured, but can't let someone else she cares about get hurt, there's no way she could bear the guilt of a third life lost. Questions crowd her head: if her gran finds out about her sneaking out and abandons the healing then surely Rowena could find another healer? Though how would she pay them without this familial arrangement? And would they need to start the cleansing again, even though her birthday's now only five days away, and the solstice just a few weeks after?

Laughter outside the window pricks her ears, male voices with the same lilting accent as Morag. Rowena gets up and, from behind the curtain, watches two men approach the back of the farmhouse down a narrow, uneven path. She assumes they must be Bernie's other two sons, the younger ones.

'I was part way through stripping it,' the taller one says, 'but Dad says you're to help me speed things up, we need to rip the seats out and then start on the panels. The wheels should be worth something too.'

'Don't see why we couldn't 'a' kept the money he had on him.'

'That was Morag's money.'

'Aye, but we're doing the grunt work while she sits on her backside,' the smaller one stops the other in his tracks by tugging his arm. He lowers his voice. 'I know Dad's sweet on Morag and everything, but does that sound fair to you? Gus had to hide his body in a ditch in the top field – his *body*, Rob. This is no game!'

'All I can say is, that girl had better be worth ...'

Their next words become dull noise to Rowena as her legs move her from the window and her body becomes heavy and pulls her to the floor: her heart thumps against her ribs; her blood runs cold; her throat constricts. I've killed Halim, she thinks, I got too close and It knew, It found me out. She rakes her nails up and down her thighs until they start bleeding, oblivious to the sting. His body is up in the top field, they said – in the field where the dead ones roam.

Rowena can tell by the stiffness in her limbs and the darkening of the room that quite some time has passed. A sharp knock at the door jolts her alert. She flings herself onto the bed, throws the blanket over her and turns to face the wall.

'Rowena, are you coming down for supper?' Morag opens the door. 'Oh, you're having a nap?'

Rowena feigns a yawn and fights to keep her voice level. 'Yeah, I was so tired after my walk. Actually, I'm not hungry so I'll have extra for breakfast if that's okay.'

A floorboard creaks.

'Hmm, well. I suppose a wee fast might be good for you but not at this stage in your cleansing,' Morag says. 'No – you should eat of the land and build up your strength. You've not been eating much as it is.'

'Okay. I'll be down in a minute.'

'Take your time.'

The door clicks shut.

Rowena winces. Rage heats her face and burns inside her

temples. I need to get to the top field and find Halim, she tells herself. The crows won't have him, like they had Drew. And I can't let Bernie and Morag get away with this.

Hair falls into Rowena's face as she slurps her beetroot and onion soup.

'We should trim that mane of yours,' Morag says, tilting her green-stemmed wine glass. 'I'm good with the scissors, I used to cut your mother's hair.'

'I'm growing it,' Rowena replies, knowing full well that some curses are bound using strands of hair. She reaches for the salt but Morag bats her hand away.

'I'll need your help with some baking tomorrow,' she says. 'I assume your mother taught you that much at least.'

'How long will I be shut up here?' Rowena asks.

Morag laughs, her teeth and lips stained blood-red from the soup. 'You make it sound as though you're a prisoner! This is for your own benefit – I need to get you straight, iron out your kinks, and I can do that better when I've got my eyes on you. Besides, you've not seen the shadow since you've been here, have you?'

Rowena shrugs.

'That's because you're in a safe place under my roof, under my protection.'

Rowena dabs her mouth to hide her incredulous expression. 'I only ask 'cause I was thinking I could help out around the farm, make myself useful and earn my keep.'

Morag looks up from her bowl, intrigued.

Rowena holds her gaze and continues. 'I noticed you're doing up the old stables – are you thinking of breeding horses again? I'm good with horses. It's in the Murray blood, I guess. Maybe I could help you get Culcrith back to how it was?'

Morag's face softens. 'I'm sure you could, child. You might have arrived under the cloud of a curse, Rowena, but you being here is a blessing for me. For this place.'

Rowena picks up her spoon before Morag can grasp her hand. 'So, what are your plans for Culcrith? It must cost quite a bit to set up a stud farm, especially in these tough times?' she asks between slurps. What she really wants to know is if it costs a human life.

The candle flickers across Morag's eyes and glances off the night-black window. 'We have our ways,' she smiles. '"Mony a mickle maks a muckle," as my gran used to say. Everything will fall into place, you'll see.'

'It's great that you have Bernie Kerr and his boys to help, I expect they don't come cheap.' Rowena's stomach twists at having to mention them. Bile rises in her gullet, but she fixes her face and skims her spoon back and forth.

'Well, you might say we have an arrangement. I've a mind to marry Bernie, in fact, so that when I'm gone I can rest in peace knowing this place will be in good, honest hands.'

Rowena masks a snort. 'What about Tessa? Shouldn't Culcrith come to her, a Murray?'

Morag swallows her wine and raises an eyebrow. 'She employed you as her wee ambassador, did she? Well,' she sighs, 'after all these years, bad blood leaves a stain. Sad but true. Sending you, though, that's a start.'

'Speaking of bloodstains, I saw one on the road out of here; looked like an animal was brought down or something. Do you get many predators around here? I read that wolves were making a return in these parts.'

There's a knock at the front door before Morag can answer. She puts down her glass and gets up.

'I finished early so I thought I'd stop by, hope I'm not disturbing you.' It's Bernie's voice.

'Not at all,' Morag coos. 'We've just finished our supper.'

There's a scratching of boots on the mat, a rustle of clothing.

Rowena sprinkles salt all over some radishes and stuffs them into her mouth, then folds some buttered bread and stashes it in the pocket of her cardigan. 'I'm done so I'm gonna head up to bed,' she says as she passes them in the hall.

'Remember to use that sleep balm I gave you, it should help clear your head of those night terrors.' Morag gives Rowena a gentle squeeze on the shoulder, putting on a show. 'Goodnight, love.'

'Goodnight, Gran.'

Morag's door is still locked, so Rowena heads to her room to wait

209

until her gran's asleep. The crude poppet she'd made out of candle wax lies on the windowsill where she'd left it. She picks the little figure up, cups it in her palm and thinks for a moment. She winds meadowsweet around it, brings her lips close to the almost-face and whispers: 'With this death flower I bind you, Morag Murray. I bind your ill intent. May your lies burn on your tongue. May your desires be always out of reach, may the pursuit of them be gruelling, and may your final breath be filled with pain. As I wish it, so it shall be.'

Rowena shivers and sits there in silence for a while, the wax growing warm between her fingers, her mouth dry and hollow now that the words have been released like moths into the gloom. She reaches all the way under the chest of drawers and tucks the little figure against the skirting board.

A creak and a click make Rowena sit up: she must have dozed off. She wipes the dried spit from her mouth, goes to the door and presses her ear to the wood. Morag and Bernie speak in low voices as the door to Morag's bedroom closes. Rowena wrinkles her nose at the thought of them together.

She waits a long time before slipping on her coat and shouldering her backpack, but when she tries the handle she finds that her door's been locked. Forcing it would make too much noise, so she opens the window instead and looks down. The sliver of moon is obscured by clouds, making sharp edges appear dull and distances harder to judge. It's only one storey up and there's a small compost heap below; doable but not easy, especially since her boots are by the front door. Rowena pulls the slipper-socks over her own socks then rolls up the blanket, straps it to her backpack and drops it out of the window first. Climbing up on the chair, she leans out and twists her body so that she's feet first, then lowers herself slowly until she's straining to hang on by her fingertips. Her torn jeans snag on the brick as she lets go and slide-drops the final few feet into a rotten mulch of vegetable scraps and eggshells. She shakes herself down and curses the stink, but at least she's not hurt. Stumbling out of the mess, she steels herself for what she might see when she reaches the top field, then grabs her pack and runs into the night.

When Rowena makes it to the top field she realises that she doesn't know what to do if she actually finds Halim's body, and it becomes harder to make her legs move. It'll be too late to get help, she thinks, but I can't leave him here on his own – and if the dead come back like my pa, perhaps Halim will stay long enough for me to say sorry? She imagines his ghost standing there, rubbing the back of his neck, looking up at the sky to growl his own curses in Arabic. Cursing the day he ever crossed paths with Rowena Murray, no doubt.

The Kerr brothers mentioned a ditch, so she approaches the edge of the field as clouds pass over the moon, strobing the landscape silver and black. A barn owl swoops low and melts into the trees – a sign that a soul has been released. 'Clean birds by sevens, unclean birds by twos,' she says aloud, 'the dove in the heavens is the bird that I choose.' She closes her eyes and takes a deep, steadying breath. The wind scratches through the leaves, and when she opens her eyes the tufted cotton-grass seems to dance along with it, like little white flames in the darkness.

Rowena takes up a small branch and uses it to dredge the ditch water and comb the cow parsley, sick at the thought of it catching on something solid. As she makes her way around the perimeter, scraping, poking and peering, she tries not to think of the horses' bones that lie beneath her feet and how they had clamoured to be heard. 'Is he down there with you?' she whispers, standing still for a moment to listen. 'I'm here, Halim ...' There's a strange hum in the air, an electric charge that makes her skin feel too tight. Every stone she kicks, every lump of uneven ground sends a wicked jolt through her nerves. What at first looks like blood turns out to be water seeping up through the soil, and a limp, upturned hand becomes nothing more than a rock.

It's a while before she hears the first whicker, but she knew they would come. She squints through the darkness and squeezes her rabbit's foot so hard the claws prick her fingers like needles. 'Where are you, Halim?' she mutters. 'What did those bastards do to you?'

Something snorts by way of reply and a hot stink of mouldering hay skims Rowena's hair. She presses on, keenly aware of a lumbering presence behind her but not wanting to look in case the horse carries her off on its back, or drags her into the water, as recounted in so many cautionary tales.

She's certain this is the right field but, finding nothing in the ditches, she wonders if they've moved or buried the body: she's already thinking of him as 'a body', she realises with a shudder. Up ahead – in the only corner she's yet to search – two blue lights are hovering in mid-air like dying tapers. Her heart lurches, bracing her muscles and nerves for something unknown as she steps towards them. They flicker and disappear.

She hears a soft padding behind her and can picture hooves pressing into the cold, soft dirt and manes rippling with moonlight.

When she reaches the corner there's nothing in the water or weeds, but on the edge of the ditch she spots flattened grass and drag lines – as if something heavy has been pushed into it. Or pulled out of it. As she bends over the stagnant water a flicker of blue wobbles over her shoulder in the reflection. She spins around quick enough to see two bright-blue eyes atop a long, muscular neck before a sudden gust almost knocks her from her feet. Something made of nothing gallops through the hedge and disappears, leaving a jagged tear in the brambles. As Rowena peers through the gap she sees the flickering light head towards the glow of the village in the distance.

An impatient hoof stamps the ground next to her – but she doesn't fear them any more: her eyes are filled with blue now, and she climbs over the ditch and through the hole in the hedge, knowing that this is the way she must go.

The pawing gets louder, a soft whinny urges her on.

Something large presses close to Rowena's back as she strides out towards Kinmuir, other shapes move at her sides and a soft thudding fills the gaps between her heartbeats. I can feel them, she thinks, they're restless. They want to run.

So she runs.

35

22 May

_____

'HEY.'

Rowena stirs and shivers from under the blanket.

'Hey there, you okay?'

She looks up towards the voice. A wavy-haired man in a brown jumper stands over her, a cigarette pinched between his thumb and forefinger. She blinks, realises that she's huddled near the back door of a brick building but can't remember how she got there. A chalkboard screwed into the wall tells her this is the Stag's Head pub.

'Is this Kinmuir?' she asks.

'Aye.'

'Then yeah, I guess I'm okay.' Flashes of the tumbling valley come to mind: the juddering lights of the village as she trammelled the earth towards it, her face stinging with air, her ears filled with static and thunder and all the world a beautiful blur ... Her chest flutters with hope as she remembers that she didn't find a body in the top field.

'So – if you're okay you'd best be moving on,' the man says, putting the cigarette between his lips. 'Here.' He fishes out a £5 note and holds it towards her. 'Maybe get yourself a coffee or something.'

Rowena wrinkles her nose, is about to say that she's not homeless before realising the truth of it.

'No? Well, in that case,' he goes to put the note back in his pocket.

'Wait!' she sits up. 'I'll take it. Thank you. And a cigarette if you can spare one.'

The man smiles and hands her both.

Rowena pockets them, rolls up the blanket and attaches it to her backpack. She notices the man eyeing her mud-caked slipper-socks.

'You sure you're okay?' he asks.

'I'm looking for someone,' she says. 'A brown-skinned guy, thick dark hair, good-looking, Egyptian accent. I think he might be badly injured and needs help. Have you seen him?'

The man shakes his head. 'Tried phoning him?'

'I don't have a phone, or his number.'

'Well, if he's injured there's a healer in the village you could try. Otherwise the nearest hospital's in Banlochry, about a thirty-minute drive from here. Or if you want I could call the police?'

She bites her lip. If Halim's still alive Morag and Bernie might twist it and pin him with trespassing, stealing or worse – and Laithness is an Iron County. 'No, it's okay. Where does this healer live?'

'See that hill over there? Follow the road that runs below it, take a left at the chip shop and then go straight on past the houses and through the tunnel of trees. You'll come to a place called Thorny-croft, that's hers.'

'Thank you,' Rowena shoulders her pack.

The man points to the pub door. 'The lavs are through there if you want to get cleaned up.'

'I don't have time, thanks though.' She moves off, then turns back. 'Can I ask one last favour? Could you please not tell anyone that you saw me?'

The man raises an eyebrow, blows out a stream of smoke, and nods. 'Go well,' he says.

By the time Rowena reaches Thornycroft her legs are bone tired and her eyes are sore from straining into every garden, nook and thicket, looking for Halim. She squeaks open the rusted gate and heads towards the cottage, its green door scratched with witch marks and framed by scented roses. Something catches her eye and she reaches between the thorns to unhook a feather – light brown at the quill point and darker at the tip, with honeyed tiger-stripes spanning the vane.

Rowena jumps as the door opens to a tall woman with curly silver hair and delicate lines tattooed along the curve of her ear. Her grey fox-like eyes flick over everything – including the feather in Rowena's hand. 'Snipe,' she says. 'Quite a rare, secretive bird. You have a lot of questions, it seems.'

'Are you the healer?'

'I'm *a* healer. Cora Durris.' She holds out her hand, roughened by calluses and encircled at the wrist by brown leather cords.

'Rachel Michaels,' Rowena says, shaking it.

Something tweaks Cora's face, but she tugs it back into a smile. 'Do you want to try again?'

Rowena's hand turns clammy but Cora won't release it.

Somewhere across the valley a dog barks.

'Rowena Murray,' she mutters.

Cora lets go of her hand. 'Now that we're no longer strangers, come in and take off your, er, slippers.'

Stepping inside, Rowena notices that the layout is much the same as Morag's farmhouse: a hallway with a dining room to one side and a kitchen to the other, with stairs in the middle and another room tucked away at the back. Rowena is led towards the latter, creaking along salt-speckled floorboards into what must be Cora's study. One wall is papered in maps, some framed, some pinned with nails in each curling corner, another wall is stacked floor to ceiling with books, and a tower of papers is propped up in the corner by the patio doors, weighted down by an old copper jam pot.

'I'm looking for someone,' Rowena says, not wanting to waste any time. 'I think he might be badly hurt. Have you treated anyone recently? His name's Halim Hosny, he's twenty, Egyptian, messy dark hair, wears knitted jumpers, always looks a bit pissed off ...' Her words stumble over the lump in her throat.

Cora indicates a battered brown armchair facing the windows and patio door. 'Easy, lass, take a breath, have a seat and slow down.'

Rowena places her backpack next to her and sits, looking out at the garden. The lawn backs onto a paddock that rolls down towards a loch, dappled navy and apricot by the morning sky.

'Can I get you a drink, a cup of tea perhaps?'

'Just water, please.'

Rowena's stomach grumbles in delight when Cora returns with a glass of water and a plate of shortbread. She takes one. 'Halim wouldn't be hard to miss,' she says between mouthfuls. 'Not in these parts.'

'Tell me more about this young man,' Cora says, taking a seat at a desk scattered with scissors, twine and things dug up from the earth. She swivels the chair left to right as she speaks. 'What's he to you? Were you travelling together?'

'We came here all the way from Pickbury in Dunfordshire. He works for my mother on and off.' Rowena looks down at her lap. 'He's my friend.'

'And you're a Murray, as in the Murrays of Culcrith?'

'My gran lives there, yeah, but I'm not one of them. I only met her a few days ago. I was sent to her to be healed.'

'Were you now?' Cora places a finger over her lips. 'There's a surprise.'

'Why?'

'Morag Murray's not a healer as far as I know. Except if you count horses – she was a marvel with them, a follower of the Horseman's Word for sure.'

Rowena remembers Gabe and his strange ritual in the old abbey, wonders how much darker it would have been with Morag or Bernie leading it.

Cora rests her forearms on the desk and considers Rowena for a moment. 'I saw your Halim.'

Rowena bolts upright and presses a hand to her chest.

'I wanted to be sure you were a friend, and not one of the ones who attacked him. I found him in a ditch up at Culcrith when I was foraging under the hare's moon. He was in a terrible way. He refused the hospital so I brought him back here to patch him up as best I could, but he'd caught a nasty fever and was in and out for a few days.'

'Can I see him? Is he okay?'

'Well, he was alive when he left here, some time last night.'

'What? Where's he gone?'

Cora shakes her head. 'No idea, sorry. Perhaps something compelled him to leave – maybe he's gone looking for you?'

'Well, did he say anything?'

'Aye, snippets, while he was rambling through the fever and fussing with that chain around his neck. Sounds like there were two men who attacked him and left him for dead.'

Rowena grits her teeth. 'Bernie and his son Gus.'

'Bernard Kerr and his boys? Well, I can't say I'm surprised, they're not known for their light touch – that clan speaks the Beast's tongue.' Cora drums her fingers on the desk, working through things as her chair sways like a pendulum. 'It's good that you and Halim got away from Culcrith. It's a place of death, a land that's turned. It's not safe for you there.'

'Cora, can you help me find Halim? Can you cast stones or check your cards or something? I can pay you, not much, but I have a few quid left.'

Cora scrunches her face as if she's just bitten into a lemon. 'I'm not taking your money, I can see how much this means to you.' The chair squeaks to a stop underneath her. 'But there's a fire in that young man, and I don't just mean the fever. Who knows where it will take him – places I won't be able to see, that's for sure. He was delirious, halfway gone.'

'Well, I guess I'll just go out and look for him the old-fashioned way, if he's sick he can't have gone that far.' Rowena dusts shortbread crumbs from her lap onto the plate. 'Thank you for saving him.'

Cora shakes her head. 'Don't thank me for that, from what I've seen he's hanging on by a thread. The only one who can save Halim now is himself.'

'Well, I have to try. I can't leave him out there, alone. I won't. It's my fault he's … ' Rowena looks up and takes a breath.

'Do you think it's wise to go looking in broad daylight? Morag will have the Kerr boys searching for her granddaughter if I know her, and she doesn't like to be bested. You should keep well out of their way.'

'What else do you know about my gran?'

'I know that you wouldn't go to Culcrith to be healed, and I doubt Morag would volunteer another mouth to feed, not with their crop yields. She must have taken you in for some other reason.'

Rowena wipes her nose and studies Cora's face, sees no flicker of a lie. She picks up her backpack and turns to go.

'Your pa must have been a good man,' Cora says, her voice soft and level. 'I assume that's who you've got tucked away in your bag there.'

A shiver snakes up Rowena's spine. Her pack is tightly shut and hasn't left her side – how did she know?

'I'm a healer for a reason,' Cora smiles. 'Wouldn't have much of a reputation otherwise. I can heal *you* if you let me, Rowena, and help you answer the real questions that you have. Besides – if you insist on heading out there won't you be needing some shoes?'

36

Date unknown

———

HALIM CAN FEEL ROOTS WRITHING underfoot as the trees bend and speak to each other in torpid nods and creaks. '*Dead 'oss, dead 'oss,*' their leaves seem to slur. '*Dead 'osssssssssss.*' The gloaming's their time, a time when no human should bear witness to their secret language and Halim's aware that he's intruding – an outsider even here. He vaguely remembers a fox-like woman with silver hair, recalls quiet rooms, his feet carrying him down a hill, a road, in darkness, compelled to return to something, or someone; yet he doesn't remember how he got here, to this unnatural forest.

In the scant light, luminous eyes peer out at him – a platinum flicker here and there, pinpricks of stars as spiders cluster in the boughs. Somehow he knows to keep moving but the air is pressing on his tired body and he trips and falls face first into the damp moss. There's no sign of what felled him, no clod of earth nor root or branch to get hooked on. The spirits are playing tricks, he thinks, they don't want me here, but I don't know the way out and I have no map. He knows that the silver-haired woman won't come to save him. Not here. He's strayed too far.

Halim's throat is thistle dry so he gets up and pushes on through layers of shadow that peel back as he passes. Wild flowers, drained of their colour, huddle in clusters wherever there's a break in the canopy. He distantly recalls a nursery rhyme about bluebells – that if you hear one ring it means you've stumbled upon a fairy gathering and you'll pay with your life – but these ones have faded and crisped into withered fingers that tickle his ankles. He looks down and wonders what happened to his shoes. He knew a girl once, running shoeless up a slope, the wind whipping at her hair ... What was her name again?

He reaches up to wipe the sweat from his brow, jerks his hand back and gasps: growing through the creases of both palms – like weeds through cracked concrete – are two white flowers. He tries to pluck them, but their thick stems are hooked in deep and when he tugs at them they lift and pucker and tear at his skin. He grits his teeth and twists and pulls until they eventually come loose, their roots moist with blood. He drops the flowers and cups his torn hands, scanning the forest for something, anything that might soothe them. The pinpricks of eyes have drawn a jagged line away into the dark and, not knowing what else to do, he follows it – and stumbles into a clearing where the air is thinner and cooler. There's a pool in the hollow with a white candle burning next to it. A sacred well, perhaps? With a shudder of relief, Halim drops to his knees, making something pop in his side – he reaches down and finds a sharp snick of bone thrusting through his skin. He tries to push the rib back in, but his palms are too tender and he's thirsty so he leaves it and turns to the water. He plunges his hands into it, scoops and gulps it down, panting and slathering like a dog. It tastes like ditch water but he doesn't care. He splashes it over his clammy cheeks and forehead, dabs it behind his ears – and then notices the stag lying part-submerged at the opposite side of the pool, its flesh already bloated and decaying as one antler thrusts up towards the sky like a lightning-struck tree. Halim spits out the water and scrambles away – staring at the small, round hole in the stag's flank as it grows wider. It seems to spread like an invisible fire, eating through the fur until the stag's skin splits open to reveal the glistening white bones beneath.

Something snaps behind him, a loud rending of twig from branch that makes Halim's heart flare up. Pressing on his ruined side, he drags his body back into the darkness and feels his way. The leaves seem to shy from his touch, so he brushes against rough bark, though it hurts his palm.

I was in a cottage, he thinks, and I left to go somewhere, but that somewhere wasn't supposed to be here. So where am I? If only I had a map …

Eventually he comes to an ancient oak with a path forking around its bulbous trunk. Its brindled branches drip with colour-less ribbons, and with no breeze to stir them it's as if the great tree is weeping. The sight of it prises something open inside Halim, a deep-hidden place of regret and shame, and he stands there, shed-ding his own silent tears. One slips into his mouth and it tastes hot and metallic, but he can't stop crying even though it's lifeblood leaking from him.

Sure that this must be the end, Halim approaches the oak to rest against its trunk and finally be still, but as he nears it he notices bits of paper stuffed into the creases of its bark. Money. He plucks a note and unfurls it like a fortune cookie. There's a number there but he struggles to read it so he drops it and tweaks out another – a coral-pink one, adorned with a fine-line portrait of an old man wearing a crown. The lines smudge and swim in the chalky light. He drops this one too, pulls out another banknote, and another and another – watches them flutter to his feet like autumn leaves until he feels a shiver up his back; the uncanny skin prickle of someone standing close behind. The smell of shoe polish and that familiar cologne, the one his father always ordered from Paris, turns Halim's stomach.

He abandons the oak and takes the overgrown path forking to the left, moving as fast as he's able. He knows that Death has caught up with him, that It won't ever stop following and It can't be outrun. Up ahead, the path narrows until it seems to disappear into black. It's getting harder for Halim to pick up his feet now, his side is screaming and feels slick as he tries to hold his broken body together. What would happen if I simply stopped? he wonders. If I stopped, and turned and faced It? If I surrendered would I be at peace?

He slows, feels the constellation of eyes on him, senses the spirits crowding each other to see what he'll do – whether he'll fight or whether he'll die.

Halim makes his choice.

Yet a question remains, haunting him like a faint but familiar echo: *Change your mind?*

37

22 May

———

'HELLO?'

At the sound of her mother's voice, Rowena suddenly loses her own.

'Hello, who is this?'

'It's me.'

A pause. 'It's late, Rowena, is everything okay? Whose number is this? How are you getting on with your gran? I hope you're not giving her any trouble after all she's doing for you.'

Cora's words vibrate through Rowena's skull: *You wouldn't go to Culcrith to be healed.* She almost hangs up, but she has to know if Halim was a part of Tessa's plan, assuming that she has one. 'I've left Culcrith and I'm not going back,' she says.

'What? Why? It's still four weeks until the solstice, you should at least stay until then to give your gran a chance to break your curse. Where are you now?'

'I'm not telling you.' Rowena grips the plastic receiver and slips another coin into the slot.

'What the hell are you playing at? Your gran and I are trying to help you and this is how you repay us? After all I've done for you, all the money it took to get you to Culcrith! I'm living on scraps here, Rowena, and I'm *this* close to being evicted. Did I really raise such a selfish bloody fool?'

'When was the last time you spoke to Morag?' Rowena asks, not rising to her mother's vitriol.

'I don't know, must have been the day that you arrived there. Why?'

'She stole the money back from Halim and left him for dead. Culcrith isn't the place you remember and Morag isn't a healer.'

'Are you drunk?'

When Rowena doesn't answer, Tessa switches to her exasperated-teacher voice. 'This is the curse speaking – it's taken root and is corrupting your thoughts, confusing you. You need to get yourself back to Culcrith and finish the healing before it's too late, before the solstice fixes it.'

'Are you not listening to me? Morag's a murderer!'

'Did you see her murder anyone? Is there a body?' A pause. 'No – so stop this nonsense. I don't know how else to help you, Rowena. Surely you want to be fixed?'

'I'm not broken, I'm not a thing, I'm your daughter.'

'So act like it. Until you turn eighteen you answer to me, and you do what I tell you, that's the law.'

'Well, it's only about three days 'til my birthday.' Rowena switches the receiver to her other ear, a fire in her belly from challenging Tessa in a way she'd never have dared before. 'What I want to know is why now? Why, after all these years of pushing me away, of tolerating my presence, do you suddenly care so much about me?'

She can hear Tessa breathing, imagines the thin line her lips make when she's angry, the way the blood vessels in her eyes become magnified by her glasses.

'Because you're a Murray, you're my blood, and you're precious, Rowena. More than you know.'

Rowena's bitter laughter fills the phone box. She drops another coin in the slot and feels her heart sink with it. 'Now I *know* you're lying to me. Why did you really send me to Culcrith, Mother?'

'I don't have time for this ... Culcrith's your family home and—'

'That's not my home, and Morag's not my family. Pa was my family and he's gone now.'

Tessa sighs. 'Look, just go back to Culcrith and I'm sure your gran can explain everything. Stick it out until the solstice and then if

223

you're still not happy I'll arrange for you to come back to Pickbury. How does that sound?'

'What's so special about the solstice?'

'JUST DO AS YOU'RE TOLD FOR ONCE IN YOUR MISER-ABLE LIFE!' Tessa's yell makes Rowena jerk back from the phone. 'I've sacrificed *everything* for you, so now it's your fucking turn!'

Rowena's life unravels in the silence that follows, and as she winds up the threads she remembers the kick of the hare, the Tarot cards in her hotel room, Pappa Red's words about the lamb and the knife, her pa's warning in the mirror and Morag's cleansing – until the truth of it lies in her hands.

'I'm to be a midsummer sacrifice,' Rowena mutters. 'You sent me here to die.' She places a hand on the glass of the phone box to stop it folding in on her. 'A blood sacrifice,' she whispers, 'to your precious Culcrith. That's why Morag wants to purify me. That's why she took me in.' It feels as though icy fingers are crawling up her chest, slowing her lungs, reaching up into her throat to make fists.

It's Tessa who breathes first. 'Once you've tasted the earth and air of Culcrith,' she says, her voice low and steady, 'it's in your soul for ever – sewn into your skin and steeped in your blood. I never really left that place, and every second away from it a hole grew inside me. And it got wider, and deeper until it hollowed me out.' She pauses. 'I was tricked into motherhood, suffocated by it, and every time I looked at you I was reminded of what I'd left behind.'

Rowena stares at the silver phone cable, coiling like a snake down her body.

'You were never really my child, Rowena, you were his, and your pa trapped me in a life I didn't want when he convinced me to keep you. You were the reason I was banished from Culcrith, but you're also my way back home: I sent you as a gift, to fix what I'd done all those years ago, to heal Culcrith. To make Morag take me back.'

The concrete floor seems to shift beneath Rowena's feet. 'You waited 'til Pa died to get rid of me. You convinced me I was cursed, made me feel like his death was my fault!'

'I did what I had to. I can't stay here, I can't live like this any more – you can't even begin to understand what I've been through ...' Tessa's voice cracks.

'Don't you *dare* insult me with your tears!' Rowena growls, her own eyes slick with them, her nose streaming with snot. 'If you want to know what a real curse is, I'll show you – I'll curse Culcrith and every creature that sets foot on it for generations to come so that nothing can ever live in that vile place again, not even you. It's dead to you. As am I.' Rowena slams the receiver down so hard it cracks. The phone rattles through all the coins she fed it as she sinks, shaking, into the corner. Her foot scuffs a brightly coloured flyer advertising 'The Nest', a new local playgroup. She turns her head to the side, leans against the cold metal and glass, and pukes.

Cora has placed a candle for Halim in the window and tucked a mistletoe leaf inside her daughter's old running shoes. She hands them to a pale and wrung-out Rowena, along with a torch, some corned-beef sandwiches and a flask of ginger-and-lemon tea. 'Go well,' she says as Rowena steps out into her garden, 'and remember – you may not be the only one out there looking for someone, so keep your wits about you.'

Rowena's determined to search through the night for Halim if she has to. Part of her even welcomes the distraction from Tessa's chilling words that peck at her brain, tugging out emotions like worms – mostly fury, sometimes grief. She crosses the paddock at the back of Thornycroft and heads through the large wooden gate towards the loch. She'll try all the trailways and bridleways of Kinmuir, using the local map that Cora gave her. The waning moon does its best to sketch out her path and the nightingales keep good conversation as she pushes on through the damp grass, blind to all of it. She no longer flinches at the flickering of moths, at the grey shadows between needles of gorse, yet she's lived with the curse too long to dismiss it so easily, and is still convinced that it's her fault Halim might be dead.

As her foot scrapes against something papery she stops and flashes the torch; is relieved to find only an adder skin. She moves the beam up as something else scurries through the darkness towards her. Round eyes flash and then disappear, followed by the salt-and-pepper fur of a badger. Rowena sighs, grits her teeth, sets courage in her chest like a stone and puts one foot firmly in front of the other.

At the loch, Cora's skiff is moored to a small wooden jetty surrounded by a skirt of mist. She looks up as her eyes catch on something dark – a figure stood thigh-deep in the water.

'Halim?' she calls out. 'Is that you?'

The figure turns and raises its dripping arms. As soon as they're free of the water their ragged fingers catch fire and become a blinding whorl of red and gold. Rowena doesn't run this time, she closes her eyes against It and tightens her grip on the torch. 'You're not real,' she says out loud, 'there's nothing there.' She counts to nine in her head then opens her eyes and sweeps the torch beam across the loch. Sure enough, the figure has gone, but the taste of ash in Rowena's mouth somehow remains.

Steeling herself, she approaches the whispering shoreline, and is rewarded with the memory of swimming with Halim – the way his eyelashes caught the droplets and held them there, the smile on his face ... Then a sudden thought strikes her like a blow to the gut: what if he's alive and doesn't want to be found? What if he's already halfway back to his parents? At least they'd be able to help him – what can I do? she asks herself. Nothing. Nothing except love him.

38

26 May. Rowena's Birthday

———

CORA WATCHES ROWENA TIE the mud-flecked laces on her borrowed shoes – even more battered and worn from four nights of walking the heath and hills around Kinmuir. 'Why don't you have a rest for one night,' she says, cradling a large tumbler of whisky, 'get your strength up.'

Rowena shakes her head. 'I have to keep looking. He might still be out there.'

Cora takes a sip of her drink, the ice clinking in its cut-glass prison. 'I'm used to walking miles, my body and joints have had time to grow into the routine and settle into the rhythm of the land. You can't just throw yourself into these eight-hour tramps each night without doing yourself some damage, Rowena. What good would you be to him then?'

She's right, Rowena thinks, I'm exhausted. Walking all night, sleeping in Cora's attic for most of the day and then doing the same again has stirred aches in muscles she never knew she had, peeled away layers of skin and bestowed countless scrapes and blisters. She knows that part of it is self-inflicted penance; a vague notion that if she's hurting too it will lessen Halim's pain somehow and prove how sorry she is.

'If he wants to be found, he'll let you know. From here or the beyond,' Cora says, pouring another whisky and holding it out.

Rowena feels as though Cora's already given up on him.

'Take those grubby shoes off and come with me to the garden, Rowena. Humour an old woman, will you?'

Rowena takes the glass and stands up. 'Why are you being so nice to me? You didn't have to help me or Halim.'

'Oh, I did though, I took an oath to help anyone who asked for it, as long as they asked nicely. And I could see how much pain you were both in – there's no way under the Mother's gaze I could have turned either of you away.'

Cora's meandering garden has a small greenhouse, a lawn with a raised bed for herbs and a large patch of scrub given over to wild flowers and weeds. Towards the end of the lawn she's prepped a bonfire.

'What are you doing?' Rowena asks as the healer starts sprinkling her fence and gateposts with a watering can.

'It's three-day-old urine. I'm protecting the space.'

Rowena tries not to look disgusted. She watches, intrigued, as Cora soaps and washes her hands over a bucket, picks up a stone bowl that was perched on the bird table and lifts it to her nose.

'Good,' she mutters. 'Light the fire please, Rowena.'

As Rowena kneels before the woodpile and takes her plastic lighter to the kindling, Cora sets out an ancient-looking deck-chair nearby. The flames catch, sending up an intense, sour aroma. 'What's that smell?'

'Rowan and other bits, some fennel shavings and chervil to get a good smoke up.' Cora takes another generous glug of whisky, sets her glass down and waves Rowena over. She picks up the bowl again, dips her thumb into it and goes to paste the contents onto Rowena's forehead.

Rowena flinches. 'Wait, what's in it?'

'Full of questions, but never the important ones! This is my nine-herb salve – well, eight plus crab apple. Stewed in moonlight and ready to go. Now stop squirming and stand still.'

Cora smudges the cold, thick mixture into the middle of Rowena's forehead, draws a line over her lips and then rubs more into the base of her throat, her own mouth moving silently all the while.

Picking up a bundle of beech sticks, she uses the leaves like a broom to sweep up the smoke, wafting it into Rowena's squinting face.

'Keep breathing, long and deep. Good, now turn the other way.'

'What's all this for?' Rowena turns and Cora wafts the smoke at her back.

'The smoke is to cleanse and loosen you, prepare you for healing. This is your eighteenth-birthday present.'

Rowena stiffens. 'How did you know?'

'Marcus Muir told me in a dream last night. Man of few words, your father.'

Rowena closes her stinging eyes and clenches her fists, annoyed that her pa chose to visit a stranger over her.

'Your mind's been elsewhere,' Cora says, seeming to read her thoughts. 'Mine's unobstructed and clear as a bell, an easy conduit. Like a lightning rod. Now, turn and face me.'

'Pa came to me once before,' Rowena mutters as her hair lifts and falls with each waft of the broom. 'He tried to warn me not to come to Culcrith, but I didn't understand. He knew that I was sent there to be a sacrifice.'

The wafting stops. Rowena opens her eyes and turns around.

Cora lowers the beech bushel and wipes a hand down her cheek, smudging it with dirt. 'So, that's what Morag had planned? Oh, lass, I'm so sorry.'

'I thought I was sent here to be cured of my curse. My mother told me that if we left it until the first midsummer after I turned eighteen the curse would be fixed and then nothing would remove it.'

The last sliver of sun disappears behind the hill, the slow closing of a bright eye.

Rowena frowns. 'Do you think I'm cursed, Cora? And if I am, can you undo it?'

Cora takes up the bushel again and waves it, slower now, like a strange rhythmic dance that makes Rowena's focus drift. 'Well,' she says, 'I am the finest healer in the Kingdom, but even I can't undo curses that don't exist. By the way, if you feel faint at any time please take a seat.'

'But if I'm not cursed, why does everyone I love get hurt or die? Why do I still get these visions and feel like Death itself is always over my shoulder?'

'Everyone's touched by death, Rowena, that's the curse of living that we all have to endure.' Cora pauses to take another swig of her drink. 'Now, talk me through your thought process.'

Rowena's shoulders slump. 'This boy I was kind of seeing, he died just over a year ago. Then my pa died right in front of me five weeks ago.' She swallows. 'Now Halim ...'

'And you blame yourself for these things? Why?'

'Because they were the only ones I ever let myself get close to and I'm being punished for it. My mother always said I was different, cursed, and there have been all these signs, ever since I was little.'

Cora pulls a face. 'And it was your mother who sent you up here to Morag? You trust her, do you?'

Rowena spits ash onto the grass. 'No,' she mutters.

'What about these visions you mention, what do you see?'

'It's a shapeshifter, a grey thing. Sometimes a bird, a spider, a shadow-man with long arms.' She shivers as smoke swirls and eddies over her head and then curls around her neck. 'I can feel It sometimes, watching me.'

'Interesting.'

'What is?'

'Grey – halfway between black and white. In your mind it's neither good nor evil, but it's something you're reluctant to let go of. You hate it, but you keep hold of it. What do you think this grey thing is?'

'It's Death, of course.'

'No.'

Rowena lifts her chin. 'What is it then?'

'Some people call it the black dog,' Cora replies, her pale eyes piercing the fire-glow. 'It's grief.'

'No, it can't be – I've heard and seen things when I've been awake. It's too real.'

'Grief is very real, lass. It can penetrate all the senses and manifest physically, coming at you like a smack to the head or a whisper in your ear.' Cora thrusts the beech bundle into Rowena's hands. 'You told me that you lost your sweetheart and then your pa soon after. Seeing those you love die in front of you is as real as it gets.'

Rowena feels light-headed for a moment, her legs unsteady.

'That's all it is? So if I let go of my grief I'll stop having the visions and the nightmares? I'll be free of It?'

Cora drags the deckchair closer. 'No, you'll never be free of it. Grief's like the grit in an oyster. It's unpleasant at first, but one day it'll smooth into a pearl, and that's what you'll carry with you for the rest of your days. You need to accept it and let that change happen.'

Rowena looks down at the bundle in her hand, notices a delicate rune scratched into the white flesh of each stick. Soon she can't tell where the beechwood ends and her own flesh begins. 'So if I'm not cursed, none of it was my fault,' she mutters, her voice paper thin. 'I didn't kill them.'

'No, lass. You don't have that kind of power.' Cora's voice dips a level, matching the sonority of the night air. 'Are you ready to acknowledge and accept this grief within you?'

Rowena feels her bones become honeycomb light, her fingertips tingle as if she's holding feathers. She takes a deep breath and nods.

'Say the words, "I see you, I accept you, and I let you go," and then throw the sticks into the fire. Say it and mean it, mind – feel the shape of the words, hear them. Don't pretend.'

The fire cracks and pops in anticipation as Rowena steps towards it. The smoke bends suddenly, an open-mouthed face arcs out of the grey and then twists away into nothing.

She looks at Cora, who nods. 'It's okay. I'm right here, Ro.'

'That's what Pa used to say.'

'I know, he told me to tell you.'

A breeze seems to blow right through Rowena as if she were a dandelion clock. Something shifts inside her and the fabric of the world changes and feels new.

'I see you.' The words become muffled by the lump in her throat.

'I accept you.' The flames quiver and refract as her eyes fill.

'And I let you go.' She casts the sticks into the fire. Their leaves curl at its touch, sending a froth of shimmering embers to join the constellations above.

Cora places her hand on Rowena's shoulder. 'Well done,' she says. She picks up her whisky glass and heads back up the lawn, leaving Rowena to her tears.

39

27 May

———

WHENEVER THE DOORBELL GOES it sends a spike through Rowena's nerves, but in the six days she's spent hiding in Cora's attic it's never been anyone but a cheery neighbour delivering eggs, or the postman with a wedge of letters from those requesting the healer's services. This time, however, there's a long conversation at the door and she can tell something's up. She creeps part way down the stairs and presses herself against the wall to listen.

'No, I'm afraid I don't recognise either of them,' Cora says.

'It's important that if you do see or hear anything you report it right away.' The woman's voice is official-sounding and firm. 'We've been informed that Rowena Murray is extremely vulnerable and suffering a great deal of mental confusion, and that the young man is dangerous and shouldn't be approached.'

Rowena turns cold at the woman's words: more lies that her backstabbing family have spun.

'Should anyone seek your help, or confide in you – anything at all – here's my number. I'm the one allocated to the case.'

'I'm sorry, officer, but as a healer I can't disclose what any of my clients say, if that's what you're asking. Do you have any leads on the young man?'

Rowena holds her breath.

'The perpetrator hasn't been seen in days,' the officer replies, 'he usually drives a livestock truck but that's not been caught on camera on any of the main roads, so we believe he and the girl are still in the area. We're going door to door first and then we'll open up the search with dogs and horses.'

'Oh dear.'

'Don't worry, Cora, we'll do our best to find the young lady and bring the man to justice – abduction carries the highest penalty so we won't rest until he's put on trial. And it'll be a swift one too, I can promise you that.'

Cora clears her throat. 'Aye, I'm sure it will.'

When the door closes, the tightness in Rowena's chest fades and she flexes her fingers – stiff from twisting the neck of her jumper.

'It's okay, you can come down now,' Cora says.

When she does, Rowena notices that Cora's usually sharp eyes have become wide and unsure, like a fox caught in the hunt. 'Thanks for covering for us, I hope we don't get you into trouble.'

Cora brushes it off. 'Come – I've made tea and saved you some smoked salmon.'

'What did the officer mean by abduction carrying the highest penalty?'

Cora tugs on her tattooed earlobe as she chooses her words. 'It seems that you've angered Morag Murray and she's found a way to punish you as well as Halim, and get others to do all the work for her.'

Rowena crosses her arms. 'What's the penalty, Cora?'

Cora swallows. 'In this county abduction carries the death penalty. And they'll not likely give a foreigner a fair trial.'

Rowena can feel the blood rushing to her feet.

'If neither you nor the police have found Halim he might still be alive, he might have pulled through; that's a good sign, Rowena.'

'I'm sick of signs. What fucking use are they if they don't help?' Rowena digs her nails into the flesh on her upper arms. 'It's all my fault. It's my fault that he came to Culcrith in the first place and got mixed up with my shitty family.'

'From what I could tell, he's a strong young man with a will of his own.'

'Well, if he is alive he won't be for long, unless I do something to fix this.'

'I know what you're thinking, lass, but you might still find him and then you can both run.' Cora's voice wavers – even she's unsure.

'No, you heard the woman, they'll hunt us down like animals and won't listen to some "vulnerable" eighteen-year-old. The police'll just see what they want to see.'

'At least give me time to register myself as your county sponsor so you won't get handed straight back to your gran.'

Rowena looks at Cora and shakes her head, never more determined in her life. 'I'm not gonna drag you into this. Anyway, I don't have the time for papers and permits – they could find Halim any second.'

Cora's face is as solemn as a judge's. 'You know what lies down this path, don't you?'

Rowena sets her jaw. 'If Halim's to have any chance out there I have to hand myself in and clear his name.'

'Don't you believe me?' Rowena gives the uniformed man behind the cold white counter her fiercest glare. 'I'll spell it out for you: My. Gran. Wants. To. Kill. Me. You can't just hand me back to her.'

The officer's moustache twitches as he taps his pen on the pad in front of him.

'For fuck's sake! Send me back to Dunfordshire then – I'll happily leave right now!'

The officer raises a bushy eyebrow. 'The system says you're not registered as a resident in that county any more.'

Rowena slams her fist on the counter, knocking over the officer's cup. 'What the fuck are you smiling at? Do you think this is a joke? Can't you see what's happening here?'

Coffee pools and starts dripping on the floor, sending up thin waves of steam. The officer doesn't flinch.

'Young lady, having known Morag Murray – a well-respected member of this community – for over thirty years myself, I can assure you that she is not a murderer.' The officer leans forward, so close that their noses are almost touching and Rowena can smell smoked fish on his breath. 'She warned us about you and your strange southern ways. Your old ways. She said to go easy on you if we found you, so, as a favour to my friend, I'll look past your

234

wee outburst and I'll even mop up this mess myself with no more bother. In the meantime you can cool off in our holding cell.'

Rowena digs her nails into the counter as the hot coffee drips onto her feet. She lurches over and takes a swipe at the officer, he dodges it so she takes another and tries to grab his tie. 'How long would I get for assaulting an officer?' she yells, her fists still balled. 'Why don't you lock me up for a few weeks? Go on! Do it, shit-for-brains! Lock me up!'

The officer grabs her wrist and yanks it hard, and when she's face down on the wet counter he twists her arm behind her back. 'It's not assault if you don't land one, sweetheart.'

When Morag arrives at the police station she makes a show of checking Rowena over, pulling her close, stroking her hair as if she were one of her precious mares. She even manages to squeeze out a tear or two as she bundles her out the door.

'So what happens next, Morag?' Rowena asks, loud enough for the police officer to hear. 'Are you gonna lock me up again?'

Morag ignores her.

'Will you bleed me over the flower beds, grind me up and scatter my flesh over the oats? Or maybe you'll burn me like a witch, is that it? Is that why you've been making all those candles and sharpening your knives?'

Morag notices Rowena looking at the beautiful chestnut horse as she unhitches it and checks the saddle. 'This one's Bernie's,' she smiles. 'Fine creature, isn't she?'

Rowena thinks about the route back to Culcrith and at which point she might make a run for it. She catches the eye of the officer – stood on the steps watching her with his arms folded, a gun holstered at his hip.

'Why didn't you tell them where you've been all this time?' Morag asks. 'And where are your things?'

'I sold them for drugs and went on a bender, filled myself right up on class A chemicals.' She'll never tell Morag about Cora – that she left her backpack with the healer and asked her to scatter her pa's ashes if she didn't make it past the solstice.

Morag gives her granddaughter a look that's somewhere

between curious and impressed. She swings into the saddle in one swift movement and holds a hand out. Rowena ignores it and jumps up herself.

With a nod to the officer, Morag jolts the horse into a trot. 'Bernie and his sons were out looking for you for days, you know, then we had to call the police in. You gave us a fright, child. And your poor mother was on the phone to me every night. Most I've spoken to her in years.'

'Why? Was she offering herself up instead? Wasn't she the one who actually cursed Culcrith?'

Morag doesn't reply.

Not wanting to wrap her arms around Morag's waist, Rowena grips the sides of the saddle as timber and grey-stone buildings bob past them. Death has captured me at last, she thinks, the cards were right after all. She leans over Morag's shoulder. 'You know that Bernie and his boys won't get away with it, don't you? Halim's parents will hire the best lawyers and bring you all down. I wonder what penalty attempted murder carries in Laithness ... That's right, *attempted* murder: he's still alive and he'll come for you.' Rowena hopes she sounds convincing.'

Morag kicks the horse, shunting them into a canter.

Let her stew, Rowena thinks. Halim's safe from the police now, wherever he might be.

She smiles and touches the charm in her pocket, the one Cora made her – powdered pearl in a hollowed-out acorn, bound in white thread.

Marin, Bernie's youngest, is up a ladder painting the stable block as Rowena and Morag arrive back at the farm. As soon as he spots them he looks away.

Rowena jumps down from the horse.

'The old stables are looking good, aren't they?' Morag says, mistaking Rowena's attention. 'We've got big plans for Culcrith now that we've been blessed with you.'

Rowena sniffs. 'And all these years I thought I was a curse.'

'You might not believe it, Rowena, but you are very precious to me.'

'You mean my blood is – the blood that you're so keen to spill in a few days' time.'

Above them, Marin's foot slips and the ladder rattles.

Morag cups Rowena's head in her hands and holds it tight. 'By coming back to us of your own free will you've saved us! You've shown us the greatest, most selfless love a person can give, and for that I'm truly grateful, Rowena, and I promise you'll not want for anything as long as you're under my roof. You're the light I've been looking for all these long, dark years.' This time Morag's tears seem genuine. 'You can stop running and rest now, child, let everything go and stand as still as the solstice sun. Litha will cleanse you at last.'

Unmoved, Rowena stares into her gran's watery-blue eyes, thinking up ways she can hurt her.

Morag releases Rowena's face and smiles. 'Love is not a strong enough expression for the way I feel about you right now.'

'"Fuck you" is not a strong enough expression for the way I feel about you right now,' replies Rowena, striding off towards the farmhouse.

40

19 June

———

ROWENA MEASURES EACH ARDUOUS DAY in birdsong – the chiffchaff and the blackbird calling up the dawn, the swallows piping in the twilight. Morag insists she should be eating more, but Rowena can't stomach the special 'wholesome' food, knowing that they're simply preparing her flesh and blood so it can be wrenched and drained from her, nothing more than fertiliser for the soil. She weaves yet another flower garland for something to do, her fingers nimble, her mind distracted as her gaze follows the diaphanous path of a sunbeam. Morag has locked the window, fixed barbed wire to the wall outside, cut the flex back from the light fitting and removed the candlesticks, but otherwise the bedroom is just the same. Rowena has thought of countless ways to kill Morag, but knows she'll never have the guts to go through with them, and if she did, what then? Even if she were to escape the Kerrs, she'd probably be caught, put on trial and sentenced to death anyway. No, let Morag have me, she thinks. I hope my blood taints the land and sickens everything it touches.

She drops the garland and goes to the window, something she does at least every few hours to scan the horizon and imagine where Halim might be. She hopes his parents have put him on a plane and flown him far away from this wretched Kingdom, but part of her suspects he might not have survived the fever or his injuries. Did he curl up somewhere to die like an animal, defeated and alone? she wonders. Am I looking for a ghost? Have I sacrificed myself for a dead man?

A knock at the door pulls her away. When it's unlocked she's surprised to see Marin behind it, looking every bit as though he doesn't want to be there. Up close, he's younger than she thought, with cropped red hair and a long, freckled nose.

'Are you taking me for my walk today?' Rowena asks, uncrossing her arms. 'Where's my darling grandmother?'

Marin's lips pinch together before he speaks as if he's worried about every word that slips out of them. 'She's busy in the top field,' he mutters.

Of course she is, Rowena thinks, that must be where they'll do it. I've seen her heft baskets of bread and milk away as offerings to lay under the turf. The solstice must be soon – is it two days? One? I've lost track.

Rowena leads the way. As she steps outside she relishes the feel of the warm, swirling breeze on her touch-starved skin. There hasn't been rain for weeks now – not since she and Halim first arrived in Laithness – and the grass has curdled yellow. Pollen debris hangs in the air, alongside the funk of tepid dung. Rowena sucks in a breath through her teeth and turns to Marin. 'Shit, it really *does* look like this land could do with watering. Maybe you could poke a few holes in me now and be done with it?'

Marin flushes red to the tips of his ears and purses his lips again.

Rowena smirks and heads off on the usual route – a wide loop around the oat field and then back behind the stables. She no longer looks for signs and shadows and hasn't had a vision in almost three weeks: fear loses its power when you know the worst that can happen is already marked on the calendar.

When they reach the corner of the oat field, out of sight of the farmhouse, Marin holds out his arm. 'Wait,' he says. He folds back some teasel and retrieves a plastic bag, from which he produces two bottles of cider. He opens them and offers her one.

Rowena takes it and frowns.

'It's made with Culcrith apples, so it's not like I'm breaking the rules, but still, don't tell anyone. Please.' He takes a sip.

She takes a sip. It's crisp and tangy. It tastes of young man's guilt.

She swigs as they walk, almost tripping over each time her head is tipped back, but enjoying what could be her last real drink. Beside them, the oat blades are rusted and spotted instead of a rich golden yellow.

As they complete the circuit of the field, Marin raises his head. 'I expect you're wondering why my pa and your gran are doing all this,' he says, plucking at the mottled grass, crushing the weak seeds between his fingers. 'It's not like they didn't try everything else – for years they had us doing all sorts of things to—'

'I don't care,' Rowena says, issuing a loud, apple-flavoured burp.

Marin nods and continues on in silence, only raising his head to bat away flies.

'Here, Marin, can you hold this for me? I need a piss.' She hands him the almost-empty cider bottle. 'It's Morag's stupid dandelion tea – runs right through me. Won't be long.' Rowena strides off between the oats, heading towards the hedge, her heart quickening. She squats for a moment in the long grass and checks that she can't be seen. Around her, the field scratches and crackles in the sticky breeze. A bird darts overhead like an arrow shot in the direction that Rowena is creeping – towards the field entrance. She gathers her wits, takes a breath and readies her muscles for a sprint.

'I wouldn't if I were you.' Marin is gazing down at her from the gate. 'Please don't make this any harder than it already is.'

Rowena stands up and dusts herself off. 'Why the hell would I want to make this *easy* for you?'

'Not for me, for you.' Marin rubs his forehead, his throat working up and down. 'We've horses that can outrun you, and a rifle too if it came to it. My brothers and my pa have risked too much already, they'd hunt you down if they had to.' He stashes their empty bottles in a rut beneath the pines. 'You might, you know, want to brush your teeth so she can't smell it on you,' he says, a shine of fear in his eyes.

'What makes you think I won't just tell her about the cider?'

Marin shrugs and looks down. 'I was only trying to make you feel a wee bit better. I'm sorry I can't do more.'

Rowena sniffs. That alcohol must have gone to my head, she thinks, as she becomes lost in the disco of light below the branches and feels like it's the most beautiful thing she's ever seen.

'How was your walk today?' Morag asks as Rowena strips for her daily herbal bath. 'It's a shame I couldn't be there, I cherish what little time we have together.'

Rowena rolls her eyes, steps out of her knickers and dips her toes in the cold water, its surface dappled indigo with vervain petals.

'All the way under, you know the drill,' Morag says as she sits on the toilet seat massaging scented oil into her knuckles.

Rowena grits her teeth and ducks under. The cold bursts through her flesh. She presses the sides of the bath to hold herself down, longer than ever – until her lungs burn and she can see Morag's shape wobbling above. When Rowena eventually emerges, her breath runs away from her and she struggles to snatch it back.

'You know, on the Continent they swear by plunge pools and ice baths,' Morag smiles.

Rowena glares at her, water dripping from her nose, her shivers practically shaking the porcelain tiles.

'Oh, stop being so dramatic, child.' Morag places her fingers on Rowena's temples and starts massaging her head. 'Sit still for a moment and try to relax, empty your mind. Let everything go ...' Her hands freeze. 'Rowena? You'd best not be pissing in my bath!' She places a finger in the water as warmth blooms through it.

Rowena laughs.

'Get up,' Morag snaps. 'NOW!'

Her skin pink and raw from her gran's scrubbing, Rowena reaches under the chest of drawers and hooks out the wax poppet of Morag that she'd made a while ago. She flicks on the bedside lamp and holds it over the bulb. The crude oval face softens and slips as the wax heats and melts. Singed dust fills her nose as she stares at the glowing filament until her eyes burn, wondering if Morag can feel this. The hot bulb bites her fingers as she accidentally touches it, making her drop the disfigured poppet. She sighs and kicks the thing under the bed.

Taking up her usual place at the bedroom window, she gazes out at the horizon, the black line of the ridge stark against red-streaked clouds. 'Red sky at night,' she mutters, rubbing her tender arms to feel the sting. The swallows draw their own lines as they spike hapless moths and midges en route to their nests. They don't scratch out messages for her in the sky any more; they don't do anything except be exactly the way that nature intended, driven on by their own wild instinct.

As she's about to turn away something catches her eye – a movement beside the stables, a shadow darker and thicker than the rest, too large to be an animal. Her heart kicks as it moves away. Was someone standing there? It couldn't have been Bernie or his three boys because they're downstairs, having supper.

41

21 June. Summer Solstice

———

GREEN, LIKE SPARKLING EMERALDS. Leaves, Rowena realises as she prises her heavy eyelids open. She's sat under an oak tree and can't remember how she got here, but the strange, metallic taste in her mouth reminds her of the vile tea she was made to drink last night, and when her brain finally catches up she realises she was drugged. A blackbird trills its virtuoso song from a branch above. It's dawn: a shifting, liminal time when the veil between worlds slips and things get through – words, intentions, blessings. Curses. Especially on midsummer morning, she thinks. She lifts her bound wrists to scratch her temple and finds another rope around her waist, pressing her spine into the tree trunk. She's sat at the edge of the top field, the haunted field. Perhaps they think her blood will run off and water the whole of Culcrith from up here?

Dotted around her, spent candle wicks sit in skirts of their own wax, next to silver bowls of water, filmy with the night's debris. Have they absorbed the will of the one who laid them? Rowena wonders. Did the moon throw its spears of light hard enough to fix Morag's words to water? She vaguely remembers glimpsing – through lidded eyes – her gran kneeling over a bowl, her lips moving. She recalls the scrape and grind of pestle and mortar. A hollow snort and a stamp of hooves ...

Rowena groans and shifts her weight to get the feeling back in her legs. There are figures out in the bone-dry field: Bernie and his boys are carting stacks of wood for the solstice fire, perhaps the same fire that will remove all evidence of her body once they're done with it.

There's a rustle and a snap of twigs to her right.

'How's our special wee lamb this morning?' It's Robert Kerr, the middle son, a lanky twenty-something with deep-set eyes and a downturned mouth.

Rowena focuses on the pearls of dew by her toes and shrugs. 'Thirsty. Hungry.' Her voice croaks through the dryness of her throat.

Robert drops to one knee in front of her and produces a roll of freshly baked milk-bread from his pocket, showering himself in poppy seeds. He takes a bite of the soft dough. 'Sorry, sweetness, but I can't share this with you, rules are rules, eh.' He spits a crumb at her as he says this and it bounces off her nose. Rowena notices his other hand twitch and rise up, as if to stroke the thick braid of hair that's nestled into her neck, but the hand drops. He gets up and strides off, cutting a swirling path through the morning mist.

She watches him in the field – inspecting the stack with his boot, adding more sand to the firebreak – and sighs, willing the sun to rise now and warm her aching body and be done with it.

'It's going to be a braw day.' Morag appears from behind the tree. She hands her granddaughter a water flask and places the back of her hand to her forehead. 'You're cold,' she tuts, laying a colourful crocheted shawl about Rowena's shoulders.

The water is flavoured with lemon verbena and Rowena gulps it down, emptying the flask.

Morag sits next to her and they gaze out over the mustard-coloured scrub as the mist finally surrenders to the sun. Rowena imagines her soul doing the same when the time comes; thinning, rising, merging with the air.

'Did you celebrate midsummer in Pickbury, Rowena?'

'Pa didn't like the old ways so he'd never allow us a ritual, but Tessa and I did a few things in secret, little offerings to protect the sheep that'd be wintering in the fields.'

Morag sniffs. 'I suppose winters are easier down south, nothing like the ones we get. Hailstones the size of fists here, trees torn up

– I doubt you've ever experienced the full force of Mother's anger. It's terrible and beautiful in equal measure. Sublime. A marvel, really.' She gets a faraway look. 'But after She's ravaged the land She leaves behind new growth, Her little gifts coming up through the cracks and debris.' She smiles and adjusts Rowena's shawl. 'Aye, sometimes you have to destroy in order to create.'

'I'll destroy you and everything you love,' Rowena says, her voice perfectly level. 'When you cut me down I'll bring you with me. If you thought Culcrith was cursed by my birth, just you wait and see what my death will do.'

Morag brushes a withered leaf from her skirt. 'The only thing you'll be bringing down is our run of bad luck,' she whispers. 'You're the *undoing* of a curse, Rowena. Tessa knew it. That's why your mother is making such a great sacrifice.'

'She's not my mother, she's a …' Rowena finds her words heavy and thick on her tongue.

'Shh, just you rest now, precious one, we've a long day of preparations ahead.' Morag smiles as Rowena's eyelids flutter and close once more.

Upon waking, Rowena shrugs off the shawl in the cloying heat. The white cotton dress Morag put her in last night is sticking to her skin and bunching around her waist where the rope still grips her. In the middle of the field the fire is lit and the Kerrs sit chatting and drinking, sending snatches of laughter on the smoky breeze to taunt her. The sun is hunkering low and the evening midges are dancing about her head: it's close now, Rowena thinks, her heart clawing at her ribcage. Don't be afraid, don't show them how scared you are.

A loud voice makes her jump. 'Away with you, Robert! Stop sniffing around – I'll do it.' Morag glares at Bernie's middle son, who beats a speedy retreat.

When Robert rejoins the others they all turn to squint at Rowena. Morag disappears behind the oak to tug loose the rope, and once Rowena's freed she rubs at the sting around her middle and arches her back like a cat. With her wrists still bound she picks up one of the bowls lying in the grass and gulps down the stale water, not caring about the bugs or money spiders. The blood swishes behind her ears as she stands and her legs almost give way: she couldn't run if she tried. Steadying herself against the rough bark, she can almost feel the pulse of the oak too, the sap flowing under her palm. She knocks her knuckles against it three times out of habit.

'Okay, child, come.' Morag takes Rowena's elbow and leads her towards the bonfire. Even the white-starred bairnswort and hardy clover have crisped up under the relentless summer heat – breaking and tearing underfoot instead of defiantly springing back. Rowena closes her eyes and walks blind, the sun heating her face like the sting from a slap. Pa tried to warn me not to come here, she thinks, but I've always been too easily led – and here I am again, being trotted through this field like a show pony. When she trips and opens her eyes she catches sight of Marin who, at pains to avoid her gaze, picks up the fiddle and starts to play one of the solstice jigs. A song rises between the men:

'The leaves are fat across the land,
The ash, the oak, the chestnut tree,
Her fruits hang heavy on stalk and stem,
Her belly is round and blessed are we ...'

Marin, like his brothers and pa, is wearing a mummer's cloak of straw and feathers, and tied to his head with animal gut is the upper part of a foal skull, streaked with coal-black lines. They're wearing executioner's masks, Rowena realises, her stomach lurching.

Morag indicates for her to sit on a low chair, crudely carved from one of the trees in the farm's courtyard: Rowena watched the boys chopping and hacking at it days ago, was tormented by the incessant, hissing scrape of sandpaper. It doesn't look like much now she's up close, and its splinters catch and tug at her dress as she's pushed down onto it. An earwig slithers out from a fold of bark between her legs and disappears again.

The folk song becomes a riot of handclaps and foot stamps, each clap jabbing Rowena's head like a bullet. She tries to listen instead for the horse spirits, and wonders if they're pawing and straining at the dirt, waiting for her to join them down there in the earth.

The fiddle skips a few notes as Morag darts over to rescue a bowl by Marin's foot. 'Careful, you lump of a boy!' she scolds. 'This took me weeks to prepare, and there's no more moonblood if it gets spilled!' She brings the bowl over to Rowena, cursing loudly.

Rowena scowls, realising that Morag must have gathered her 'moonblood' from the cloths she was given to line her knickers, and that the herbs and wild flowers she was sent to gather when she first arrived in Culcrith have helped create the very ointments and spells that will become her undoing.

Morag dips her fingers in the bowl. Rowena shrinks back and tries to knock her away, but Morag holds her firmly by the chin and paints a cross over her sweat-slick brow.

Rowena's bloodshot eyes stray to the horizon. There's nothing there but a darkening froth of hedgerows twitching with roostings.

'Quiet!' At Morag's word the singing stops, leaving only the soft crackle of the fire.

She stands over Rowena and begins circling the crude wooden throne. 'This young woman, born of this land, we return to this land,' she says, dripping liquid from the bowl as she goes. 'With the permission of our ancestors, we'll plant a new seed here today and cleanse the land with fire so that it may grow and bloom. Culcrith demands balance, and so we return to the soil the one that should never have been. This is our intention.' She glares at the others until they repeat the words.

'This is our intention.'

'Look!' Gus, Bernie's eldest, points towards the farmhouse. 'Is that coming from the stables?'

Morag stops moving.

Everyone turns to see a thick column of smoke.

'Might just be a small wildfire in the scrub,' Bernie says. 'Marin, go check it out, and be quick about it.'

Marin ditches his fiddle, mask and cloak and runs full pelt down the slope.

Bernie, Gus and Robert are restless as they eye the dark plume and swig their ale. Rowena can see their bodies tighten and thrum with a dangerous energy.

Morag, however, eyes the streaks of light that waver along the ridge to the west. 'We can't wait too much longer,' she says, her tongue clicking in her sticky mouth. She carefully unwraps a woven crown of yarrow, vetch and fern, places it on Rowena's head and tucks a stray hair behind her granddaughter's ear.

Rowena sits silent and still, numb to the full-sky beauty of the sunset above their heads. She makes herself hollow, turns out all of her feelings and thoughts in the hope that they'll be sacrificing nothing but a husk and the spell won't work if it's not really her …

'Something's not right,' Bernie mutters. He gets up and starts pacing. 'The boy's taking too long.'

As he says this, smoke whooshes up into a great grey leviathan directly above the stables.

'That's no wildfire, Pa,' Robert mutters.

Gus stares at the brightening glow. 'Holy shit, do you think Marin got our horses out?'

'Both of you stop your gaping and get down there!' Bernie yells, spit flying from his mouth.

The two brothers take off.

Morag grips Bernie's arm. 'We can't wait,' she says. 'We've come too far, we must do this now before the light dies.'

He casts a glance at Rowena, his red face snarled up with alcohol and adrenaline. 'You sure about this, Morag?'

Morag raises an eyebrow. 'You sure you still want a piece of Culcrith, or should I sign it over to my useless daughter and see what she makes of the place?'

As they're bickering, Rowena slowly rises to her feet, driven by a calm desperation.

'Look around you, Bernie. Scraping by and surviving isn't enough, we need to *thrive*. And believe you me, this land is as thirsty and ready as we are.'

Bernie lowers his mask and adjusts his straw cloak.

Unnoticed, Rowena picks up Marin's fiddle, raises it above her head and brings it crashing down onto the back of Bernie's skull with a satisfying CRACK. He yells and falls to his knees. Moving without thinking, Rowena picks up a shard of the wood and holds it like a dagger above him, ignoring the slice it's making in her palm.

'This is for Halim,' she says, as she plunges the shard into Bernie's side. The flesh gives, and she can feel things moving aside as the point sinks deeper.

Bernie grabs Rowena's bound wrists and looks up at her, his eyes round and shining like a rabbit in a trap. He plucks the shard from his side and sprays red across her white dress.

Sickened, she stumbles back. A heartbeat later, Morag strikes her hard across the face, sending her sprawling in an explosion of pain.

Bernie groans. 'There's too much blood, I think I'm bleeding out.'

Morag looks to the dimming sky, and then back to the stables.

'Morag? Help me?'

She shakes her head. 'Not right now, there's no time.'

'Well, then you'll have to get your hands dirty for once, won't you?' Bernie growls as he rolls onto his leaking side.

Morag picks up Marin's discarded straw-and-feather cloak and ties it around her shoulders, swamping herself in a mottle of brown and gold. The skull mask becomes even more chilling when it's filled with her cold blue eyes.

Rowena's chest tightens as fear fills the void left by adrenaline. 'You're losing your farm,' she gasps, sitting up. 'Look – it's burning! Aren't you supposed to be saving Culcrith?'

'I *am* saving it,' Morag says as she moves closer, the straw rustling with each step.

She draws a silver knife from a lambskin sheath.

Bernie's whimpers become weaker.

Rowena claws handfuls of dried grass, trying to get to her feet.

'It'll be quick and painless, child, I've done it plenty of times on the animals. You'll not feel a thing. I promise.'

Behind Morag, the light from the solstice fire seems to darken as something slips in front of it. A shadow-man, with long and ragged branch-like arms, stands silhouetted against the flames.

Rowena draws a sharp breath and smiles. 'You came for me!'

42

———

HALIM HOLDS A FLAMING BRANCH in each hand, his inscrutable face partially hidden by a thick beard. The sky seems ablaze with a second sunset as he moves closer.

Rallying, Rowena manages to get up, but Morag grasps her braid and jerks her head back – almost wrenching it from her shoulders. She curls a strong arm around Rowena's weakened body and holds it firm against her own. 'You – not a step further,' Morag hisses. 'Toss those branches on the fire there and I'll let her go.'

Rowena feels the bite of the blade at her throat, a warm trickle of blood down her neck.

Halim hesitates.

'Don't do it, Halim, you know she won't keep her word.'

'Blessed be the Mother that provides, and brings the meadow to bloom,' Morag's low voice rumbles against Rowena's back.

A single tear escapes as Rowena tries to slowly slip her bound hands under Morag's arm without tempting the blade deeper.

'We seek your energy and protection on Litha,' Morag continues, 'as the sun travels on its longest path and as the last light fades.'

Halim raises the branches like swords.

A deathly pale face appears over his shoulder.

'Halim – behind you!'

He spins around barely quick enough to dodge the downward swipe of the foal skull as Bernie lurches towards him, teeth bared in agony.

As Bernie collapses at Halim's feet, Morag continues the ritual, her voice and blade remaining steady. 'By the power of the sun, these sacred herbs and this precious blood, I ask that the light shine again on Culcrith even as the dark days approach.'

Halim stands over Bernie's hunched form. He topples him with a nudge of his foot and touches a branch to his cloak, dubbing him with fire. It catches in seconds and flickers to life, feeding at first on feather and straw, and then on skin and flesh.

Bernie hardly puts up a fight: he moans, his drained body twitches, and then he becomes still – surrounded by veins of fire that continue to creep their way across the bone-dry grass.

Rowena can hear them now, coming for her, the drumming of hooves in her ears – louder still as she manages to edge her fingers between blade and skin. With a sharp jolt of her body and thrust of her arms she pushes away from Morag and stumbles towards Halim, ignoring the throbbing wetness of her neck. She snatches one of his flaming branches – a second before Morag launches at her and knocks her to the ground. They both land hard, breath exploding from their mouths.

Morag wheezes and presses all her weight onto Rowena, the foal-skull mask slipping over one eye. 'May this blood wash away the blight on this land and may the soil be RENEWED ...' Her words elongate, and then strangle into a scream as the branch that Rowena holds to her back does its work.

Morag rolls away, contorting and twisting her body as smoke writhes around her, a freakish and desperate dance trailing gold and grey ribbons. No amount of spinning or thumping can stop the flames eating their way across the straw and up her body, and Rowena watches, slack-jawed, as her grandmother claws at her neck to undo the knot of the cape.

The hideous, stomach-churning noise that comes out of Morag lasts only until a bright collar of fire creeps up over her face and is sucked into her mouth and nostrils, snatching away her breath. Her fingers still grasp the knot of the cape even as they blister and blacken, even as she crumples to the ground, her hair fizzing into nothing.

Halim drops his branch and stares at the smouldering bodies of Morag and Bernie.

The land got its sacrifice after all, Rowena thinks; the lamb became the knife. She feels the ground drop away as Halim lifts her. With some effort, she raises her hands to the flower crown on her head and tosses it into the fire.

He carries her away from the blackened mess, the stifling heat and the bacon-smelling smoke, to the hole in the hedge at the far corner of the field. He pushes them through it and sets her down on the other side. Tearing the hem of her dress, he wraps a strip of material around her bleeding throat and another across the blade-torn fingers of her right hand. Only then does he untie the rope at her wrists.

'I'm sorry I'm late,' he stutters.

She looks at him then – sees that his face is covered in the yellow ghosts of bruises and that a scab has grown over his lip, puckering the skin under his matted beard. 'You're here, you're really here,' she says, her voice thin and strained. She goes to touch his cheek but he shies away, so she puts her hand to her neck instead and wonders how deep the cut is.

'Save your energy,' Halim says. 'We need to get out of here before the brothers return.'

'Marin, Bernie's youngest boy, went to check out the stables, didn't he catch you? It was you who set fire to them, wasn't it?'

Halim's brow tightens. 'I knocked him out before he saw me and left him in there – I knew the others wouldn't be far behind so I didn't have time to move him. I did what needed to be done,' he insists. 'I had to draw them away from you.'

He puts his arm around Rowena and helps her up.

She glances back at Culcrith for what she hopes will be the last time and notices a scattering of tiny blue lights – is sure that she sees horses nosing the shadows around the fire, flicking manes of smoke as they weave in and out of the dusk.

Heading towards a glade, Rowena and Halim reach a pollarded willow, its branches like splayed fingers from a thick knuckle of wood. A handsome chestnut horse is tethered to it.

'That's Bernie's mare,' Rowena mutters.

Halim shrugs. 'It was the biggest horse I found. Are you able to ride?'

She nods, ignoring the coldness spreading through her limbs.

Holding his ribs, Halim climbs into the saddle first, wincing from the effort.

Rowena gathers up the tattered skirt of her red-streaked dress and places her bare foot in the stirrup. Waiting a few seconds for her wooziness to subside, she swings herself up and he nudges the horse into motion. As they stomp over the flattened wire fence and wind their way down a steep slope Halim leans his body back into hers to keep their weight even. She picks catchweed from his jumper and holds him as tight as she can, trying to ignore the jagged, gummy stitches in the back of his head and the taste of blood in her throat.

A chattering laugh makes his whole body tense. 'What the hell was that?'

'Just a grouse.'

'Is anyone following?'

She shifts around in the saddle. 'No.'

'*Khara!*' Halim sighs. 'Where do we go now? We're fucked.'

'But we're alive,' Rowena mutters. She closes her eyes for a while and rests her cheek on his shoulder, feels it rise and fall, tries to pretend that everything's okay.

'I suppose there is one place that criminals might go unnoticed,' Halim sniffs. 'Do you know the way to the Wilderness?'

'I know a place we can get maps,' she says, her breath stirring the curl of hair behind his ear. 'I also found your woodworking book and kept it for you. We need to stop at Cora's – head towards the lights of that village.'

'Who's Cora?'

'The healer who dragged you out of a ditch and saved your life. Don't you remember?'

He shakes his head. 'It's all a blur. I know I was in a room some-where but I left.'

'Where'd you go? I was out looking for you so many nights, not knowing if you'd survived the fever, especially out there on your own.'

'I honestly can't say. It was so dark. I must have walked for miles. My father appeared, and that's when I knew I was lost, truly lost – I wanted to be anywhere but there, with him. I woke up in some woods, built myself a shelter the way you showed me and slept for what felt like days.'

'The police were after you, I had to turn myself in to prove that you hadn't kidnapped me.'

'I'm sorry, Rowena.'

'I'm not. I couldn't let them catch you.' She feels tremors through his spine but can't work out if he's crying or if it's the gait of the horse.

They ride in silence for a while.

'I was watching the farm trying to figure out what to do,' he says eventually, 'waiting for the right time to get you out of there. I guess I waited too long, coward that I am.'

'You're not a coward! You came back for me! You returned to Culcrith after they tried to kill you, when you could have just flown back to your parents.'

'No, I made my choice and that path is closed to me now.'

Rowena raises her head. 'What do you mean?'

He wipes the sweat and grime from his face. 'There's something I didn't tell you ... I suppose I was embarrassed by my privilege and what you'd think of me. I was promised quite a bit of money when I turned twenty-one, a substantial share of my parents' wealth.'

'That's great. What will you do with it?'

'Nothing. To claim it I would have had to pledge to return and work for my father before my twenty-first birthday. I couldn't do it. I turned twenty-one three days ago.'

Rowena frowns. 'Why couldn't you do it? It seemed like you were pissed off with this life. You told Morag you were going back to your parents.'

'I thought about it. A lot. The past few months it's been weighing on my mind, especially as things got harder and ... more complicated.'

'So what happened?'

Halim grips the reins tighter. 'You happened, Rowena.'

Before she can reply, he kicks the horse into a canter and the heath softens and blurs beneath them.

43

21–22 June

———

IT'S TRUE DARK BY THE TIME they reach the healer's cottage in Kinmuir and Halim can barely hold himself up from the soreness in his chest and the tiredness in his bones. He hesitates at the front gate with the horse, piecing together the vaguely familiar features of Cora's face now that his head's free of fever. The healer stands barefoot on the path, staring, and behind her a single white candle flickers in the window. She touches the pendant hanging at her neck. 'Rowena called you out of the woods, I see.'

'It's okay, you can trust her,' Rowena whispers. 'I know it's hard to believe right now, but there are some good people in the world, Halim.'

Cora beckons them off the road. 'You've been through hell, I can't even begin to imagine. Don't tell me what happened, though – if I don't know I can't testify.' She nods towards the horse: 'You can put her in the paddock out back.'

'We just came to pick up Rowena's things,' Halim says, clasping the reins. 'It won't take long.'

Cora waves a hand in front of her face as if swatting midges. 'You take as long as you need. Wash that smoke from your skin and get some food and rest for the onward journey, you've a long way to go.'

Halim frowns. What does she know about their journey? He hadn't thought much beyond getting Rowena away from Culcrith.

Her eyes glistening, Cora steps forward and studies Rowena, touches her fingers to her bandaged neck. 'I'm ashamed to admit I was only expecting one visitor tonight – yet here you are, in the flesh, a ghost no more.' She smiles, and then takes up the horse's reins herself and leads them down the side of the cottage. 'I went to the police,' she confides as they brush between the fir trees, 'not long after Rowena returned to Culcrith. I told them that Morag Murray was holding her against her will, but when they went to investigate there was no one in – said I was wasting valuable police time.'

'We must have been out for my daily walk,' Rowena mutters. 'That or the pigs were lying and didn't bother calling round at all.'

Cora turns, her face pinched and serious. 'I also travelled to the Black Isle to make an offering at St Dandoch's Well. I thought about calling on Morag myself, but if I'd raised suspicions I knew she would have made things worse; the signs … weren't good. I should have done more, I should have had hope. I'm sorry.'

'It's okay, Cora. You've done so much for us already.'

Cora shakes herself. 'Well, there's fresh-brewed tea in the pot or something stronger in the decanter – with it being part way between night and morning, I wasn't sure which you'd prefer.'

After his turn in the shower, Halim joins Rowena and Cora in the ramshackle study, his damp hair sticking to his forehead. Rowena has a thick poultice strapped to her neck and her hand is now properly bandaged.

'I laid out the arnica and aloe for you,' Cora points to two clay pots on her desk. 'And Rowena's bag's over there. You'll see I slipped in one of my old compasses and a special map – a rare one that sets out the lands you now call "the Wilderness" in more detail. I've marked the parts you'd do well to avoid, such as the old Doom Park, where murderers and so-called witches were dumped in unmarked graves. Those places aren't for settling.'

We're murderers, thinks Halim, touching his aching ribs. 'So we have a plan then?' He still feels dazed, as if his soul is out of phase with his body and his voice doesn't belong to him.

Rowena nods. 'All those days locked up at Culcrith made me yearn for the Wilderness even more. That place can be anything we want it to be, we can make our own way, see where the wind carries us. Besides, the Kingdom's got nothing left for me – I've no family, no home.' She bites her lip. 'Neither have you by the sound of it.'

She's right. His truck and his inheritance are gone and he's lost his passport – everything he knew and relied on. There's no longer a comfort zone, no contingency plan or well-marked route, only unfamiliar terrain lies before him now.

'What does your gut say?' Cora asks, as she pours Halim a generous whisky.

He gives a small shrug. 'It says we're out of options.'

'Maybe the Wilderness was your destination all along and you just didn't know it? Perhaps you and Rowena were supposed to go on this journey together, to save each other?'

Halim takes the tumbler and grips it tight, thinks back to Rowena's Tarot reading – the cards that showed the two of them together, bodies falling from a tower ...

'You both need to let go.' Cora's voice brings him out of a fug. 'Shake off everything that's holding you back and see what remains. Then you'll know what's important, what it is you truly need.' She glances between the two of them. 'Well, I'm off to get my beauty sleep. There's fresh bread, eggs, and a cheese-and-meat platter in the fridge, take whatever you need.'

'Wait,' Halim holds out his hand. 'I never got to thank you for all you did for me; my head was addled, and I was so broken and angry I must have—'

'No need to explain, son.' Cora smiles, takes Halim's hand in both of hers and shakes it. Her grey eyes narrow as she leans in to whisper. 'Promise me you'll look after that girl?'

Halim swallows and nods.

'She's in foal, by the way.'

Halim pulls his hand back.

'Aye, that fine chestnut mare will make you some good coin where you're headed,' Cora winks. 'You should leave before daybreak, put some distance between yourself and these parts. It's not safe for you here.'

Rowena gets up and kisses Cora on the cheek. 'Goodbye, Cora. Thank you.'

Cora nods, then clicks the door shut behind her.

Halim downs the whisky in two gulps. It burns his throat and leaves a lingering hit of smoke that makes him think of Bernie and Morag. He gags, puts down the glass, rushes out into the garden and dry-heaves over the grass. He spits and wipes his mouth on his dirt-crusted jumper.

Rowena heads over, cupping her damaged hand, trails of pink glistening down her neck from the poultice.

He sits, and then lies back on the lawn and gazes up at the stars. The more he looks the more they reveal themselves, unfurling across the endless black, making everything that just happened seem so small, a footnote in the hundredth volume of the universe. Hot tears slide down his cheeks as his chest rises and falls.

Rowena lies down next to him. Her fingers find his and fold over them like petals. 'It's over,' she says. 'We did what we had to. And now we're free of them all, everyone who betrayed us and let us down.' Her voice trails off and Halim can tell that she's crying too.

He fights the numbness that his mind and body are trying to push on him, desperate to feel and remember every second of this moment with her, even if it hurts like hell.

44

A New Day

———

THE DAWN LIGHT TWEAKS and gilds the landscape moment by moment and mile after mile as Halim and Rowena stand on a plateau above a vast valley. Bell heather bursts red on the slopes below them, sending up a heady scent and a fawn-coloured cloud of pollen that catches on thermals and swirls up the mountainside.

Halim smiles at Rowena, hoping that she doesn't notice the shallow gradient of it. 'Do you want to climb higher?'

She looks out at the view and shakes her head. 'No, this is perfect.'

As if on cue, a golden eagle appears in the apricot-dappled sky, drifting in a widening gyre above their heads. They watch the immense bird scan the scree for its next kill. It hovers for a while and then dives like an arrow, disappearing behind an outcrop.

Rowena touches her fingers to her throat and sighs.

Halim realises he can't read her any more: on the road she never bothered to hide her feelings, her sharp-edged highs and blunt lows, but here ...

He gathers rocks for the cairn while Rowena finds a sheltered spot near a cushion of pink flowers. She kneels, lights the candle, drips wax onto one of the flat stones and stabs the candle in place.

'You ready?' Halim asks.

She nods.

He takes out the plastic urn and places it in front of her. The candle flame stops flickering and stands tall and proud.

'Pa would've liked you,' Rowena sniffs. 'He'd probably be amazed that someone as clever and respectable as you stuck around with me this long.' She looks up at Halim, the red line on her neck already scarring. '*I'm* amazed, to be honest. You could leave at any time, you know; I wouldn't blame you, not after all the shit I've dragged you into.'

'Do you want me to leave?'

She wipes her nose with the back of her hand. 'I don't need you to look after me.'

'No, but maybe I need *you* to look after *me*? I don't know what the fuck I'm doing out in the wild – would you leave me alone to go hungry and die out here? What if I ate the wrong berry or something?'

A smile threatens her lips. She turns back to the urn, unscrews the lid and begins to pour Marcus Muir's ashes on top of the rowan leaf she's laid out to mark the spot.

Halim marvels at how a man can be reduced to such tiny pieces, and then suddenly remembers the fires of Culcrith and shudders.

'Pa,' Rowena says as the mound grows like sand in an hourglass, 'I set your body free to rejoin the earth, to run into the rivers, to rise up into the clouds and nourish the soils to grow once again. And as I let you go, know that I also keep you with me.' A tear splashes into the ash, darkening it. When the urn becomes light in her hands she sets it down.

Halim undoes the chain around his neck and lays the dog tag next to the pile.

'Isn't that gold worth something?' Rowena asks, her eyes wide.

'Not to me.'

He helps her lay the stones, one by one, over the mound, creating a new sacred place in the Wilderness, a place for the two of them to mark on their map.

Rowena stands, approaches the edge of the plateau, the breeze lifting her hair like a red-gold Medusa.

Halim's never seen her stay still for so long.

Eventually he joins her there.

Below their feet the sheer drop is broken only by a few wiry saplings that somehow cling to the rock at diagonals. In the distance a pale line cuts through the valley, marking out the gap between mountains – a boundary of water, not steel.

'It's going to be all right,' he mutters.

'How do you know? Don't tell me *you've* started seeing signs now?'

'No, but we're together, we'll see each other through. We'll be okay.' He's saying it more for himself than for her, he realises.

Rowena rubs her arms and shivers. 'But what if getting there takes too long? And what if "okay" isn't enough?'

He resists the urge to put his arm around her, sensing an invisible barrier between them. 'We're like those saplings down there,' he nods. 'We've been battered by the wind and rain, burned by the sun and defied by the rock, yet somehow we pushed our way through the cracks, and we're still standing.'

As they watch the brightening day, their fingers graze one another – perhaps stirred by the updraught.

'I feel like I've shaken off a weight today,' Rowena sighs. 'I've left pieces of myself up here.'

Halim turns to her. 'So now we see what remains.'

Acknowledgements

———

Lots of love to my nearest and dearest for believing I could make this book a reality: James, Karim, Arden, Julie, Lissy, Cassie, Lou, Tina, Vicky, Mia and Louise. Huge thanks to my agent John Baker for seeing something in me and being an enthusiastic champion of mine. Thanks to Calah and Leonora, my sage-like editors at Serpent's Tail (even though they nixed my original ending). A shout out to designer Harry, copy-editor Mary, proofreaders Jane and Salma, managing editor Emily, the marketing and publicity team and everyone else behind the scenes at Serpent's Tail who went on this journey with me.

Thanks to Bobby and Co. at Spread the Word, who do great work in finding and nurturing under-represented voices, and to my fellow London Writers Awards 2019–20 graduates – many of whom got published before me and spurred me on through sheer jealousy. Thanks also to the Curtis Brown Creative Summer of '17 WhatsApp group, which has provided endless encouragement, 'tea-spilling' and laughs.

Finally, I'm grateful to you, reader, for choosing this story and staying with it to the very end – and if you're a writer yourself, remember that everyone has a different path, and you'll hack your way through the 'no's' to find yours in the end.